More books by Alan M. Clark,

available in paperback, ebook, and audiobook

Of Thimble and Threat
The Door that Faced West
Say Anything but Your Prayers
The Surgeon's Mate: A Dismemoir
The Prostitute's Price
A Brutal Chill in August
A Parliament of Crows
Apologies to the Cat's Meat Man
Mudlarks and the Silent Highwayman

Praise for the writing of Alan M. Clark

"Crime and horror wrapped in a wondrous symmetry, made all the more terrifying by its factual basis, *A Parliament of Crows* has it all. Read it!"

—F. Paul Wilson, author of Cold City

"In a publishing landscape where everything has been done...to death, comes something marvelous, frightening, and new—*The Surgeon's Mate: A Dismemoir*. Alan M. Clark has birthed a masterpiece that oscillates between bone-deep confessional and hide-your-eyes-horror."

—Charles Atkins author of *The Prodigy*

"*Of Thimble and Threat* is a terrifically absorbing read. A mature novel and superbly researched. The image of silver in the blood was woven expertly and made the ending luminous and poignant."
—Simon Clark, author of *Vampyrrhic* and *Night of the Triffids*

"Clark proves himself to be the ultimate double-threat, his prose every bit as evocative and compelling as his art. Steeped in Victoriana *Say Anything but Your Prayers* is a worthy edition to Ripperology."
—Steven Savile, author of *Silver* and *London Macabre*

"In *Jack the Ripper Victim Series: The Double Event*, Clark's attention to details of the era reveals a class system where a poor woman alone is all but doomed to an early grave. Readers will come away touched by these profound portraits of desperate women and shocked by not just the crimes which ended in their demise, but the greater crimes of a society that offered them no hope. This book is a must-read; be prepared to be horrified."

—Nancy Kilpatrick
Author: The Power of the Blood series
Editor: *Danse Macabre* and *Expiration Date*

From the review of *A Butal Chill in August* in *Ripperologist Magazine:*
Everything about this novel inspires admiration. It reveals terrible things about the world of London's poor, yet it is a work of great beauty, ceaselessly entertaining and compellingly readable. The rigging of a ship burning in the fire at the London Docks 'sparkles like a spider web dripping with dew at sunrise'. When we finally meet Jack the Ripper, he emerges from the darkness like an ordinary man, smelling of sulphur and soap. *A Brutal Chill in August* is a triumph.

From the review of *Apologies to the Cat's Meat Man* in *Ripperologist Magazine*:
Alan M. Clark is not the first author to find the victims' lives irresistible, but he has no equal when it comes to writing vivid and intellectually provocative stories about them. This is storytelling of the highest quality.

Fallen Giants of the Points

a novel by Alan M. Clark

IFD Publishing
P.O. Box 40776, Eugene, Oregon 97404, U.S.A.
www.ifdpublishing.com

ISBN: 978-1-7342978-6-7
Printed in the United States of America

Thanks to Jill Bauman, Melody Kees Clark, Lisa Snellings, Langley J. West, Linda D. Addison, Mad Wilson, and especially Rose Prescott, who shared with me her vast knowledge of the lands and the ways of the West.

Note from the Publisher

Many slang terms appear in this book. An attempt has been made to make the meaning of those terms clear through context within the narrative. Even so, the reader can find most of the slang defined in a book published in 1849, *Vocabulum, or, The Rogue's Lexicon: Compiled from the most Authentic Sources, a Dictionary of American Thieves' Cant*, by George W. Matsell. The book is available for free in a Project Gutenberg EBook that can be downloaded or read online. https://www.gutenberg.org

Fallen Giants of the Points

a novel by Alan M. Clark

Publishing

Eugene, Oregon

Introductory Note

Brother and sister, we have decided to work together to make a record of our childhood experiences. Since our stories follow much the same course, we've agreed to make a single tale of it while contributing our own separate chapters. Therefore, like an object described by two viewers, the reader will find some overlap in our descriptions.

To tell our story properly, we have taken a long, careful look at the past, particularly at the children we were between the years 1843 and 1849. We've revisited and compared memories; the good, the bad, and the indifferent. Though we have better understanding and better language now, we've tried to portray the world as we knew it during our early years, and to use words and notions as they may have occurred to us then.

The narrative has been edited by our dear friend, Tessa Angelo, a school-marm in San Francisco, California, and practically a mother to us. She has tamed our language some, but since our English was stewed up in Five Points, New York City—a burg full of immigrants of all colors and creeds—dear reader will find some curious and colorful phrasing in the narrative.

—Alta Mae and Cedric Brewer
San Francisco, California, 1873

Cedric—1

The things children believe! The wildest fancies become conviction so easy. And with the power to charm and amuse, what dangers those notions pose are not easy to foresee. I know my sister, Alta Mae, and I held notions in childhood that might have turned deadly. This account will show how we gained and lost a fear and hatred that could have turned us into killers. Indeed, the same fear and hatred in another almost killed me.

I am Cedric Brewer, born 1838 in Five Points, New York. In my early childhood, I mostly lived on the streets with my sister, two years older than me. Grown now and not prone to the nonsense I held in childhood, I yet remember believing my parents were giants. In 1843, my older brother, Egan Brewer, a young man fifteen years old at the time, gave me this lie and many more to believe. I was five years old, my sister, Alta Mae, seven. She believed the lie too.

"Our Ma were a giant prostitute known as Gaying Bay," Egan told us. "She died shortly after giving birth to you, Cedric, and fell dead along Little Water Street. People took up inside her."

"They lived inside her?" Alta Mae asked.

"Yes—still do—but you have to understand she were made of houses."

Alta Mae looked at Egan as if she didn't understand.

"We've visited her corpse many times," Egan said. "It now looks like houses along a dead end."

"The Cow Bay tenement?" she asked with a quizzical look, tilting her head this way and that.

"Yes, so named because of the way Papa treated her."

Alta Mae gave Egan a withering look, her lips drawn back. "She couldn't move if she were houses."

"Little girl," he said with a big loving smile, "there are more things possible than you've known or seen in your short life."

She shook her head slowly, as if unsure.

Egan nodded, his face open and truthful, or so it seemed.

Alta Mae frowned, squinted at the bright sky, then nodded to show she understood.

And, so, I took his words as true.

The Cow Bay tenement was indeed two rows of houses along a dead end, each connected to its neighbor by underground tunnels. The place sheltered hundreds of the wretches and criminals of the Points.

"Our papa, also a giant, were a drunkard named Colt Brewer," Egan said. "Though he ill-used her, he did love Ma. Upon finding her dead, he commenced his last bender. Drank so much, he too fell dead not far from Ma. Much the same sorts of people took up inside his corpse with the thought that their need for drink might be well-served should they make his drunkard heart to pump again. They never did get it started. Cozy enough inside him, though, they remained."

Later that day, Egan took us to a rough cluster of buildings that looked somehow jammed together. I'd been there before. The place had once been a brewery, and was now a tenement called the Old Brewery. "This were our Pa," he said.

In the largest chambers within, now apportioned into rough lodgings with sleeping pallets, Egan pointed out what he said were Pa's dried up organs, truly old brewing equipage.

Again, Alta Mae gave her looks and asked her question, but in the end she seemed to accept that the Old Brewery was our father.

And, again, I believe what she seemed to believe. My five year old idea pot could hold the notion more readily than hers, it seems.

Egan was a scout and messenger for the Bowery Boys, a crew of some renown in the Points. The gang had started out as firemen and had always reached for political power. When older, I would learn they called themselves nativists. Mostly of English blood, their politics say the only people of worth are protestants born on the soil of the United States. Indeed, they believe that only that sort should be allowed to vote in elections. They would have their own political party in the Know-Nothings within ten years. Egan got his opinions from the Bowery Boys, and we got ours from him.

With no schooling at the time, my understanding of the world had been hopelessly muddied with the beliefs of the fools in the Points. I can liken it to trying to grow up while looking at life through a lead pipe nearly clogged.

In 1845, when I'd become seven and Alta Mae nine, I had begun to understand how much big brother lied to us.

Hell, he'd had me believing I'd swallowed a spoon that slipped into my knob to give me the hard wood. No doubt that greatly amused him.

Yet I still loved him and kept looking to him for guidance, as did Alta Mae.

Egan took advantage of our trust and betrayed us. He sold us to sweat shops in the cellar of the Old Brewery. Separated from Alta Mae, I found myself imprisoned in a factory room with other children and made to toil for scant victuals.

Both my sister and I had known little but hardship and hunger on the streets of New York. At the least, I told myself, I remained safe and fed each day, there in Papa's rotten gut. I could only hope Alta Mae fared as well or better.

Alta Mae—1

Alta Mae Brewer is my name. I was born in the year 1836, in lower Manhattan's Five Points. The only family I knew were my little brother, Cedric, two years younger, and my big brother, Egan, eight years older than me. Neither short or tall, big brother had a thin frame, and a round, red-cheeked mug with pale blinkers, green some days, blue others. Cedric, a smaller likeness to our older brother, had clear blue blinkers, and though I did not know why, he'd always been more pleasant to look upon than Egan. They both had the same tightly curled dark brown hair, as did I, though a bit paler.

Creatures of the street, none of us ever had a home when young.

In one of my earliest memories, we're staying the night in the cellar of a tumbled down house with two women who pretend Cedric and I are their children while begging during the day. Palliards, they call that sort of beggar. Egan is upset because they have rubbed sores on our arms and faces and scratched small, bloody wounds in our skin with needles, all to make us more pitiable. With the warmth, summer must have come. We're pleased that Egan has discovered an abandoned partial pail of beer to share with us for a supper. I think he drank most of it. He gets puffed up, maybe feeling proud he'd found something for our bellies. "Little ones," says he, posing like a strong man, "you have Egan, the clever, brave, and able, as your protector. I'll always do my best to defend and provide for my kin."

That's pleasing to the ear. We always feel better to have him nearby. And he does protect us for a long time.

But as we all grew, he became shit at it. Cedric and I admired him for what he did for us early on, when we were all trying to get by on the street together. He taught us a lot of the things parents might teach their children, like how to hoist from markets and shops, and to buzz the pockets of our betters in crowds.

I remember him at his best, taking care of us while we were sick, once finding an idle brothel bed for us to rest in. When the prostitute it belonged to returned and saw how wretched sick we'd become, she slept in a chair so as not to disturb us.

"'Tis my sway with people like that prostitute that helps us get by," Egan said, "and that is a virtue of my service to the Bowery Boys." By that, he argued for the right to spend more and more time away from us. More like arguing with himself, as we'd always done our best to take care of ourselves.

Concerning his own wrongdoing and the crimes we got up to, he told us that until the United States government took up the nativist cause, we should regard those profiting from the world as we found it fair game. He most often told us what we wanted to hear, and if he couldn't decide what we wanted, he'd give us lies that helped us feel better about ourselves. Sometimes, he seemed to amuse himself, seeing what lies we'd believe.

One of his gave Cedric problems. I would only learn of the lie years later when he had grown older and thought to explain why he'd always been pulling on his knob, something that had confounded me each time I saw it.

"Me and Eagan were eating soup at a street kitchen, and I lost my spoon," he told me. He would have been about six at the time.

A year earlier, Cedric had found the spoon on the street. We rarely ate with anything but wooden spoons, so he was pleased to have it. He carried the thing with him thereafter, proudly using the spoon every time he ate.

"I told Egan it were missing, and he says, 'When you picked up your bowl to drink from it, you didn't remove your spoon. You swallowed it down with your soup. Little boys are prone to do that.'

"I got upset. 'I've lost my spoon?'

"'You haven't lost it,' Egan says, trying to put me at ease, 'it's in your gut.'

"'Won't it hurt my insides?'

"'No, its edges are all smoothed. Most times spoons lodge

in the bread bag. Sometimes it'll escape from your stomach and you'll feel it move into your knob, making it big and hard. You just rub it a little and the spoon will let go after a time and move back into your bread bag.'"

Even as little brother told me that story, I reckoned Egan had probably taken the spoon to sell.

Because of what big brother said, Cedric reached to rub his knob a lot, even in front of folks in the street. Sometimes he'd have it out of his breeches. When he was still little, those who saw him do that gently asked him to put it back, or they'd just giggle and point. The older he got the more often he'd get outrage.

"You can't be pulling your knob out in front of people." I told him. "They don't show you theirs and they don't want to see what you have."

"But the spoon!" he said.

Again, I didn't know what he meant until years later.

He agreed to stop, but he'd forget himself from time to time, and then, there it would be, where anyone could see it.

We truly loved Egan, even after we learned how often he lied to us.

By 1845, he spent most all his time doing the bidding of the Bowery Boys in their fight to keep the Irish Catholics from over-running the Bowery and nearby neighborhoods. Always someone wanting to move in on those parts, though there is no more miserable place for common folk.

That year, Cedric and I were most often on our own or with other small children of the streets in and around Five Points. Not that I thought of myself as small at nine years of age. I might have joined one of the all-girl "little" gangs, but then they wouldn't have wanted Cedric around. At seven years, he'd been too young for the "little" gangs. If I wasn't there for him, he wouldn't have had anyone looking after him.

We earned a crust however we could, at our worst competing with the rats for scraps off the fishing boats and barges at the waterfront, at times making ourselves sick just to put something in our empty bellies. Often what went down came right back up again.

Avoiding the coppers was easy enough—too many guttersnipes for them to take notice of two more.

We feared the missionaries. They did God's work, taking children from the streets and putting them in homes.

"You get sold into service that way," Egan told us, "you might as well be doing polly in the block house." By that, he meant picking oakum in prison. Most of the homes children got put into offered poor shelter, skilley or gruel for food, and a master or mistress with hard labor for the child to do.

"Children put into Catholic homes become slaves," Egan said, "often blinded and made dumb to keep them obedient. The young and tender are eaten."

If we saw man or woman toting a Bible, we gave them a wide berth.

Egan didn't trust many different sorts of people and he made certain to tell us his reasons, some, I have to say, just odd.

"You've heard the Germans jabber," he said. "Their language is the devil's own tongue, full of ugly noises. Even speaking God's English, the German cove will make it unpleasant to the ear."

Saying "cove," he meant simply "man," whether he thought highly or poorly of the fellow.

Egan also told us to avoid blacks. I was maybe six years old when Egan pointed out a black cove with a lump in his lower lip and cheek.

"Now, watch him a moment," Egan said.

The black fellow sat in a buckboard outside an iron monger's shop. He looked to be waiting for someone inside to come out and join him. After a moment or so, he spat on the road.

"You see that?" Egan asked.

I did. The spittle looked brown, just like the man.

"The black man is born with a corruption of the spirit that darkens his skin," Egan said. "Some try to rid themselves of it, spitting it out, but the corruption keeps coming back. Don't trust the black man for nothing."

Not long after, I learned about chewing tobacco, and knew

he'd pulled my leg. Still, a pig-ignorant child, I kept my distrust of blacks and had nothing to do with them.

God's English! Corruption of the spirit! I'd never known Egan to enter a church. I know what he was about now I'm grown, but back then, we were warm tallow in his hands and he molded us how he wanted. Egan made clear to Cedric and me who we should tolerate and who to turn away from. "Don't get into fights with them now. You can do that later once you're older and stronger. Stick with your own, and you'll be fine."

When Egan began to lose interest in protecting us, it seemed clear that what he'd done for us had, in part, been driven by guilt. With time, the sting of that failed to move him.

Winter of 1845 stung deep and hard, bit our feet and hands something terrible. Our ragged shoes did us little good until we stole adult socks to wear over them. That would hold them together for a while. We feared the nights, as we had to try to find warm walls and chimneys to cozy up to, or areas above or near enough to boilers, and competing with other children doing the same.

Near dawn on a morning in December, Egan, still asleep, answered my knock upon the door of the tiny, wooden lean-to shed where he slept. He hired the use of its floor from a blacksmith so he'd have a warm place to sleep at night and so he could have a girl with him if he found one. The brick back wall also belonged to an oyster cannery. The cannery's steam pipes kept the bricks warm. The air in the shed felt miserable in summer, cozy in winter.

"One day you'll awaken, but we won't," I said through clenched ivories. I shivered and quaked in the cold air, hugging Cedric to me to steal as much of his warmth as I could. That winter, I'd got angry with Egan for not helping us any more than he did, yet I tried not to show that for fear of driving him away quicker.

Even with his sleepy squint, I saw Egan glaring at my black eye and spilt lip. "Where'd you get the half-mourning?" he asked. "You been fighting again?"

He didn't think girls should do that sort of thing, even though his gang went up against gangs of girls as willing to maim and kill as any other roughs. Indeed, I'd seen Hell Cat Maggie in a street brawl with the Bowery Boys. Fellow must have thought her a man before he kicked her cunny. He looked surprised when she didn't go down. She leapt at him then, tore his mug open with her metal claws. Hooked an eye and pulled it from the socket, she did. Maggie was a Catholic, and a member of the Dead Rabbits. Even so, I couldn't fault her for wanting to protect her own. I liked to think I might be that tough one day.

Grinning, I said, "Had to fight to keep our sleeping spot."

Big brother didn't like my answer. He combed his curly brown locks with blackened fingers, yawned and scratched his scalp, then checked under his nails for chatts.

"Can we come in?" Cedric asked. I could hear his ivories chattering.

Perhaps also hearing that, Egan's blinkers grew wider with a look of worry—the sting of that guilt, I suppose. He tolerated me since I spent much of my time looking after our younger brother. Egan had always taken more care with Cedric, possibly because he was a boy.

Big brother moved aside to let us in. Pulling on his sit-upons and donning his coat, he said, "Stay here and I'll see what I can do about getting you something to eat. If the blacksmith comes and wants to give you a hard time, tell him who you are, and he'll back off."

Once he'd gone, we lay in the bundle of rags he used for a bed and slept.

—⁓—

He returned to say, "Come with me to Papa and I'll get you two something warm for your bellies."

Eager for food and warmth, we followed him.

Saying "Papa," he meant the tenement, the Old Brewery, as he'd had us believing it was our deceased father. Yes, goosecaps that we were, we'd swallowed that along with the one about Ma being the Cow Bay tenement. Somehow those notions stuck, even though by 1845 we'd learned better.

I remember some of how I'd found my own truth in his lies about the tenements when I was little. I saw the head of a figure in each of two windows set close together in the Old Brewery's main building. As they moved about, as if together, I thought of them as Papa's blinkers looking out at me. Never mind he was supposed to be dead. Two sets of five privies along the North side became Papa's toes. I pictured him wiggling them and startling folks inside doing their business. The long brick parts, set close together with a corridor between, I had as his legs. Along the west side, a couple of splintered sheds, with boards poking out this way and that became his hands and fingers. In the largest chamber, which I knew to be his gut and chest, stood the old abandoned brewing equipage: a giant copper tank, vats, and barrels. They had to be Papa's bread bag, sweetmeats, and giblets.

Although a harder task, I had like notions about the Cow Bay tenement as Ma.

On occasion, I had dreams about them being up and moving around, sometimes strolling through the city, hand in hand, if not fighting. They towered over the people in the streets, doing their best not to step on folks. Papa, always drunk of course, wrecked houses and shops when he stumbled and staggered.

Sometimes folks fell out of Ma. Saw a cove and his prostitute, in the midst of passionate missionary hogmagundy, fall from a window in the house of her bosom. Dreamt once that Ma and Papa paused to kiss, and a man ran up to a tap in Papa's ankle and drew off a pail of whiskey.

The sad fancies of a girl who longed to know her parents.

Once I knew he'd told a tall tale about Ma and Papa, I'd asked Egan to tell me the truth, but he always had something more important to do. Began to suspect he knew something he didn't want to tell me.

Egan led us through the wintry morning to our destination. We struggled to keep up. Hadn't rained for a while, so the streets were easier to walk with the mud frozen, as long as we steered clear of the icy sheets of horse piss. In that neighborhood, people usually kept their heads up and moving about to watch for danger. That cold morning, everyone had bundled up as best they could; hands in pockets or arm pits, huddled into their collars, hats pulled low.

As the sprawling structure of the Old Brewery came into view, so the smells of the place reached us, one of rotting grain still clinging from its time of brewing. Then came the reek of offal, some from the work of butcher's shops inside, their castoffs collected in a couple of half beer tuns.

Folks said that not a few human corpses, chopped and torn to look like the castoffs went into the tuns as well; residents of the tenement's main chamber known as the Den of Thieves who died on their own from disease or from the abuses of their mates, or those lured to their deaths in Murderer's Alley, a back lane that ran along one side of the Old Brewery. The maggoty, fly-ridden mire in the tuns and its reek discouraged interest in the contents. They got filled until the smell grew mondongo, and the landlord had to hire a dray for removing them to the East River. The tuns got dumped to feed the fishes, were washed out, and returned to the Old Brewery for more. No telling how many human corpses went that way into the river over time.

Passing through the main entrance of the place, the odors of unfettered human life added to the reek; a mix of stale urine, sweat, hogmagundy, spilled slops, and vomitus.

With all that, the place had kitchens for those who could pay, though the victuals weren't much to brag on. Egan fed us a stew of salt pork and cabbage at Mama Mercy's Kitchen, a place I thought of as located in Papa's shoulder.

Afterward, he took us down to the boss of the factory rooms, a man named Malcolm, a fat-arsed cove with thick lips and bulging blinkers. Those who saw us entering the cellar looked at us as if we'd been added to the menu.

We didn't know what we were in for, Cedric and me. Our bellies full, we'd grown sleepy. Egan had a quiet talk in a muddy cellar corridor with Boss Malcolm while a couple of his young roughs stood by, twins by the looks of them. I could not hear what big brother and Malcom said, just the murmur of the boss's blustery voice, and what sounded like Egan trying to bargain.

Cedric leaned against the brick wall, slid down it to sit. The wet filth at our feet discouraged me from joining him. He had to pull his legs in tight to keep from being stepped on by those coming and going along the corridor. Some, mostly men, slowed to get a good look at us. A few showed too much interest. Ill at ease, I turned away from them.

Weary of seeing those keen eyes, I got curious about what lay behind the heavy wooden doors. I had lifted the thick board that barred one when the Boss pegs me with his bulging blinkers, says, "In a hurry to help out, are ye?"

Startled, I dropped the bar and it fell back into the metal brackets with a loud thunk.

He turned back to my older brother. "Five years," said those fat lips. He held out a purse of coin, bounced it in his hands so the metal inside might be heard.

Soon as Egan took that skin full of honey, the roughs grabbed our collars.

Slow to know what was happening, I didn't put up much fight at first.

Egan walked off with the Boss.

Cedric spoke up first. "Egan," he said, almost a question.

Surely, Big brother would call to us to follow and the roughs would let us go.

What did I know at nine years?

Egan kept walking.

Kicking and screaming, Cedric and I tried to get away, but the roughs' grips were iron.

"Don't leave us," I cried at last.

"I have debt," Egan said. I barely heard him over the howl Cedric sent up.

Big brother, our protector, left the Old Brewery that day without looking back.

The roughs dragged us away in the other direction, further along the corridor, then down swaying, creaking steps to a nearly empty lower passage in Papa's stinking bowels. The rough that had me stopped, while the one with Cedric kept moving. I clawed to get to Cedric, as the cove with him unlocked a door, opened it, and shoved him inside. Took a lumping for that, I did. Yet I was more upset about losing my little brother. To give me that anointing, the rough had taken his hand off my collar. That gave me a chance.

I stomped his foot hard as I could and shoved him backwards. He fell in the slippery mud, and struggled to get up. I ran toward the door Cedric had gone through. Seeing a ring of keys on a hook beside it, I knew I'd never find the right one and get the door open before I got caught. The other rough spread his arms and legs wide to block me. I leapt for the opening between his left arm and leg, curled into a ball, and rolled to my feet behind him. Now both roughs were coming for me, but they had more trouble in the mud than I did.

"Let him go," said one to the other. "He won't get far. The tunnel is fallen ahead. He'll have to come back this way."

They thought me a boy. And why shouldn't they? Wasn't a particularly dimber girl. Dressing as I did, in what rags I could find to keep warm, woolen cap on my head, pulled down over my hair, I'd hidden what prettiness I may have possessed.

I ran on until the light gave out, then felt my way along the walls. While afraid the ceiling might fall down on me, I feared the roughs behind me more.

Because I remembered that warm cathouse bed from when Cedric and I had been so sick with chills, I believed for the longest time Egan must have had good reasons—more than just debt—for what he did to us that day. I could not fully admit to myself otherwise until years later.

Cedric—2

I was thrown into a darkened chamber that held maybe ten other children. The door closed and I heard a key turn in a lock.

Lived and worked in that cellar for an unknown long time, I did. Lost count of the days. "Five years," the Boss had said to Egan as he paid him.

The Old Brewery had been built nearly a century earlier beside a lake called the Collect Pond on what at the time had been the outskirts of New York City. The establishment, known as Coulter's Brewery, grew with the city and in much the same untidy manner. The original building began to sag and lean, another was built to shore it up, then another, and so on until a cluster of buildings stood together, in some ways holding each other up and roughly fitted into one. Tunnels connected the wet and sometimes flooded cellars.

Other businesses, a tannery, a distillery, and such like, took up around the Collect to use its water and exhaust into it. With time, the lake turned so fouled, the city filled it in, yet the new ground remained marshy. Anything built there sagged, shifted, and often collapsed as the ground sank. A perilous gamble, only the worst landlords bought into those parts. First the down and out made their way there because rents were low. Criminals, the accomplished and the petty, followed.

The crossings of Anthony, Cross, and Orange Streets formed the Points. New York City grew to surround and swallow the neighborhood. A wonder it did not choke and spit it out right away. Instead, those parts got to be so dangerous, the coppers wouldn't commit their men to patrol it. The Five Points rookery was born, given time and room to fester and grow.

They say the financial decline of 1837 put several of the large establishments out of business, Coulter's Brewery among them. The place ceased to brew and turned into the tenement I knew.

With the law loath to enter the Points, many wanted criminals, those fleeing indenture, or absconding from ships and militaries, chose to lose themselves in the Points. Many disappeared into the Old Brewery.

The premises of other large businesses that had closed around the Points also became tenements to house the growing numbers of poor. They had names that suited: Brick Bat Mansion, The Barracks, Jacob's Ladder, and Gates of Hell.

That year, 1845, Irish Catholics, fleeing the potato famine in Ireland, muscled their way into the Points by the thousands. Some had got into the tenements showing their usefulness. Egan said they brought with them many ne'er-do-wells or much worse: ruthless criminals.

With over a thousand people living in the old Brewery, mostly criminals of one sort or another, and the growing hatred between Protestants and Catholics, nearly every night saw one or more murders in the place.

The Cow Bay tenement, a long deadend alley of houses, each connected to the next with tunnels dug beneath the ground, had its share of murders too, the corpses buried in the floors and walls of those underground passages.

Despite the bodies being hidden, all that murder was common knowledge. But when it came to the tenements the law always had its tale down. The few times the coppers entered the Old Brewery— usually chasing someone wanted they'd got wind of—they did it in groups numbering thirty, forty, or more. Always became a great calamitous fight, with deaths on both sides.

A good thing I didn't know half that history when I got trapped there or I'd have lost more heart than I did. I had little hope of getting away. I'm not certain the coppers even knew about the factory rooms in the cellars. If they did, perhaps Boss Malcolm paid them to blink.

Some of the other children in that room with me—eight or ten at a time—said they'd been there for years. Tender, little things, they were, misshapen, had rotten and missing ivories, and bowed legs. I'd a dread of growing that way with time.

However long, I did my time there without seeing the light

of day—just lamp light. Full dark at day's end, after the overseer collected our work, and left, locking the door behind him.

The darkness at night was a thick thing that discouraged movement. Even if I felt something crawling on me, I let it alone unless it bit. I learned to sleep through the long, dark hours, even with the noise of footfalls and knocking about, shouting and wailing, fighting, and possibly the sounds of death coming through the ceiling from the Den of Thieves above.

I remember a few of the children, girls and boys. Sally Six Finger had lost a finger on her left hand and had an extra pinkie on the right. I question that recollection because I'm not certain I ever got a good look at her hands. Otherwise, she was just a raggedy, dark-eyed girl with a button of a nose. The Roach Prince, a pale skeleton of a child, hunted even in the dark, and shared his catch. Ghost Pocket, a ginger-haired girl, never got caught with the goods she buzzed off the overseers. And then there was William Buckets, with his wide bone box always reaching for a smile and his matted locks that he'd stiffen with mud and shape to look like a hat with a brim. He made me laugh twice. Don't remember what about, but joyous moments in that dull place, all the same. Most of the other children weren't there long enough for me to remember them—got sick or lumped senseless and taken away. Each time one went out, a new one came in.

I learned quick not to brag about my Papa housing us.

We huddled together for warmth at night under thin blankets. A tub to take up our slops sat in one corner—also emptied and used for bathing a time or two.

Food was gruel or skilley with mysteries, as we called them. Became a game to make guesses about the extras. Never a winner, though, since we had no way to find an answer.

By day, we prepared, fitted, or finished objects sold in shops, much of it trimming and smoothing ivory or wooden parts to fit into metal ones. I recognized the pistol grip roughs I smoothed 'cause some of my brother's crew ran with pistols. I suspected some of the parts I trimmed and fitted were for toys, games, or furnishings for the homes of the well-to-do, a world I believed I'd never see. Most often I did not know the purpose of the objects I helped to make. Had my curiosity, but the overseers forbade talking during the hours of toil, and no one else in the room would have had answers for me.

The overseer lumped us if we soiled our work, a difficult thing to avoid in Papa's muddy gut, especially when the rain from without worked its way in and we had standing water.

Overseers did come and go, all cruel, some worse than others. The more kindly ones didn't last.

An overseer, Samson his name, a fleshy English fellow missing a hand, told us, "This is what awaits ye beyond that door." He waved his stump in the air, and I thought he meant to lump us. He'd struck me with that boney nub once before after he caught me stroking my knob—hurt worse than any hand I'd had laid against me. But, no, he only threatened on that day. He banged on the door with the stump, said, "Cannibal mucksnipes await in the tunnels outside. They took my hand back when I were a lad doing yer work. Got away, I did, or they'd have had me deeper in the tunnels, to half-drowned rooms where they amuse themselves seeing how much they can cut off a child before he meets his maker." He scowled at each of us in turn. "Enjoy your toil and be thankful ye're kept safe from the worst."

I remembered the hungry gawping of those I'd passed on my way down into the cellar—something like the gaze of those men in the street that would pay me a penny to coax the spoon into my knob.

Whilst Samson didn't scare me, I still couldn't get past him and through that door.

I thought of Alta Mae, tried to picture her in my mind. Rawboned, pigeon-toed, and knock-kneed, she moved in an ungainly manner, her head down, green blinkers peeking through a pale brown mop of tiny curls. As I remembered her, she had more the look of a gawky boy. If she'd carried herself better, she might have been dimber enough.

I worried for her safety. Thought I heard her a few times when the door opened, her voice among those of other children in other rooms perhaps. That might have just been the longing to be with her.

Alta Mae—2

Just raw dirt this deep in Papa's bowels. Then chunks and piles of dirt. I moved around them and deeper, hoping there remained enough space in the fallen tunnel to allow a wee girl to pass through. I prided myself on squeezing into tight spaces, sometimes for hiding from those after me, sometimes for pilfering. I'd once slipped through a black iron fence into a boneyard to collect a few items left graveside by mourners, a bit of food to eat and flowers I sold. Took skin off either side of my head to get through. The place had been guarded when open and locked up tight at night for over fifty years, ever since medical men caused a riot over stealing the dead and ottomising them.

Another time, having smelled the rotting refuse of a fruit shipment in a warehouse closed for the night, I crawled through a drain that ran from under the building to the street. I came up into the warehouse through a grate in its floor. That bruised pear meat was well worth it. Sweet! Got a bit drunk on the bits that had begun to ferment.

The dirt piles got larger and closer, till there wasn't hardly any room left and I crawled on hands and knees. Still, I couldn't go back with them roughs waiting for me. If I were to get out and sneak back in to free Cedric, I had to go forward. I pushed on until I slithered through thick mud, bits and pieces falling on me from a ceiling just inches above, the air thin and wet. Panic choked me a few times as if the ceiling had indeed come down. Got through it, though, until finally, I was well and truly stuck, unable to thrash about even while my panic told me to. I could not move. Fear forced a scream out of me. Now, I wanted those roughs to come get me, yet that didn't happen. I could hear nothing but my own ragged breathing, knew I would die there alone, crushed and suffocated under the earth.

Weeping as I thought about my waste of a life, I decided that perhaps without me to help, Egan might take better care of Cedric. I thought maybe I stood in the way, that my little brother would be better off with me gone.

Even so, I took a deep breath of the thin air and held it, not wanting to let go of life.

Then it occurred to me to ask, *Why care?* Both frightening and comforting, I found no answer. Frightening since it said my life was of no account. Comforting because I could let go the fight. I'd a big blue-steel spring inside me I kept wound tight, just to have the life in me to keep Cedric and me going. At least, that's how I imagined my pluck and drive.

Letting out my breath, I could feel that spring unwinding. I took long slow breaths after that and let myself settle further into the mud, my new home, my final resting place.

I must have slept some because I dreamt of Papa sitting on a giant privy seat alongside houses in Mulberry Street. The seat stood as tall as the houses. Made of brick and stone, papa's mug had the all-overish look of someone costive. People in the streets appeared alarmed to see the peaked roof of Papa's head, so high above us, tearing clouds in two. They pointed, gaped, and cowered, some running away.

His shuttered window eyes blinked, the great double door of his mouth opened, and I heard my papa's voice for the first time. "What's to stare at?" he said. "One day there'll be sky scrapers aplenty here."

And that's when I felt the breeze. Hardly there at all, yet it cooled the sweat on my face. I knew I had awakened and could feel that spring inside winding up again. The air came from behind me and moved in the direction I headed. An opening to the outside lay ahead, if I could just get to it!

All at once, it came to me why Papa had looked so costive: I backed him up.

"Shit me out, Papa," I cried.

Moving slowly, I scooped what blocked my passage, mud from beneath me and loose soil from above, and moved it along my sides and legs until I'd got it behind me as best I could.

This I did for hours, while it seemed a day or more. Long enough my hunger returned and began to gnaw at me. If I got stuck and afraid, I repeated, "Shit me out, Papa!" And each time I found myself inching forward into small gains I'd made. Light ahead encouraged me. Not certain it was more than fancy at first. Then there came a time when it became a certainty. I believed I saw dim shapes outside. With that, I feared the ceiling collapse more because I could see my escape.

The thought that I heard rain soothed me a bit.

Doggedness and calm, I told myself, as I wormed forward. Breathing fresher air by the moment and finding a few more inches to move my limbs were the sweetest of victories. I got back upon my knees, then to my feet, moving forward in a crouch toward an opening spattered with falling water. I smelled shit and knew Papa had done as I'd asked.

Beyond, I could see a giant hole with broken pieces of dwellings in it. I'd come out part way down one of the sink holes that had opened up in the Collect. The pit had swallowed some houses and a shop with a sign said, "Bertram & Co Dry-goods." The newest sink hole had opened up last week. I'd not gone there to give it a look. Though tempted to search the ruined premises below for valuables, I had the urgent need to escape.

Felt warmer out than when I went in. The rain had taken away some of the chill.

I clawed my way up the loose, wet soil, avoiding a reeking hollow in the side of the pit. The smell told me it was a privy vault that had torn open as the ground fell. That's where the smell of shit came from.

Got to the lip of the sink hole, poked my head up to look around. Sagging dwellings surrounded the giant pit, one partly fallen in. Dusk or dawn, but couldn't tell which with the overcast. Saw a dim glow low in the sky between what looked like a small church and a cottage, yet I didn't know East from West. No one about, perhaps fearing the unstable ground.

Sure enough, as I crawled over the lip, the edge gave way. I tumble down, thirty or forty feet. Landing on the shake roof of one of the swallowed houses, I broke through, tearing the skin of my right leg from ankle to knee. Too sudden, I didn't feel the pain at first, not until I tried to work my leg out of the hole I'd punched. Then it was all I could do to keep quiet, so's not to draw notice from someone who might wish me ill. Got my leg out and rested some, pouring the pain out through tears. I saw my foot had become crooked, broke somehow. I lay upon that roof for some time, my stomach aching to be fed. Had no notion how long since my meal of cabbage and salt pork. I had to get out of that hole.

Once I'd gathered myself together, I started to climb back up the side of the sinkhole. I chose to go up the dryer side, one protected from the slanting rain. Took some time without the use of my right leg. Had to pause now and then to let go more pain. Through it all, I began to scheme how to get Cedric out of Papa's gut.

Though frightening to consider, I figured the best way would be to go back in the way I came out. Unlikely anyone would expect such a thing. I'd have to heal up first. In the time that took, someone might close the passage, or the sinkhole might be filled in. I'd have to improve my lock picking skills to get into the factory room. I'd have to find a weapon to take with me to fend off any roughs in there with Cedric.

Again, I poked my head up to see above the rim and someone grabbed my left ear. Hurt so bad, I didn't choose to fight but with my voice.

"Stop your caterwauling before someone worse hears and comes for you," came a woman's voice.

I took her meaning and kept quiet as I could, hoping she meant no real harm. She let up on my ear, grabbed under my arms, and hauled me up. I sat near the edge of the pit, worrying it might give way again. She crouched down beside me, her hand held ready to grab my ear.

"What were you doing in my house?" She asked. Had a fierce look about her, her brown blinkers circled with white, and her plump cheeks a hot red.

Yes, she frightened me. I'd also been struck dumb by her odd words and just stared at her. She was an old woman, forty years and more. Had a round mug with deep set blinkers, black brows, and a hard mouth. Graying black locks poked out of a wet, stained bonnet. Her sodden chemise and skirts plumped out like she ate well.

"Weren't in no *house*," I said. "I *fell* in the hole."

"Saw you, I did," she said. "You pulled yourself out of a hole in my roof"

"Made that hole when I fell. 'Tweren't bigger around than my leg."

She rose and looked down into the pit, then nodded.

"Even so, you come with me," she said. "You're just the little thief I need."

"Can't walk," I said, gesturing angrily at my right foot. "Broke it on your house."

She took a look at my foot. Soon as she touched it, I gulped breath to scream, but held back. She backed off, rose, and lifted me so I could lean on her.

"I'll see you fed, cleaned, and housed at my brother's lodgings," she said. "You'll need time to heal, and I'll see to that too. Then you'll owe me a debt of service."

I'd become too weary, cold, hungry, and miserable to argue, though I had my fears.

We made for the gap I'd seen earlier, between the little church and the cottage. The brightness higher now, I knew a new day had begun.

Cedric—3

Excitement came when the toil in the factory room changed from one sort to another. We looked forward to those changes. My favorite was cutting patterns from heavy cloth, perhaps for upholstery. Somehow that reminded me of stuffed dolls.

I had to content myself most of the time with what happened in my head. I fancied persuading the other children to help me kill the overseer with our sheers or whatever tools we used on a day. Not much of a plan, since the door locked from without, and we'd just be stuck in there with a dead man until a new overseer arrived. Then we'd all be in for it.

Odd that Egan, who had done so much to protect the liberty of his family, had robbed us of freedom. Yet something Egan had said the week before I went into the factory room helped me escape my confinement, in a manner of speaking.

"What you have in your idea pot," he said, tapping my forehead with a finger, "your thinking, is all yours. Nobody can know or have anything to say about it unless you tell them."

He'd been speaking that day of the different sorts of people he thought deserved scorn. Although immigrants—blacks, Catholics, and Jews—were the ones he hated the most, truly he looked with a jaundiced eye upon anyone moving in on our neighborhoods. "Many don't share my beliefs," he'd said, "and I am but one man, so most of the time, I don't reveal to others my feelings. Within my thoughts I have true liberty. I can think what I want."

Again, he tapped my head, "In there, you are free to do whatever you want, believe as you please, and sometimes it's best to keep the thoughts that are important to you to yourself."

I know now that he needed me to share his opinions of others. He just didn't want me to express those opinions in the wrong place and suffer a lumping. Whilst I had little experience hating, I did swallow most of the beliefs he fed me. With scant knowledge of the world, they went down easy as pap.

As I said, we'd had that talk maybe a week before I went into the factory room. Once I'd been there for a time, I took his words a different way. I decided that my thoughts, especially recollections, could give me back some of the liberty taken from me; that I might still wander the world outside in memory.

Each day, I tried to remember and picture what I missed from being outside. Since I'd come in from the cold winter, I thought of how I'd be missing the coming spring-time warming, the changing light in the sky, and birds—especially birds. At first the recollections came easy, if tainted with the bitter feeling of want denied. With time, though, I had difficulty in picturing what I wanted. Life outside the room had become a dream, hard to hold onto.

Then I remembered a fallen nest I'd discovered one spring with little blue eggs in it, and that no one could tell me how the mama bird made them blue. I held onto that one because of the powerful curiosity it put in my head and chest.

From then on, I looked for memories that held strong feelings.

I remembered Egan treating me like an equal and playing games with me. I beat him a few times, and when I did, he told me I was smart. While I suspected he allowed me to win on those occasions, that only made it better.

I recalled the generosity of a woman on the street that I didn't know giving me a candy stick one Christmas Eve. Don't know why, but I gave half of it to a waif girl who kept glancing at me as I licked the sweetness. She gave half of that to another little boy. Felt good to see them smile.

I remembered the great fire in New Street that summer of 1845, an adventure that began with an explosion maybe a mile away from where I stood in Rose Street. Alta Mae and I ran toward an orange glow that rose high into the sky. We dodged through people running this way and that, suffered cuts to our feet through our ragged shoes from the glittering shards of broken window glass in the streets, even blocks from the fire. Closer to our goal, we saw fire engines drawing water from the pond in Bowling Green Park, and firemen spraying it from hoses, trying to douse the flames.

I thought the fire and the rolling smoke beautiful that night, then felt all-overish for liking it once I learned that thirty people had died in the fire. The next night, I lay on the trampled grass in Bowling Green Park, watching fireflies rise from the Earth into the air. A great mystery to me, I counted thirty of them, no more, no less.

Had a dim recollection of one wintry night when the pain of cold in my feet had got so bad I thought I'd die. Must have been about six years old. Me and Alta Mae went to stay with a prostitute Egan said knew our mother before she died. I wanted to ask her questions about Ma—what she'd been like, what it was like to be with a giant—but I never saw the woman. Alta Mae said, "She is ill. We must leave her alone."

In no shape to press the matter, I sat, trying and failing to pay no heed to my misery. My sister set about to warm us. She found nothing to burn in the fireplace. At last, Alta Mae bundled me into her shawl, pulled the straw mattress off the bed over us, and hugged my feet until the pins and needles were gone and the feeling returned. We kept each other warm beneath that musty mattress, as the house remained dark and cold all night. I've never had warmth to comfort me quite like that again.

I recollected many such moments to aid my escape to the freedom within, while I toiled away the hours and days.

As time passed, even the strong memories did not offer enough liberty. I yearned most for the warm sun on my face and hands, smiles, and laughter. Precious little of those last two in the factory room.

Alta Mae—3

She gave her name as Carlotta Angelo. "I prefer Carla," she said. "My brother's name is Paul Romano. He's gone to sea. I've been staying at his lodging since my house fell in."

When asked, I lied and gave my name as Lesley.

Mr. Romano's lodgings were a single, crowded room in a crooked, midling-sized house on the edge of the Collect.

Inside, I came face to face with some of what Egan had given me to fear. The chamber had two beds, a little table and chair, cupboard, wood stove, and a set of shelves beside a small curtained window that faced a thin alley. Three figurines sat upon one of those shelves, Catholic saints staring down as if trying to decide how much work they might get out of me before I gave up the ghost, or whether I'd be better served up as a meal. The powerful fear came in an instant, brought on by what Egan had said of Catholics. My thoughts scattered like rats frightened from a rubbish pile.

That moment, I'd have fled back out through her door had I been able to walk.

I tried to tell myself Egan had said a lot of things not true, but I reckoned he'd had his reasons, and that some truth a nine-year-old girl might not quickly grasp had perhaps been hidden in his words.

And then the oddest thing: I wanted to like two of those saints, though I knew I shouldn't. I recognized them from some I'd once seen in a shop window. The shop keeper, a nice man in an apron, smoking outside his establishment, had told me something about each of the saints as he pointed to them in his window. My favorite was Joan of Arc, because she looked strong and proud, safe and invincible in her armor. As threatened as I felt on the streets much of the time, I wanted to see myself that way.

I also liked the one the shopkeeper called Saint Francis the sissy— yes, that's what I thought he'd said of the little man surrounded by animals. I didn't understand how he might be a sister to anyone. I liked Saint Francis since he had the animals as his friends. They got so close to him! Magic, that. I'd always wanted animals to like me, except for rats, maybe because I'd had to compete with them for food and had once been bitten.

Knew an angler who might have pilfered the saint figurines for me, right out of the shop window with his hook on a stick and string. I was wondering what I could trade him for the service when Egan came upon me, caught me looking at the saints.

"Catholic idols!" he said, grabbing my arm and nearly pulling it from the socket in his hurry to get me away from there.

Well, here they were again, looking down at me from the shelf. And like I said, I wanted to like them, and knew I shouldn't.

Sadly, I not only believed Egan's lies, I'd begun to see his way of things, his desire to see our people win out over the hordes of foreigners coming to our shores. He was for abolishing slavery so all the blacks might be sent back to Africa, and he had a hope for a Protestant Church of America.

Carla sat me on a bed and turned away toward the cupboard.

On the counter beneath, I saw knives, and for a moment I knew she would carve me up for her supper. I shriveled into myself, feeling small and helpless. Yet, she did not reach for a knife.

"Some tommey," she said, turning back and handing me a goodly portion of a small loaf.

She'll fatten me up first, I decided, even as I tore the bread from her hand to feed the great and growing hollow in my gut.

Hungry as I'd got, my red rag was dancing to the tooth music. Chewing and swallowing, I knew that if she'd a mind to fatten me up, I'd have some time since I'd never been more than a slip of a girl. I would enjoy the food while I could.

"You are filthy," she said. "Stand and lean against the wall, so's I can place a blanket to protect the bedclothes. Then you can lie back and rest, and I'll make ready your bath."

I did as she asked. After placing the blanket and helping me back into the bed, she pulled a wash tub from beneath the other bed. With it half filled with water, she had to have considerable strength to move it. She dipped a deep pot in the tub to fill it, and placed that on the stove, then dipped more into a basin. With a clean rag, she washed the cut on my lower leg, doing a good job of removing the dirt and smeared blood, but leaving the scab alone.

"You won't need stitches to close it," she said, trying to catch my gaze.

I didn't look her in the eye.

"While the water heats on the stove, you rest. I have ciphering to do." She sat with her back to me at the small table, opened a book, and took up a pencil.

I watched her for a time. She remained at it longer than I expected, and I decided she must be doing more than the simple ciphering most women did.

Despite my fears, I became drowsy and fell asleep.

I slept unmolested and awoke to find Carla pouring steaming water into the tub.

She saw I'd awakened and helped me stand. "I'll continue my work whilst you bathe. I borrowed from a neighbor fresher slops for you." She gestured to the far bed. Draped over the footboard were clothes befitting a boy. She handed me a lump of slippery and returned to her book.

As I peeled down to my birthday suit and washed with the soap, she never turned to see she'd been wrong about me. No hardship wearing boy's rigging—had done most of my life. Better for moving in a hurry or sneaking about.

Couldn't remember the last time I'd had a bath. The warmth got me sleepy again, but something told me I had to get done before she got a look at me. I finished and dressed.

A black cove walked in just then. I let out a cry and backed up toward Carla. She turned and held my shoulders, said, "That's Ivan, is all. He ain't gonna hurt you."

I thought him terribly bold and ill-mannered to burst in on a white woman.

"Forgive me, Aunt Carla," he said. "I didn't mean to barge in like that. I should have knocked."

He was tall and wide in the shoulders, bundled in a heavy blue coat against the cold outside, black woolen hat pulled down over his ears and brow. His dark mug had creases up the cheeks, a broad nose, and a round, full mouth. He put his open hands out to his sides in a way that lessened my fear.

"No, we're finished," Carla said.

He looked about thirty-five years old, so I wondered was she truly his relation, or merely dubbed "Aunt."

"Here for my penny whistle," he said. "Had some time and thought I might blow me up some earnings."

From the cupboard, Carla retrieved a tin whistle and handed it to Ivan.

"You should stay with the Charles's for a time as I've got this boy, Lesley, here with me."

Ivan eyed me with no threat to it, and nodded. "Pleasure to meet you," he said.

He put the whistle to his lips, blew three notes, and went back out.

If Carla was indeed his aunt, then maybe Ivan belonged to her brother, the seaman, Paul Romano, perhaps a son from a union with a black woman. From their words, I'd got that Ivan lodged there too.

Had I slept in his bed?

If he were just now asked to stay somewhere else, that meant he'd remained a lodger, even after his father left. He'd been living with Carla alone.

Did they get up to horizontal refreshment?

I didn't like to think of it. With two beds, maybe not, since they wouldn't have to pig together.

Still, a woman on her own—I had to wonder how she got on so well.

"Are you married?" I asked.

"No. My husband died many years ago."

She'd be beholden to someone, but I didn't know how to ask her about it.

"I have to find my brother, Egan," I said, thinking that if he would help me, I wouldn't have to stay with Carla and Ivan. I don't know why that seemed a good idea. Big brother had just sold Cedric and me into slavery.

Though I should have done, I hadn't stop loving Egan. At the time, in some way I cannot now fathom, I believed he didn't know what happened after he walked away from us in the Old Brewery, and that the Boss must have misunderstood, or done what he wanted with us, heedless of Egan's wishes. And I thought all that in spite of him saying he'd betrayed us because of debt.

"Rest yourself," Carla said. "You can find your brother later."

"I also have to help my little brother escape from one of the factory rooms in the belly of the Old Brewery."

"You'll help me first," Carla said. "Then you can have your family reunion. We have to get you healed up so you can work off your debt. I'm taking *good* care of you."

Although she'd said before that I'd "owe her a debt of service," I hadn't truly considered what she meant. First chance I got, I pocketed one of her knives. Thankfully, Carla didn't seem to notice it missing.

—⁓—

Other blacks lived in that lodging house as well; the Charleses—a woman, Neve, and her girl child, Joela—in a room directly across an entrance hall, and the Mohammeds—a man, his wife, and five children—living in a room at the end of that hall. I could hear the children coming and going, their rumbustious play, and the full-grown arguing at night.

I'd known of such mixed dwellings, like the Den of Thieves in The Old Brewery and certain cellars beneath Cow Bay, where blacks and whites mixed and made mulatto children. Yet I'd never thought to go to those places, let alone think of taking up in such chambers. I'd known a cove, wed to a black woman. Never spoke of her with him, though. I'd also known mulatto children on the streets. Much like any others except for their looks. I reckoned the white part of them made them decent.

With what Egan gave me to believe, I feared that being in that house with blacks put me in great danger. He'd said of their kind, "Don't trust the black man for nothing."

Helpless with my damaged foot and needful of Carla to see me through—for at least a week or more until I could find Egan—I knew there was nothing for it.

Carla introduced me to Miss Charles and the Mohammeds. As they showed little interest in me, some of my fret lifted.

Miss Charles—Neve—and Ivan were rather familiar with each other. Dimber in her way, she had a certain grace.

After that first hunk of tommey, when Carla offered me victuals, I took little so I wouldn't plump up and look tasty. I did that for a week before deciding I needn't fear her as a cannibal just because Egan had made warnings about Catholics. He had told me the black man chewing tobacco spit brown corruption, but I'd seen the dark spit from whites chewing too.

Despite believing I owed her a debt, Carla didn't treated me like a slave, and instead more like an indentured servant.

Still, in my idea pot, I held myself apart from her. She was a Catholic, and they were simply wrongheaded. Truth be known, I knew little about it, having never gained an interest in religious matters.

Carla worked for certain undertakings in the Cow Bay and Old Brewery tenements. Six days a week, she left the lodgings and remained gone for some hours in the early afternoon to meet with those that employed her.

She went to church each Sunday at St. Mary's in Grand Street. "Once you're back on your feet, you can go to Mass with me," Carla said. With the look I gave her, she didn't make the invitation again.

Following the meetings with her employer and after church on Sundays, she stopped at market before returning home with victuals to make a good meal. I'd never eaten so well.

Ivan, Neve, and Joela ate with us in the evenings. He brought out a larger table and four chairs from Neve's room and placed them in the hall. Carla brought her chair out and served us all soup and tommey most nights.

I'd been with her two weeks when she said, "I want you should go through the hole you made in my roof and find something got swallowed with my house. I'll tell you more once you're made well enough to do the job."

What she said didn't frighten, yet I had my concerns about how long before I'd be able to do as she asked.

At a supper in January, Ivan said, "Got word from Papa."

Carla's blinkers grew large. She clutched his big hand, showing eagerness for the news.

"Seems Captain Wallacey and the Destitution have carried him around the Horn and up to the Bay of San Francisco. Says he likes what he sees in California and will stay a while to learn if he can make a better place for us there. He's looking at two towns, Yerba Buena and San Jose."

"That's the ends of the earth," Neve said to Ivan. "You won't go there on the *mere* chance of a better life."

"*Won't* I?" he said.

"Well" Neve said, full of pout, "me and mine ain't going with you."

Carla took Ivan's hand in both of hers. "I'd go if Paul believes we can do better there."

Ivan merely nodded, and we went on with our meal.

Neve did not speak or look at Ivan or Carla for the rest of the meal.

—∞—

In my second month with her, Carla warned that the sinkhole had been getting wider, her house slowly covered over as the sides of the pit fell in.

I still couldn't walk, and said as much.

"You are not a lazy boy," she said, with an anger growing in her dark blinkers, her black brows bearing down. "I know your sort. I see them b'hoys every day. The streets are full of snotters, divers, and sneaks like you. You have the sand to do what I need done. You would not have gained your age on the street had you not been strong-willed and good at mousing. I have been good to you. You *will* help me!"

I got up, standing on one foot while putting little weight on the other. Even then it hurt.

"Now, take a step toward me," she said.

As soon as I tried to use my bad foot, I cried out and fell to the floor.

41

Spitting mad and using a language I didn't understand, Carla shouted and gestured wildly.

When her anger was spent, she helped me back into my bed, said, "We'll give it another week."

—∿—

Once that week had passed, Carla brought home crutches for me.

I tried them out. "These lifters won't help me crawl into your house."

"I suspect your foot is recovered more than you'll let on."

"I do not deceive you," I told her.

"Still, you must make the effort."

Thinking I didn't want to repeat the pain of the week before, and fearing that what recovery I'd had would be lost each time I hurt my foot, I didn't move fast enough for her.

"Your sort would prefer to lie than ever tell the truth!" Carla raged.

The anger that took hold of her! She grabbed me, hauled me off the bed to my feet, and let go. I cried out and fell back upon the bed. I reached for my broken foot, and wept. She took a bedroll strap hung on the wall and whipped me across the legs and backside with it.

"You owe me!" she shouted. "Get to your feet."

The strap bit harder and my trousers split in the back.

"My savings are in that house. Without them, I'm at low tide."

To stop the whipping, I tried to do as she asked, but again fell, folding up on the floor. I made for the safety of shadows under the bed. She grabbed my legs and pulled me back. Scrambling to get away, I upset the jerry beneath the bed and got a face full of reeking piss. We fought, and with my good foot, I landed a blow to her middle. Enraged, she grabbed the band of my trousers and yanked. They tore, and she fell back with the tatters in her hands. Part way under the bed, I turned to face her.

Looking at my backside and beneath, where I expect she'd thought to find boy parts, her eyes grew wide. Carla's bone box hung open. Her features softened, and she began to laugh, a deep hearty one.

I didn't know what she found humorous.

She rose slowly, touched my good foot. "Oh, girl, get you out from under there. I won't whip you again."

Still afraid, I didn't move.

"I see you ain't pretending. I will give you more time."

She laughed again. "Is Lesley your true name?"

Smelling of cold piss, I slid cautiously out from under the bed. "No, I am Alta Mae."

Regardless of my sodden face, hair, and clothes, Carla took me in her arms and hugged me. "I'm sorry," she whispered in my ear.

I didn't want her to hug me. I didn't trust she was sorry.

"Don't tell Ivan and the others I'm a girl," I whispered.

"We'll keep it between you and me."

Perhaps unwittingly, she called me "she" in front of Ivan and Neve not long after that, so the truth came out.

—⚞⚟—

Daily for another month thereafter, she tried to persuade me to go down the sinkhole, but not overmuch. Then, helping me to and from the pit, we began making trips each afternoon to look at her house, as if that would somehow encourage me. The first time, I saw that the hole in her roof have been enlarged.

"Some one got in." I said.

"They will not have discovered my cache."

The sides of the sinkhole had fallen here and there, covering more of her roof. The dry-goods shop I'd seen before had already gone under.

—⚞⚟—

One evening, as she worked at the table on one of her books, I asked her about the ciphering work.

"I am a bookkeeper for a man that runs businesses out of the Cow Bay and Old Brewery tenements," she said. "The money they take in, the money they pay out, I record all of it so they know how well they're doing and what they may owe. It requires that I do maths to find the right totals."

"They trust you to do that?" I asked, thinking it a man's sort of work.

"Yes. I have a good reputation for my ability to read, write, and do maths—skills most in the Points don't have."

"You can read too?"

"Yes." She grew still for a moment, as if thinking. "Do you want to learn how to read?"

I didn't know how to answer. Believing I would never have the chance, I'd never considered the question. Now, I had to wonder if I could learn such a thing.

"You have time as you are healing," Carla said.

Thinking there must be some hidden reason she'd want to do that, I held my tongue. If I took her offer, might she somehow teach me the wrong words so that I would be gummed into becoming Catholic?

"It will help you to get on better in the world," she said. "Jobs that require reading pay better and there are fewer trying for them. Taught my daughter, Hetty, to read."

She saw I had questions about that.

"She died two years ago at the age of eight. She would be about your age now." Carla grew misty-eyed telling it, and turned away for a moment.

Could that be her reason for taking me in? Did she want to pretend I'd become her child? If that was what moved her, I decided I shouldn't be too afraid.

Carla wasn't beholden to anyone but her employer. She had landed a job that paid her well enough to have decent lodgings, to keep us well-fed, and to feed Ivan, Neve, and Joela much of the time as well.

If reading and writing could do that for me, I wanted it.

"Yes," I said. "That would be most generous."

She looked pleased.

I still didn't trust her altogether.

—⚬—

One day we arrived at the sink hole to find that rains in the night had tumbled down much of one side steepness, and the roof of her house had been hopelessly covered over with dirt.

Carla stood looking down into the pit for the longest time. She shifted from foot to foot, frowned, and grimaced. I feared she'd go mad on me again. Shaking her head, she closed her blinkers for a long moment.

"Your money," I said sadly, because I'd taken to her some, against my better judgement.

With a far-off look in her eyes, she worried at her lips with a finger. Her mouth twitched at the corners. She took a deep breath, let it out, and dropped the hand to her side. All this telling me she reached for some way out of her loss.

"I can reach high tide easily enough," she said, as if speaking to herself. "What he's holding should be as much or more than the stake that went down the sinkhole. Yet I'd counted on having much more."

She fell quiet again for a time.

Then a crooked smile broke free, wrinkling up the flesh around her left eye. "But if I took the whole thing…"

I tried to catch her eye.

"Never you mind," Carla said. "It's not your funeral."

"Will you be turning me out?" I asked, fearing she no longer had a use for me. I'd be easy prey on the streets with my bad foot.

"No, girl, I could not do that to you."

I had folded the knife I'd taken from her into the waist of the skirt she'd given me to wear. Taking it out, I said, "I stole this from you."

"I know. You needed something to make you feel safe. You may keep it if you like."

"Truly?" I asked, and she nodded.

I'd had a frustration on the street, keeping a knife. Always ended up selling mine or trading it for food. A good, sturdy knife, this one. I became determined to hold onto it, though I knew I'd thought the same about knives in the past. Now that I didn't have to hide it, I could make it ready for quick use. I would find a piece of leather to work into a sheath for the blade, so I could carry the knife in my pocket.

I'd have thanked her if I'd been any good at such things.

45

"I were thinking I should get your little brother out of the Old Brewery," Carla said.

"You could do that?"

"Will take some thought, but, yes, I think I can. Boss Malcolm, who runs the factory rooms, is my employer."

My opinion of Carlotta Angelo was changing fast. Still, something told me not to be gulled into liking her.

"We could take him with us," she said.

"Where are we going?"

Carla didn't answer. She just smiled.

With time, I suspected she meant California. I had no cause to want to go there. She didn't have to know that yet.

Another six months would pass before I knew more about her plans.

Cedric—4

I cannot say what my time in the factory room did to my spirit; cannot find the words or don't truly know. Waiting for release, I pushed many needs and fears away, hoping to leave them unfelt. I can liken it to walking barefoot on sharp stones. I have to slacken my soles so the rocks don't bite so hard, and know that smoother ground is ahead. Or I can say it's like holding my breath to go through a flooded pipe, as I did once to break into a closed-up fish market shop. I could not do it and give in to my desire to gulp breath or fearing I'd get stuck. No, I could only go forward. All that while not knowing when it would end, and despair reaching to take hold of me. Perhaps the trick of surviving the factory room was indeed to slacken my *soul* so that being trapped didn't bite my spirit so hard.

These are not words I could have used at the age of seven, nor could I have explained my thinking. Being as honest as possible about the little boy I was, I try to look at the world the way he saw it, remember what he believed. Much of what bemused me then, including how I felt and why, are no longer mysteries, and I can write about that time with the greater understanding I have today.

Now that I'm grown, memories of the factory room haunt me still. I find myself there in dreams, sitting in the dirt, trying to trim something to fit into something else. Sometimes I think those are the moments I escaped into fancy, dragging me back to insure I fulfill the five-year contract.

Alta Mae—4

Early August of 1846 had come, and I'd got good enough on crutches to get out of the lodgings, go to market with Carla, and see a few friends, such as they were. I say it like that because some, like Leigh Bottoms, a girl about my age with a mop of flaxen hair, treated me different to see me out of rags. The past winter, me, Leigh, Cedric, and Aggie Thomison had spent many nights in a crawl beneath Teller's Inn in Cross Street, huddled up against the establishment's broad fireplace foundation. Even though we'd been out of the wind and the stone ash dump below the hearth gave off some warmth, we'd shivered against each other to stay warm. Leigh had also been my confederate in buzzing crowds. Being a rum blowen girl, she'd been good at drawing the eye while I did the dipping.

Saw her in Mulberry Bend. There I am on those bloody lifters, and the first thing she asks is for me to give her money.

"I don't have any," I said.

"Where'd you got your togs?"

By then, I'd a mind to tell her nothing, and just looked at her.

Did she have it that I thought I was her better? Won't ever know. She walked away with her conk in the air. I wanted to give her a nose-ender, but I held my anger.

Later, I decided that if we switched places, like as not I'd have said and done the same as she did, seeing a friend in nicer clothes as I went hungry and barely got by.

Also saw Bobby Maze, a young sneeze-lurker of some note, and a good friend of Egan's. Big fellow for his seventeen years. Had friendly blinkers in a pitted mug. Always smelled of cheap snuff. Would give me a dip if I asked. Never too good to talk to me, even on the streets where we might be seen.

Seeing my crutches, he asked, "Why the lifters?"

"I fell in the new sink hole at the Collect."

He laughed until I said I'd been healing up for months. "I'm sorry," he said. Still, he snickered some.

"Almost healed," I said. "The lifters just keep me from turning my ankle." I smiled since I didn't want him to know I'd got huffed by his humor. "Have you seen Egan?"

"He didn't tell you?"

"Tell me what? Ain't seen him since he sold Cedric and me into the factory rooms in the Old Brewery."

"Did that, *did* he?" Bobby smiled grimly, looked at his feet, and shook his head. "I was wondering should I be proud of him for what he done or think him a fool. Now I've decided."

"What are you *on* about?"

"Egan, he signed up to join Colonel Stevenson's regiment of New York Volunteers. He's off to the fight against the Mexicans in California. Told him he were mad, as he'd miss all the excitement here if he left."

Bobby didn't run with the Bowery Boys, but he always threw in with them in a street fight.

"You truly didn't know?" he asked.

"I've been bed ridden, healing a broke foot, staying with a woman."

"She dress you in that smicket?"

Wearing a skirt, blouse, and bonnet on that day, something unusual for me, I nodded.

"Looks good on you," he said, doubtful.

"I hope you're getting by, Bobby," I said more huffy than I meant to, and said my goodbyes.

Troubled by what he told me about Egan, I tried to tell myself it was for the best because big brother had done Cedric and me great harm. For all that, he remained the only family we had in a place where bonds, even if fragile, were earnestly needed. I had to think about forgiving him.

Two days later, Carla said, "You been moping about long enough. What troubles you, girl?"

I didn't want to tell her.

"I see it," she said, lifting my chin with her hand, "giving out

49

what's your business leaves you feeling unprotected. That's fine as long as what you're keeping inside ain't chasing you in circles."

I couldn't see any harm in her knowing, and told her what I'd learned from Bobby about Egan.

"You know I'm working on a plan to get to high tide," she said. "Once I go through with it, I'll be leaving in a hurry. Ivan and me will travel to California to join Paul in San Jose. Before we leave, I'll fetch your Cedric out of the Old Brewery. I thought you two might go with us, maybe find your Egan there."

A joyous thing to hear she'd get Cedric out so soon. Carla smiled to see me smile, but then she must have seen the unhappiness grow in me as I thought about her suggestion.

"What about going with us?" she asked.

My first thought, a foolish one: *I can't up and leave Ma and Papa.* The truth: I didn't want to think of leaving the Points, the only place I'd ever known.

I'd grown used to eating regular, having a warm bed each night, and all else Carlotta Angelo provided me. Still, I'd always thought I'd go back to the streets in time. I didn't dread that. Just the way of things in my life—my lot.

Yet now came a chance to cast lots again. I'd come to like living with Carla. I had to allow that I'd become quite taken with her, even though she was the Catholic aunt of a black man. I told myself Ivan would be no danger to me as long as he respected Carla. He would not go against her wishes.

And Egan—he was family, and I had a need to join him, even while the thought of that gave me a disquiet. Because I knew we'd grown to be a burden for big brother, I could forgive the thing he'd done. Even so, until he proved his trustworthiness, I'd be careful with him.

Pondering these things with a long silence, I'd looked away, and now Carla tried to catch my eye. I decided I should show my willingness before she withdrew the invitation.

"Do I have a choice?" I said, forcing a smile. "Will Cedric, once you help him? I never done the thing you wanted. Your house went down too fast and I were so slow healing up. I reckon I still owe you a service."

Had to give myself that false sense of duty to push back on my fear of leaving the Points.

Carla didn't seem to notice. She nodded and smiled. "Next Tuesday, then."

Cedric—5

The sound of a key turning in the lock on the door awoke the overseer. "Back to work," he said, his voice groggy from sleep.

The door opened and a cove's voice from without said, "Matron here to find a boy."

"Not one o' mine," the overseer said, holding the door to prevent it from opening further.

Since I sat near the door, he had to shove me aside.

"You open that door, Seamus!" came the voice from without, followed by a banging and shoving. Seamus slipped backwards on the muddy floor as the door slowly swung inward. When it had opened far enough, Seamus gave up the fight and stood back.

"Damn it, Brass," he said, "I got quotas to meet. Boss Malcolm will have my bawbag if I'm short again."

The man that stood outside the door had an old woman with him. "Can't be helped," he said. "Were one of our own had her nephew sold into the room by a lad, Egan Brewer, didn't have the right to do it. This here's Mrs. Carlotta Angelo, Boss Malcolm's bookkeeper. Cedric Brewer is her nephew. You in there, boy?"

I could see the woman and didn't know her, so I was slow to speak up. Seamus didn't know nor care about our names.

"I can't haul Egan Brewer up to the Boss to answer for it," Seamus whined. "He joined the New York Volunteers headed to California to fight the Mexicans. Tarnation, Brass, you're putting me in a hot stew."

Hearing Egan had gone west, my heart sank. I decided that if I left the factory room, I'd have no help getting by. A foolish concern, because if my brother had been about, he might well have sold me into service again. In the midst of this brooding, I couldn't help wondering if it would be possible to find Egan in California.

No telling what had happened to Alta Mae. She might still be in one of the other rooms.

William Buckets, seated beside me nudged me with his elbow. "Go!" he said.

I looked at him, shaking my head like a fool.

"Don't worry," he said, "I'll save your spot." His smile grew so big, I saw four big gaps in his ivories.

The fellow without, Brass, I decided, had heard what Buckets said.

"That you, Cedric?" he asked me. He turned to the woman. "They're always so filthy it's hard to tell one from another. That your boy?" he asked, pointing.

"Cedric," she said, "Alta Mae is hoping to see you soon. Come on out."

Hearing my sister's name like that, my blood sped up and I got dizzy, but that was all I needed to get me moving. I rose on my wobbly sticks and made for the door. Brass caught me and helped me through.

I turned and bid farewell to Billy Buckets, as I called him. He gave me another smile. I never saw him again.

Then the woman hurried me up the passage to the creaky wooden stairs, and out. My legs, hardly able to keep up, folded a few times on the stairs. She lifted and carried me the rest of the way. I could see she meant to hurry.

"Alta Mae?" I said.

"I have her hid away, healing up from a broke foot." she said. "You help me, and you'll see her this very day."

Again, my heart lifted.

Outside, she set me on my feet. Summer had come. I felt the sticky heat. The light, the colors, the sounds, became almost more than I could bare. My eyes and ears were drawn this way and that, a most unsettling thing.

Mrs. Angelo had not got me across the muddy street before I cringed in fear of a wagon coming toward us at an even pace. I had nothing to fear from it. Had stepped out of the way for prancer, wagon, and carriage all my life. Yet my idea pot gave me fear all the same. I knew I would not get out of its way in time.

Before I could think to stop her, Mrs. Angelo lifted me again and carried me across. She set me down next to the wall of the distillery across the street from the Old Brewery. I'd always fancied Papa, a known drunkard, probably liked having his liquor so close, even in death.

Mrs. Angelo huddled with me against the wall, offered me bread and cheese. With that to draw my heed, I let go my fear, and feasted.

Alta Mae liked to say that eating while aching with hunger is dancing to tooth music. That it was. I've never eaten anything better since.

Mrs. Angelo then took me into a Aog's Mercantile in Little Water Street, across from Ma. Whilst inside, she pointed out through the door to an alley between two of the Cow Bay houses. "Unseen, I want you to go through there to the back lane and search the privy at the end to the right for a box or a hide full of darby." She gave me a heavy apron too big for me, said, "Wear this so you can hide your findings beneath."

Feeling more fit, I questioned that she should tell me what to do. "Why don't you do it?" I asked.

She lifted a hand to strike me, thought better of it. "Because if I'm seen, someone might try to stop me. Nobody here knows you, I expect."

"There's danger, then, and the darby—coin is it?—don't belong to you."

"Is part mine. There's no danger for you as long as you're quiet about it—just a b'hoy and his toilet. I know you and your sister have spent plenty of time getting by on the streets. Don't tell me you never took something ain't yours. Do this quick, so I can take you to Alta Mae. You come back without it and I won't."

Not a surprise to me that a grown stranger might take command of a child's life since I'd just got free of that sort of thing.

"I'll be here in the mercantile buying a portmanteau and waiting for you."

For Alta Mae's sake, I didn't think I should do otherwise. I left the shop, crossed the street to the back lane, and entered. Cautious, I went all the way to the end, my wobbly legs still giving me grief over taking them for a walk.

Beside a door to a building on my right sat a lone privy. I entered and secured the latch. Light coming through a hole near the ceiling fell on the shit hole and lit the scattering of bugs buzzing around it. The walls were weathered boards nailed in place. None moved when I gave them a try. The floor was brick, mortared together, so no place to hide anything there. The bench looked solid on the side. The seat swung up on hinges for easier cleaning. Lifting it, the reek hit me in earnest, and I stumbled back. I turned away from the smell and the buzzing, took a deep breath, and held it as long as I could whilst looking down into the privy vault and along its sides. Had to do that again and again until I got more used to the odor.

About three foot down along the privy's back wall, I saw an odd board that had no purpose being there, one that looked pegged in place rather than nailed. Had to lean down deep toward the vault to reach it. Weak in the legs, I lost my footing and fell forward into the opening. My right hand caught the back wall, but slipped in the mire until my elbow smacked it hard, stopping me. Got a skeery vision of being stuck down in the slops, calling for help until someone happened by to pull me out. To right myself, I kicked out with my left foot toward the door, striking hard enough to open it. Fretting I'd made too much noise, and whoever Mrs. Angelo feared would come after me, I pulled myself up and out quick. I turned and latched the door shut again.

My second try, I bent down into the opening while hooking a foot around an upright in the left hand wall. Still, I could barely reach the board. Was damp, bespattered with shit, and fairly tight. I worked first one peg, then the other loose. Nothing else held the board and it slipped away and fell. A small place behind it had a nail with a cord tied to it. Spattered and caked as it was, I hadn't noticed the cord running down into the privy vault until I pulled it free. I hauled away on it, and heard the prize break from the slops below before I saw it. A piece of hide tied into a pouch came up as I tugged; a large, weighty bag. If all coin, it would be a bene swag haul, even if slathered with slops.

Could run off with it, I knew, and eventually find Alta Mae. So much could be done with that money, yet I could only think of buying things to eat and maybe letting a warm place to sleep. None of that would be as good as seeing Alta Mae that very day.

I could not keep hold of the slippery bag without tying it around my waist with the long cord. Having made certain the shitty parcel hid well under my heavy apron, I opened the privy door, and returned to Aog's Mercantile.

Mrs. Angelo turned up her nose at my smell. "Did you fall in?"

I didn't answer because I didn't want to give her anything. *Let her fret*, I told myself, and stood by, my hands hidden under the apron.

She took me by the shoulders and shook me. "You *did* find it."

The clerk behind the counter looked at us cutty-eyed, and Mrs. Angelo *did* look to fret a bit.

She grabbed my ear and had me outside in the street quick.

"You *must* have."

Though not a question, I knew I had to answer. She'd clapped her dark blinkers on me and wasn't going to let go until I did. That tempted me to bring the hide out from under the apron and shove it at her, muck and all.

"Found a large purse full of coin," I said ill-mannered, "and a lot of shit." I lifted the apron to give her a look.

She took my right hand, the cleaner one, and led me away toward the Collect. Then she walked on ahead, putting some distance between us, and I struggled to keep up. Thought at first she just made me hurry, until I got a fuller head of my own unwashed reek mixed with that of the filth-dipped hide of coin. The smell had driven her to walk far ahead of me. She knew I'd follow to see Alta Mae.

Since I had to trade it for my sister, I kept a tight grip on that purse.

A frenzy of flies tormented me if I got too close to the horse pies in the road. Some left pies to follow me. Loath to draw stares while thieving, I feared that others in the street might take too much notice of me, even though the people of that neighborhood were used to the muck end of things. Few paid me any mind, and those that did, hurried away.

More and more, the street had a mix of blacks and whites, and when we arrived at a leaning wood frame house, I saw a black man waiting out front beside a wagon in the yard. Mrs. Angelo walked up to him, getting awful close to say something I couldn't hear. He smiled and touched her hand.

I heard Alta Mae calling me from the porch of the house. She leaned in the doorway, propped on a crutch.

I dropped the hide of coin, and ran to her, yet stopped short. Not because I smelled like a nest of turds. No, forgetting that, I'd have hugged her there and then. Since we'd not done much hugging in the past but to keep warm in the night, I fell suddenly sheepish. My gut turned over and I flayed the floorboards with the tommey and cheese I'd eaten earlier. I turned away from Alta Mae in shame.

Heard her crutch on the porch, and then she stood beside me. "I'm sorry you're not well," she said. "A terrible thing they done to you."

I didn't understand how what Egan did to us had become *a terrible thing* they *done to you.* Not wanting to make a bother, I kept that to myself.

Of course, I'd wondered what had happened to Alta Mae. I looked up, and she must have seen the question in my eyes.

"I got away from them the day they took you," she said. "Crawled down a tunnel, fell in a sink hole, and broke my foot. Carla took me in, give me time to heal. I been trying to find a way to get you out since. Then Carla…well, you know, since you're here now."

"I don't like her," I said.

Alta Mae spoke almost at a whisper. "She has a temper, but she got you out."

I turned away. "Who is she? What does she want from you?"

Alta Mae didn't answer. Felt her hand on my shoulder. "There's more to eat when you're feeling better. Your bath awaits."

"In her lodgings?" I asked.

"I worried over questions like that at first too. Did me little good. She did want something from me I couldn't do. I am none the worse for not doing her bidding. You'll see she's not a bad sort. I cannot tell you everything right now."

My sister helped me up, took me inside to a room on the right where a steaming wash tub sat waiting. Just before Alta Mae shut the door, I saw Mrs. Angelo and the black man enter the house. The woman tried to hold the hide of coins at arm's length, her head tilted away from it. They went into a room across the hall and shut the door.

"Who's the black man?" I asked.

Alta Mae put her finger to her lips to shush me. "Never mind that. Carla deals with him."

I didn't tell her about what Mrs. Angelo made me do, and I hadn't yet said anything about Egan going off to California because I hadn't figured out whether I thought that cause for worry or good riddance.

Alta Mae—5

Sure enough, when Tuesday came, so did Cedric.

Upon arriving with Carla, he hurried to greet me on the porch. I feared he might knock me off my crutches. Ashamed to say, relief came as he turned away to hash. And *not* because I feared the fall. The sudden feeling that I'd failed Cedric left me unworthy to hug him. Worse, after he'd finished his mess, he got small and quiet, like *he* thought the same.

I told him what happened to me, and he had few questions about it.

Seeing his unease came from anger at Carla and being troubled about Ivan, I grew calmer.

I'd prepared him a bath, and as he soaked, I answered his questions about them, and told him about Egan going to California with Colonel Stevenson's regiment of New York Volunteers.

"An overseer in the factory room said that about Egan," Cedric said, "and though I want to find him, what he did to us...."

"Yes, and you suffered the worst," I said, "but he is family and we must forgive him. I've decided we should join Egan in California."

Cedric had a sulky look and became quiet like he did when he wasn't taking news well. I chose not to tell him about us traveling west with Carla and Ivan.

"Come out once you're dressed and we'll go," I said.

"To California?" He still looked troubled.

"Yes. Don't take too long."

Ivan had hired a wagon and two, which stood in the yard awaiting our departure. Cedric remained in the lodgings while we loaded the wagon. I jumped up into the bed of the thing, waiting for Cedric to join us.

Cedric—6

Alta Mae always made out that I did as she said, even though I'd changed her mind plenty of times. To get my way had always been a fight that left us both with hard feelings.

Since Alta Mae had made her decision about going to California to find Egan, I had to decide if wanting something different was worth the fight.

I trusted she'd thought it through, yet I was of two minds about her idea, neither a comfort.

Sitting in the bath she prepared for me, I tried to decide what I thought about our big brother. I remained drawn to him. He had been obliged to us as family before he decided to earn off our misery. Did he regret what he'd done? Alta Mae meant for us to forgive and forget. Could I do that? I knew that if we went west, I'd have a long time to get used to the idea, and maybe think of ways to work it out with him.

Or had the time come for Alta Mae and me to be on our own hook? I leaned toward that since, lately, that's mostly what we'd done. The difference would be that we'd not keep trying for big brother's help because it wouldn't be there. We'd have to think about how to get on for a year and more. That meant getting off the streets, finding paid labor, lodgings, all while dodging those who would want to claim us for their own use; the pious, who would put us in homes as labor, and the kidsmen that would run us hard with their bands of child thieves. A difficult undertaking, the more I thought about it.

So that left deciding whether staying and making a life in the points would be harder and more frightening than going west. The more I thought of it, the more I began to see some good in going to California; something new in a place where folks were fired to go. I reckoned the growing towns would have plenty of paid labor and commerce, and the citizens, many of them rubes, would therefore occasionally have wages in their pockets.

My ability to see the world had little improved—that clogged lead pipe I looked through hadn't cleared much. I didn't know that, nor that it mattered. I knew little of the dangers of the West; the lawless towns and people, the vicious animals, and the savage Indians. Yet I had survived hardship; I'd endured suffering and found my way out of it—by luck, certainly—but that gave me a bit of courage.

Alta Mae had said she'd wait for me in the yard in front of the house.

The bath had gone cold. I got out and dried. As I dressed in the rigging Alta Mae gave me—newer togs than I'd seen in a long while—I felt changed, new somehow. I put on the shoes and socks she'd left for me, and I felt ready.

A looby kid at perhaps eight years of age then, I went to join Alta Mae, figuring she'd packed up what we'd need, and we'd just walk away down the street, heading west. In my happy mood, I dismissed thoughts of hardship and hunger. With the warm summer nights, how hard could it be? We'd beg, borrow, and steal all the way there.

Alta Mae—6

By and by, Cedric came out, looked at me funny, and asked. "Where are they taking us?"

"We're all traveling to California," I said. "Carla has a brother, Paul Romano, there."

Cedric stood, hands on his hips, red-faced stroppy. "I ain't going with those people," he said. "Get down from there and go with me."

"No, I'm going with them, and you should come too."

Cedric rarely went against my wishes. He stared at me, his mouth working to find words that didn't come. Tears grew in his blinkers.

"No," he said at last, stomping a foot into the dirt. Cedric had grown little, and got so thin in the eight months he'd been locked away. He looked weedy and helpless, and that gave me an idea.

"Then you'll be all alone here. Small as you are, with no one to protect you, how long before one of the missionary ladies catches you and puts you in a home, maybe a Catholic one."

Carla looked curiously at me.

Cedric danced back and forth on his thin legs, grimaced and held his left knee for a moment, biting his lip.

"Weak as you are from months working in the dark, you won't do them much good," I said. "Like as not, they'll give up on you and serve you for supper one night. That'll be your end."

Carla hid her growing smile.

In a conniption fit, Cedric fell to his knees and pounded the ground with his little fists.

I'd never seen him so torn. Now tears gathered in *my* eyes. "I reckon I'll cry about it now," I said, allowing the upset to catch in my voice, "since I won't know about it when it happens."

"Please, don't go," he wailed. "I'll do anything if you'll stay."

Ivan's blinkers grew wide and his brow corduroyed as Cedric went on with his pleading and blubbering. Carla looked about, perhaps to see if those in the street were growing alarmed by the loud squall.

"I won't know," I said sadly, "because I'll be in California with Egan."

Sobbing and wiping away his tears so he could see, Cedric looked up at me. I think he saw my will would not be shaken. A moment later, he got up and took a trembly step toward me. I jumped down and quickly gathered him into the wagon. He collapsed between the two trunks in the bed with us and went on weeping into the crook of his arm.

Ivan drove us into the street.

Eager for the journey and still fearful of what lay ahead, dismayed to have played Cedric so, but glad to have him with me, my stomach was a carcass full of quivering worms.

Cedric—7

What I discovered in the yard out front surprised me—the wagon I'd seen upon arriving, now loaded, Alta Mae in the bed, Carla and her black man on the seat.

The fight with Alta Mae turned out to be over whether we'd go with them or on our own. I *did not* want to go with that sly woman. She got me out of the Old Brewery to serve her own schemes, and I didn't trust she wouldn't make me do more. One thing to take risks for myself, another to be forced to do it for another.

Untouched by any of my arguments, Alta Mae's eyes remained cold-steady, and I lost that fight. In the end, I told myself I could not let her go off with those strangers unprotected. If she expected to get to California, she'd need me to see her there.

—∞—

We headed first to Albany, New York. Never having been more than a few miles from the Points, I had no notion how far we'd go to get there, let alone what it would be like to go all the way to California.

Wagon and all, we boarded a barge at the Hudson River. A steamboat would tow the barge upriver. Other passengers with their wagons, carriages, or simply their baggage also boarded. Some looked to be of a higher station, and others wore togs not so different from our own. Considering my clothes, I grew puffed up on the notion that someone not destitute might mistake me for an equal. That would be the first time in my life that might have happened.

Then I saw that because we had a black man with us, the only passengers willing to greet us were a black man and his mulatto woman companion. Like we carried the pox and everyone could see it. Took the wind out of my sails.

As we set out, afraid I'd fall in and drown, I huddled in the bed of the wagon under blankets. The ride became steady enough once

64

the steamboat took up the slack from the cables and moved away from the dock. The sounds of water slapping the hull, the horns of other boats in the distance, and the cry of gulls overhead, drew my interest. I poked my head up to look around, got curious enough to conquer my fear, and climbed down from the wagon.

Although I'd seen steamboats at dock and in the distance on the river, until then I'd no good notion of how they took the water. A wet affair. Water, spraying from the great wheels and thrown by the wind, spattered us. The din of noise didn't stop. I thought the steamboat would become tired and have to rest. Worked for a short time, I did, in a lathe shop, sweeping up the shavings. The lathes ran from a steam engine that had to be shut down from time to time and fed oil. Don't know how the steamboat, big as it was, kept it up for so long.

Alta Mae stood at the stern of the barge, she said to watch the water foam, yet the biggest foam came off the big wheels of the steamboat in the opposite direction. I thought she watched the city growing smaller in the distance. She had a sad look when she turned my way.

Good, I decided, maybe she'll want to turn back. Of course, that couldn't happen until we'd arrived at Albany. By then, I figured, her sadness would have lifted. I'd set my mind on going where Alta Mae went. Without liking it, I tried to settle into that purpose.

She grew dauncy, stumbled to the taffrail, and flayed over the side. Carla came to her aid, and I overheard Alta Mae say, "I'm afraid I may be with child."

"No, darling," Carla said, chuckling. "You're just seasick."

"We're not on the sea."

"All the same…"

I didn't like Carla calling my sister "Darling."

Mrs. Angelo and her black man, Ivan, spent most of their time standing in the stem, looking past the steamboat in the direction we headed. Alta Mae had said he was her nephew. As close as they stood, I feared they might be lovers. He looked a little pale for a black cove. Probably not pale enough to be a decent sort.

Once the newness of travel wore off and day had been replaced by night, I grew bored and returned to my sad state of upset. Again,

I hid in the wagon under blankets, and must have slept until roused to make room for Alta Mae.

"Where are they?" I asked.

"Carla and Ivan are sleeping under the wagon," she said.

I listened to hear the sounds of hogmagundy, but heard only snoring.

Whilst awake, I noted that the overcast had cleared and the stars fairly poked out of the sky. I'd never known there to be so many. I watched their beautiful glimmering light until I returned to sleep.

—⁂—

In the morning, clouds had returned and with them rain. Ivan secured a canvas over the wagon to help keep us dry.

We arrived at Albany and transferred to a packet boat on the Erie Canal. After removing our belongings, Ivan had returned the wagon to a cove waiting for it.

The day went on dreary and wet, with much rain.

Fool that I was, I said and did as little as possible to make certain the others knew I remained unhappy.

We set out, our packet boat pulled by a team of mules. The numerous passengers were of the lower stations, perhaps thirty in all. Carla got friendly with some of the women, Alta Mae at her side. I didn't like that either. The boat had a large cabin on it with windows open to let in the air. Smelled good outside most of the time.

Ivan and I joined many of the passengers in spending time on the deck atop the cabin. We kept to ourselves, and I put some distance between him and me.

With nowhere to go, I whiled away my time looking about at the scenery, listening to the birds, seeing things I'd never seen before; a snake slipping through the water in rippling, spreading "S" shapes, a furry beast that swam, blue birds, and red birds. My favorites, the black birds with split tails, flit this way and that quick enough to catch flying bugs. Geese passed over in numbers I'd never seen before, great spear points in the sky, some so low and close to us the honking of the birds drowned out other sounds. The land all around changed as we moved, from tilled earth and crops, to hills with jutting rocks and some marshy places, to forest, and much more, nearly all of it green!

Ivan caught me looking about with my bone box hung open and my blinkers gone wide with awe at what I saw. He smiled and nodded his approval. I swiftly pulled a scowl over my mug, and he chuckled. I hated him for it.

If Carla or Alta Mae looked at me, I'd turn away and huddle into myself. I would not let them believe I had decided we did the right thing. I would not let myself think that either.

We passed beneath different types of tall bridges and through locks that could raise and lower boats into parts of the canal with differing water levels.

Most delightful of all, we passed over brooks and rivers on canal bridges filled with water. A thing to see! I overheard passengers talking about them, a cove telling his woman companion, "Bridges that carry water are called aqueducts." I didn't hear proper, and believed for the longest time they were called *aqua ducks*.

Our packet boat stopped to pay tolls. We also stopped in small towns along the way, to let passengers off, take new ones on, and to switch out the teams of mules. We had the chance to go into those towns for supplies or to stay the night and catch another, later packet boat, yet we did not leave the one we rode.

At night, everyone onboard had a small pallet inside the cabin to sleep on. We also all huddled inside during the rain. I was in out of the rain on our second day when Ivan caught me in the corner of the cabin with my hand in my pants. He moved to sit between me and others, and spoke in a whisper. "What are you doing, boy?"

"Not that it's your funeral," I said, "but I've a spoon in my gut that gets into my knob and makes it stand out. My brother Egan told me to rub it to make it go down."

"What in *Hell* are you *on* about?" His blinkers pinched in like he'd stubbed a toe or something.

Though I'd become a bit frightened, I explained, "See, I swallowed a spoon when I were very little. Egan said lots of boys do that without meaning to."

"You ain't swallowed no *spoon*" he said, looking more like he'd grown angry. "If you *had*, you'd've *choked* to death."

With the growing fear of Ivan, the spoon had left my knob.

He had me trapped in the corner and I couldn't see past him well. I remember how small my voice sounded as I asked, "Why, then, does it get big?"

And what had looked like a scowl spread into a smile. He chuckled, covering his mouth to make it quieter. "You are a queer sort, Cedric." He chuckled some more, and I thought he teased me now. Yet his next words came out warm and friendly. "Don't worry about it getting big. It's a good thing." He patted me on the shoulder. "I'll tell you about it sometime."

Relieved he wasn't going to hit me or whatever else I'd feared might happen, I just nodded.

"Don't be touching yourself like that around others. People don't like to see that."

Again, I nodded.

After a time, the rain stopped and we went back out.

—⁂—

We spent four nights onboard. On the evening of the fifth day, we stopped in the city of Buffalo. The steamboat that would carry us on Lake Erie wasn't due to arrive until the next day. At the dock, Carla hired a hand drawn cart with large wheels to load our belongings onto. We stopped for supplies at a mercantile. I was glad to hear Carla tell Ivan to stay outside while we went in. Concluding her business with the clerk, she asked, "Is there a place nearby where a family might sleep out under the stars."

His hooded blinkers cut toward Alta Mae and me. Carla slid a coin across the counter to him.

"Yes, he said, "but you take a chance of inviting danger."

"I am good with a pistol," Carla said. "I shouldn't worry."

He directed us to a small woods at the edge of town where we found a spot in the trees to fetch up for the night. Ivan made a lean-to using canvas hung from the tall wheel of the cart and a tree on one side and secured to the ground with spikes and cord on the other.

Carla collected wood and made a fire. She handed out fresh baked tommey and some cheese from the mercantile. Tasted good, and the fire gave a welcomed warmth. Couldn't help wondering what Carla would want for it, and that led to thinking she probably kept a tab of all she provided, including the travel costs, and one day Alta Mae and I would be given a big bill or she'd ask us to do something at great risk.

As we settled in for the night, each with our own bedroll, I watched Ivan. I saw that he had four pistols in his jacket when he adjusted them so he could lean back at ease. He also kept a rifle among our belongings. I'd seen it tucked between the trunks in the wagon and then in the cart. I imagined getting to one of those barking irons before he did and putting a hole in him. Having so many of them, I figured he must be good with barkers and that discouraged me from such flights of fancy. Still, I worried what he should do with them.

My fancies and worries weren't doing me any good, so I tried to set them aside and watch the fireflies. Since I thought of their lights as tiny signal lamps, I always wondered what they might be saying to each other. As one got close to my arm, I didn't fend it off as I might have done other witless beasties.

Closing my eyes, I listened to the forest sounds: insect songs, twigs and branches rubbing together, and the settling of leaves.

I searched high and low to find sleep. Not certain I found it before a rustling noise awakened me, and I smelled tobacco mixed with something sweet. Though afraid to, I reached to touch Ivan's shoulder some feet away. He sat up quick, a pistol in his hand, and I cowered down.

From the direction of the noise, further sounds came, a scampering among the brush, moving away.

Ivan got up and dashed toward the sound.

I'd heard of bears in the forest. He'd be no match for such a beast. In that moment, I knew the black man stood as our only protection. I hoped he would not be harmed; a selfish wish, my concern being for Alta Mae and me alone.

Ivan returned, saying, "Whoever it was, got away."

Mrs. Angelo and my sister had been awakened by the commotion. Carla sniffed the air.

"I smell something too," Alta Mae said. "Is that..."

"Vanilla," Carla said.

"Only a fool would try to sneak up on someone in the woods

while smoking aromatic tobacco," Ivan said. "Must have been someone lives nearby, just happened to cross our path and we scared him as much as he did us."

"Or he didn't know any better because he's a city fellow," Carla said.

"Why would you say that?" he asked

She didn't answer, and Ivan let it go.

With time, we all settled back down. I did not think I would sleep.

—◊—

Surprised to find myself awakening around dawn.

In the day that followed, Carla seemed to be the one who'd had little sleep in the night. Her eyelids drooped, and she was slow to speak when spoken to. Ivan led us in packing up to leave, as she stood about, head in hand.

We located the dock and our steamboat and resumed our westward journey. Carla took a seat right away, drowsing on and off.

I had to wonder what had kept her awake in the night. My idea pot kept telling me it might have had something to do with what I'd taken from the privy at Cow Bay.

We would go to St. Louis Missouri and winter over before traveling further west. I had little notion of what that would mean in distance and hardship.

Early on, the travel by water had been easy and pleasant enough, if at times unsettling to my bread bag and shoulder loaf.

The night we'd had an intruder disturb our camp off the road in Buffalo, I'd had a dream that Ma and Papa were striding across the land, headed west. Each step took them half a mile. I drew comfort from the thought that they'd be in California when we got there.

The Steamboat that took us across Lake Erie was much grander than the one on the Hudson. Even so, I'd become so weary of travel on water and the sick feeling it gave me, I found little pleasure in it.

Since I'd been mostly off my feet for more than a week, I'd gained extra time for my injured foot to heal, and felt fit again by the time we reached Toledo, Ohio.

Cedric remained mumpish toward us, and his mood improved but slowly in the next leg of our journey.

In Toledo, we hoped to gain passage on the Wabash and Erie Canal. Turned away from numerous barges too full of goods and passengers to take us, Carla grew impatient. I could see she wanted to hurry.

"Ivan," she said, "secure us a wagon and two."

The man who made the sale to Ivan advised him not to travel through the Great Black Swamp in Ohio. We set out instead heading west through Michigan toward the northeast corner of Indiana.

"After the intruder at our camp in Buffalo," Carla told us, "we shall be quiet and more careful at night." She kept looking back over her shoulder as we moved along.

Ivan must have sensed something was amiss. "Everyone keep an eye out for high pads," he said. "Speak up if you see anyone suspicious along the road."

Rarely saw anyone we might have called a bandit. Occasionally, we passed persons going in the opposite direction or we caught up with some moving slower; travelers, and square countrymen, perhaps going to market.

Ivan had a rifle and several pistols, and made certain Cedric, Carla, and I knew how to load them. He shared out supplies for the loading, and we practiced to learn to do it swiftly. "You keep some of the powder, wad, and shot on your person," he said. "If I drop a gun after firing it, be ready to pick it up and load it."

Cedric seemed pleased with that. I remembered Egan had a no-account pistol at one time, but he'd never let his little brother near it.

Had I not been so boney, I would have ridden in the wagon more easily. The roads being heavily rutted, we had a bumpy, jolting ride much of the time. Ivan did his best to avoid the ruts, and a few of the times he failed, we all had to get down from the wagon and help the team pull it free. The creaking, rumbling contraption tossed Cedric and me about, even though we'd set the trunks, Carla's portmanteau, and my carpet bag in the bed to wedge us in place. Even with the blankets beneath us, the hard wooden bed and especially whatever we leaned against—the side boards, the gate, or trunks—jarred us hard enough to raise bruises.

At times we'd had enough, and walked for a while, yet the pace became too brisk within less than a mile.

Spending our time seeing new things in the forest helped us endure the rough ride. We made certain to point out to each other anything seen moving about. Occasionally we startled deer and others animals on the ground. I saw a ginger-haired wolf at a distance, and something that must have been a pig. Many times, we merely heard something large moving through the brush in a hurry and saw nothing, even if we strained to get a look. Even more life appeared up in the trees than on the ground, small furry creatures and many different sorts of birds. Bird and insect song came from every direction.

I note these things common to forests because, for one raised in the Points, the discovery of so much life was bewitching. In the city, I'd known little of animal life beyond horses, dogs, cats, and birds. Of cattle, swine, and fish, I'd mostly known their flesh as I ate it on the occasions I'd been lucky enough to have meat.

The land had some small parts with tall grasses, and some cleared, tilled soil with crops near small towns. Tall trees covered the rest. I remember wondering if we'd ever see the end of them. The forests grew so thick, even in full sun, the leafy treetops shut out much of the light and darkened the forest floor. Dawn and dusk of each day, the green of it all so much the same in the dim light, I feared I might miss hidden dangers.

We stopped in small towns along the way to buy supplies. Carla hurried us in and out of those towns in a way that told me she feared being seen. She had a troubled look about her much of the time.

About ten miles beyond a small town called Hillsdale, two men bearing pistols and having long, fat blades in their belts, stepped from the cover of brush along the edge of the road. Raising their pistols toward us, their aim stalled the moment they found themselves facing Ivan aiming two pistols at them. He'd done that so fast, I hadn't seen it coming. Glancing over at Carla, I saw she had the rifle aimed. I had to wonder about their readiness. Although surprised enough by Ivan's speed, I wouldn't have expected such steadiness from Carla, at her age. My own hand had gone slower to the handle of the knife in my pocket.

When the would-be bandits had first stepped into the road, they'd looked something like madmen, as if they thought that should rattle us. All in their eyes, it didn't wind the blue-steel spring in me. I'd had much worse give me the evil eye. Rough-looking fellows for those parts, I expect. Nothing we hadn't seen before in the Points.

The larger of the two, a black-haired, dark-eyed cove, was dressed in stained buckskins and a planter's hat with a bent brim, as if he'd slept in it. He looked like he'd been about to speak, but remained silent upon seeing Ivan's pistols, his bone box hung open.

The other, a middling-sized fellow with pale eyes, a scarred chin, and a head of wild red hair, dressed in black canvas togs and had a red bandanna, too easy to see in the green forest. He looked like he might make a try despite the odds, until Ivan said, "No." Quietly as he'd said the word, the two heard it well enough and they backed down.

I didn't have time to be afraid since it seemed we'd come upon them so fast. Yet I got such a good look at them because we moved past slowly. Gave them a steady gaze, I did, and Cedric did too. They looked confused, and I figured they were used to having their way with farmers carrying their goods to market. They lowered their weapons as we passed, Ivan standing and turning with his pistols, Carla keeping a bead on them. Our team pulled us on by, and we left them behind. I don't think they had any desire to follow.

Following that, I caught Cedric gazing at Ivan now and then with a thoughtful look, as if sizing him up anew. I think he liked what he saw.

As we made camp one night, Ivan asked Cedric, "Will you take charge of building and lighting our fires each night?" He offered a box of spunks.

I knew little brother would be excited to have the job, but he just nodded his head without looking at Ivan and took the matchbox.

Even so, Cedric's distrust and scorn for the black man let up some after the bandits.

Little brother's dislike for Carla remained. If anything, it deepened. By the time we got into Indiana, his brooding had got to be too much.

"Tell me what has you so ill-tempered," I said.

"You won't want to hear."

"Still, I'll listen."

Cedric pulled on a face, said, "She made me steal something from a privy beside our Ma in the Points. That fellow sneaking into our camp in Buffalo might be the one who we robbed coming to get her. It were a lot of money."

"We don't know if that were man or beast," I told him. "Might've been a woman returning home after meeting up with her lover." I laughed as if we spoke of a lighthearted matter.

He looked at me with his blinkers squinted up hard. "She's up to no good, and we could be the ones to suffer for it."

"Even if you're right," I said, "we've long since left him behind."

"We should hope…"

—⚬—

I did not want to believe him. Even so, his words troubled me enough over a couple of days that I decided to talk to Carla about it. I didn't find the right moment until we'd got well into Indiana. While helping her break down our camp from the night before, I told her what Cedric had said.

She turned to me angrily. "I don't answer to you, and certainly not the b'hoy."

I let the matter go with the idea that I should talk to her when she'd fully awakened—she tended toward grouchiness in the mornings.

—⚬—

The next day, I tried again as we made camp in the evening. We were laying out our bedrolls. Cedric busied himself collecting wood and building a fire. Ivan had unhitched the team, removed their tack, and was busy hobbling them.

When I brought it up, Carla gave me an angry look meant to discourage, but I went on. "Cedric doesn't like not knowing what's behind the risks he's made to take."

"He is an orphaned boy," she said, glancing with caution at Ivan, and keeping her voice low. "He doesn't have a choice."

Her manner told me Ivan didn't know about the theft.

Again, though I now shared Cedric fears, I let the matter go.

—⚬—

At our next camp, while Cedric and Ivan spent time at a stream, looking to catch some fish, I brought it up again. Carla was adding stones to the campfire to hold up a pan in hopes of frying their catch.

"We just want to know about that hide full of coin," I said. "It's stolen, ain't it?"

"Oh, it's the two of you now, is it?"

"Yes. He's my brother, and I must look out for him."

"He benefits from what I had him do, as do you. You two are fed and kept safe."

"We will share your risks, just want to know why. If someone is coming for you, we should know about it."

The twitch in her lip told me she hadn't expected we'd put together the theft from the privy with the intruder to our camp in Buffalo.

"He did the job for me you couldn't do. You said yourself you owed me."

"You're telling me Cedric got your savings out of the house in the sinkhole, and he says he got them out of a privy."

"No," Carla said. She shook her head, took a deep breath, and let it go. Some of her anger went away with it, and she looked at me squarely, as if trying to decide if she should be honest. She set down the stone she held.

"Boss Malcolm has a brothel in the cellar of one of the Cow Bay houses. I am, well…I were the bookkeeper for that and the sweatshops in the cellar of the Old Brewery. I got the tallies from the girls each day, and ran totals on the services rendered, while the brothel's cash carrier, a cove named Lowell Carson, would provide me with the collected funds to match. Coming up short a few times, he suggested I adjust my totals to match what he give me. The first time, it weren't enough to trouble me, but he did it again and the amount were more. I adjusted my totals again. After that he began to do it more often, the amount slowly increasing. Quickly, I didn't want to protect him without getting a slice. I made a deal to work with him to skim the honey and split the take."

I knew of Boss Malcom. Everyone in the Points did. "Didn't the Boss see funds were missing?"

"No, our take being such a small amount of the whole, he didn't notice, yet the funds grew into something large over time. Lowell were the cash carrier for our scheme too. We'd put the skimmed funds in a small purse that he'd pocket, and I'd take the rest, along with the rigged books to Boss Malcolm. A bit of a dandy for the points, Lowell got to fretting over our designs. He asked me each time we met if I thought the Boss had got suspicious. Fearing Boss Malcolm might send some roughs to search his office or lodgings, Lowell would talk of the need to find just the right place to hide our growing pot of money. Two years ago, I asked for my half, and he agreed that at our next meeting he'd hand it over. Sure enough, he kept true to his word. Sitting there in his office, I noted a privy smell about the coins, even as he give them to me in a purse. I hid the purse in my house two years ago. That were what I wanted you to retrieve for me."

"What were the funds in the hide from the privy?"

"What had accumulated since the first time we split the take, two years ago."

Carla smiled, then chuckled before continuing. "The day we saw my house had gone down the hole for good, it came to me while we stood there looking into the pit that Lowell had always needed to visit the privy right after our daily meeting. We always met at one o'clock, following his midday meal, so I hadn't made much of it. I would get up to leave, and he'd often say something about needing the privy before leaving out the back door of his office to the lane running behind the house. So, standing on the lip of the sink hole, I made a plan to find out if my suspicion were right. The next day, at the end of my meeting with Lowell, I went out the front of the house, walked through the side alley to the back lane, and watched around the corner to see if Lowell had indeed gone into the privy. There were just the one privy there at the end of the lane, right next to the door he'd gone through. I thought he'd already be inside by the time I got there, so I waited to see him leave. Took a while, yet he finally come out. When he did, he looked about cutty-eyed, as if making certain no one had seen him. That's how I knew he hid our take in that privy somewhere."

Carla placed a hand gently on one of mine, looked at me carefully, and said, "We're using those funds to get away to the West. In his last letter, one I received shortly before we left the Points, Paul said that the Bay of San Francisco is a place of good fortune, that there's much to do, plenty of possibility. I've never known him to take to a place as much as he's done with California, and he's been to many parts of the world."

I couldn't help smiling to see her eagerness.

Carla gripped my hand and lost her smile. "I thought taking the full darby a rum bite, but we may have a problem."

"You think Lowell Carson is coming for you?"

"No, Not Lowell. He has brother, Fletcher Carson, who protects the girls at the brothel, makes certain there are no deadbeat clients. Fletcher also works for a shylock, breaking people who don't pay up their loans on time. He's a big fellow with a chunk of his left cheek missing. The one on his face," she added with a grin. "Folks say it was taken by grape shot when he were in the British Royal Navy. His whole mug is terrible disfigured. He's a deserter, came to the points before Lowell did."

"Is he as frightening as he sounds?" I asked.

"He is, and I don't mean to make light of it. If he's after us, we have something to fear."

"Would he come all this way?"

"I don't know," Carla said. "I worry because of what we smelled that night in Buffalo. Fletcher Carson smokes a pipe with a sweet-smelling tobacco, one that smells of vanilla."

"Just how much money did Cedric take?"

"Close to seventeen hundred dollars in coins of all sizes, some of it foreign—Spanish, British, and French mostly. Lowell had converted all the soft, the bank bills and other folding credit, into gold and silver coins, probably fearing that if shit got to them, they'd be worthless. Were all your brother could do to carry it."

Again she smiled, and this time I didn't like it. She had not been fair with Cedric.

"You know I'm going to tell him about this."

"Yes."

"Why did you keep it from me?"

"Giving out what's my business leaves me feeling vulnerable, something like sleeping in a room with the door and windows open. Always been that way. I keep my business to myself until I'm good and ready to share it. You're the same way, and I try to respect that. I still don't know anything about you from before I grabbed your ear at the sinkhole."

She'd said that about me before and she was right.

"You tell your brother all about it and make certain he knows to keep an eye out for Fletcher Carson. He ain't like those jinglebrains that tried to rob us on the road a few days back. No, he's a Jack cove, and would be ready and quick. He'd try to get Ivan first, leaving us defenseless."

She saw the fear that gripped me with her words. "Don't worry about Ivan. Like his father, he's a sea crab. Started out in life a ship's boy for the pirate, Benito de Soto, and learned the trade of killing at a young age. Fletcher turns his muscle on deadbeat clients, people not known to give as good as they get. Ivan is more than a match for Fletcher in a fair fight. I've told him about my fears."

I knew nothing of the pirate, yet I heard her confidence in her nephew.

Carla was a woman with a fearless fortitude, I decided. Where she got that, I didn't know. I suspected she'd had a hard life and survived much that would surprise me. Although I had little to hide but petty thievery, I had no intention of telling her about my life. Because of what she'd said about sharing her own business, I knew better than to ask about her past.

Even so, as we went on with preparing the camp, I watched her with new curiosity. For an old woman, she was indeed something different. I found myself holding her in high regard.

Cedric—8

I had equal parts love and hate for Egan.

He'd been a father to me when I was little, finding ways to get me fed and keeping me safe in moments I thought I'd been done for. His pale green eyes had the power of jewels to draw my own blinkers, as I looked to him to know my way in all things.

He'd also taken me from the world and put me in the dark of a factory room to toil away my days with little to keep me company but my hopeless thoughts and those of the other children with me. That would have gone on for years had Carla not taken me in thrall for her scheme.

Perhaps I hated her to make smaller my hard feelings toward my brother. I suggest that since, looking back, I might have willingly helped her if I'd been given a choice.

As I said, I would have been about eight years old at the time. Hard to know for certain since I don't know my birthday. At that age, I could not have found the words to reveal these things about myself. Nor could I have so easily explained my thinking, yet what I write here gives a good idea of how I felt, and makes some sense of the bigoted, brooding little boy I'm putting on the page.

Egan had won my heart at an early age, as I suppose most older sibling may do with their younger ones. He played games with me he wouldn't make time for with Alta Mae. We played knucklebones, a game I could carry in my pocket. Egan kept a bat and ball for knurr and spell. Playing that, we broke some windows and had to run for it a few times. That was truly the most fun part of the game. Later on, once he started sleeping in a tool shed and had a place to put things down, he kept a set of dominos, and we found rules for many games with those.

He could also be mean as hell. One time when I'd been about six, I saw him with this skinny, dark-haired girl. They were eating apples and talking on a stone wall at the edge of the Cow Bay property. Hungry, I came up friendly and wanting to say hello, maybe get some of his apple. Egan told me to stay away, and I must've got a hurt look because the girl laughed at me, said, "Who is this stray?"

"He's the town bummer, is what he is," Egan told her. "Follows me around and tries to take what's mine."

He picked up a rock off the top of the wall and hurled it at me hard. Struck me in the forehead. She laughed again. I turned away and ran so they wouldn't see my tears and the blood dripping down my mug.

Egan had just begun to move away from Alta Mae and me then. We held him back, I knew, while he tried to make his life better. Plenty of times he pretended not to know us. He forbid Alta Mae and me from coming close to him when he was with the Bowery Boys. A hurtful thing, but I tried to understand.

Even so, we saw him in a street brawl between the Bowery Boys and the Dead Rabbits in Mulberry Street. Must have been fifty or more to a side. The street had cleared quickly of anyone not wanting to take part. The coppers, knowing about the coming brawl, had assembled a block away in either direction. As they'd done with past gang fights, they would only step in if the savagery threatened to spread to more valuable properties.

Egan and his armed crew had the most color. With their red shirts, they already looked bloodied. He stood like a man, all seventeen years of him, holding the bat we used to play Knurr and Spell. The Dead Rabbits, in their ragged secondhand finery, looked like ordinary criminal roughs. All teeth, wild blinkers, and sweaty pink mugs. They bore arms much like the ones the Bowery Boys carried. Some had cudgels, others had weapons for cutting. Both sides also had objects to throw, yet the first volleys that flew between the gangs were curses. Not long after, broken bottles joined the oaths, followed by brickbats, and paving stones. Cries of pain by those struck set the two parties moving. A great roar went up from both, and they ran at each other, the combatants beating their enemies with bricks and clubs, cutting and stabbing with iron and steel.

Afeard for his safety, I tried to keep my eyes on Egan. Became such a tumult, I lost him. Saw a sword swinging wild, cutting red tracks through Dead Rabbit shirts and trousers, saw a Dead Rabbit with a cleaver, swinging at a red shirt. Because of the color, I couldn't tell if he made the cut.

Egan's weapon, our bat, appeared. Saw it held high before it came down hard on a fellow's head. The one with the cleaver came at big brother, slashing toward his gut. Egan took a cut to his left arm to stop it, then swung the bat to block another slash. He lost the bat, rolled onto the ground, and stood up holding an iron rod someone must've dropped. The cleaver came at him again, and Egan held it off, turned swiftly, and swung the rod. The two weapons slammed together with a ring of metal I easily heard over the tumult. The Dead Rabbit's grip on the cleaver shuddered, and he nearly dropped it. Egan swung again, braining the fellow.

From behind, a coward struck big brother in the head with a copper's truncheon. I cried out to him as he fell, and tried to go to his aid. Alta Mae held me back, and finally had to hold me down.

Once the fighting ended, we discovered Egan lying in the road, bloodied above the left ear. Blood-spattered Bowery Boys took him away, though we told them he belonged to us.

We worried needless through the night. Saw him the next day in Little Water Street. He said he was well, but for a headache and the pain in his left arm. He showed me he'd had twenty-six stitches to close the cleaver wound. "Bobby Maze done me up," he said. "Got me corned enough I hardly felt them go in. Said he were sorry to miss the brawl, and that stitching me up were nearly as good."

Bobby Maze, a fellow with a pocked, yet handsome mug, was an old friend of Egan's, good at rolling the well-heeled after throwing snuff in their faces. As they sneezed and carried on, he'd relieve them of their valuables.

Big brother seemed glad to see us in a way he hadn't for a long while. Seeing he yet lived, a powerful dread had lifted.

"Found our bat in Mulberry Street," I told him. "To keep it safe, I hid it in the downspout toward the back of Farley's Bucket Shop."

He gave a big smile, said. "When my arm feels better, we'll have a game. It'll be a fizzing game with a bat that's seen battle." He clapped me on the shoulder too hard, but I shrugged it off.

He'd tossed an exciting notion into my idea pot, and he stirred it in by mentioning it a few times over the next couple of days, saying the bat would have extra power for all the blows he gave the Dead Rabbits with it. After he'd healed up, I asked him about having a game nearly every time I saw him. Egan never again had time to play knurr and spell with me.

I did wonder who won that brawl in Mulberry Street since no one said. In the end, perhaps it didn't matter. Both sides had said they would not be trod upon by the other, and I suppose their deeds made that known, if it wasn't already. They had delivered that message to one another many times before and would do so again and in some much greater battles in the future.

Watching Egan in that fight, I couldn't help thinking I could never be that brave, that I would surely stop dead before stepping into such danger. Swamp me if I didn't still cry when I cut my finger. Proud to have him as my brother, Egan had my admiration and my love, despite his now-and-then cruel streak. To my mind, he stood as tall as would those giants that were supposed to be my parents, should they get to their feet.

As we traveled, I'd come to miss Egan more and more. If he'd been with us, we would not have had to deal with Carlotta Angelo.

Well into September now, we camped just outside of Terre Haute, Indiana. The next day, we would arrive in the city with the hope of finding passage on the Wabash River. From there, we would find our way into the Ohio River, the Mississippi River, and finally to St. Louis, Missouri.

Sitting by our campfire, waiting for a meal of beans and johnnycakes, I tried not to enjoy the warm feeling that came from the thought that I'd be reunited with Egan in California. The question of his loyalty to us remained. What I expected might regain our trust escaped me, yet somehow I knew I would not let that get in my way, that I'd embrace him and allow his sway over my life again in a heartbeat. I was milk and water when it came to my older brother.

Alta Mae had told me about a scheme Mrs. Angelo had had with a partner, Lowell Carson, to bilk funds from Boss Malcolm.

Carla had indeed used me to rob that partner. Now, Carson's brother, a cove named Fletcher, had come after us, just the sort of thing I feared.

At least Carla had brought a strong, capable man with us. Ivan had easily fended off the two bandits that tried to rob us. He did indeed have a way with barkers. Though I didn't trust him fully, and would not ask anything of him, he'd taught me to load his flintlock pistols—three different types—and his percussion cap rifle. He taught me something of fishing by requiring my help at the task. We feasted on the fish we'd caught. Rarely had I eaten so well, and I thought that becoming a fisherman might be the life for me.

Without me asking for it, Ivan had begun to teach me how to move through the forest silently while hunting, and how to listen past the closest forest sounds. He showed me how to know one animal from another by their footprints, droppings, and something he called spoor; a scent left behind, the height of a broken stem, twig, or branch, and the path an animal might choose.

"After supper," Ivan said, "I'll teach you to fire the rifle. What do you say?"

I was delighted, but would show no eagerness to him. "Yes," I said carefully, "that would be a good thing."

He gave a twitch of a knowing smile. In that moment, I believed he saw me as a lowly creature that had done little more to get on in life than beg and steal, and that I would easily take from him without showing gratitude. Little did I know, I merely saw *myself* that way.

Damn him. How could he be that smart? Hadn't Egan told me the black man had brains little better than an animal? A fice dog, he sat whittling away at a long, forked branch, as Carla and Alta Mae prepared victuals for him. Where was *his* gratitude?

Yes, I'd got in a pucker. I hid that away because I wanted his lessons.

Alta Mae, stirring a pot of beans and salt pork, paused to say, "I want to learn too."

"No," I said, "this is for men. You wouldn't be able lift the rifle."

"You ain't a man," she said, "yet you're learning. You won't be able to lift it either."

Carla, flipping Johnnycakes in a pan, winked at her. "Stir!" she said sternly, gesturing toward the pot of beans.

"Yes, you may learn as well," Ivan said. "This fork will help you both hold the rifle steady." He held up the forked branch, now pluck free of its leaves and twigs. "I'll also teach you rules for handling firearms that help prevent dangerous mistakes."

Alta Mae gave Ivan a big smile.

Whilst my surliness deepened, I knew better than to make trouble if I wanted to keep gaining from his knowhow.

—⚹—

Alta Mae didn't like firing the rifle. She couldn't hit anything. She complained about the loud noise, and that the weapon's butt cracked into her shoulder too hard. I suffered the same and didn't do any better. Even so, I stuck with it. She tried a pistol, then returned to camp to help Carla.

Once she'd gone, Ivan asked, "You still having trouble with that spoon?"

He laughed at me, and I turned to leave.

He grabbed me by the arm and turned me around. "Please bide a moment."

I wanted to kick him, but again decided I'd rather learn from him than make anger.

All serious, he said, "That ain't no spoon in your staff of life. It's supposed to get big like that sometimes. When you're a boy, that staff has a mind of its own, and grows large at the worst times. Once you're grown, though, and with a woman, you'll need that."

What did being with a woman have to do with it? I reckoned he just didn't understand. "When it stands out, it's hard like something's inside, and I can't make water, just like there's a spoon stuck in it. What do you say to that?"

"I know *I* don't have a spoon in me," he said, "yet mine does that, especially if I see a bugarooh woman."

He told me all about how men and women made love, as he put it, how good it would feel once I finally did it, having children, and such like. I'd thought hogmagundy little more than two naked bodies rubbing against one another.

"How's that any less far-fetched than what Egan told me?" I asked.

"Perhaps it's not. Life is a mystery. Little boys swallowing spoons don't enter into it."

Shrugging him off angrily, I returned to camp.

I got Alta Mae alone and told her what Egan had told me, and what Ivan had said.

She laughed at me too!

"That's why you're always yanking on it!" she said, her eyes wide.

"Shush, Carla will hear." I swallowed some of my anger. Didn't feel good going down. "Yes," I allowed, whispering the word through clenched ivories.

She held me by the shoulders, looked me squarely in the eye, said, "What Ivan told is true. I knew most of it. What I didn't, fits with what I did know." Then she frowned. "Egan lied a lot, and had fun teasing you and me both. Were a cruel thing at times. I'm sorry."

"I know he did," I said. That was possibly the first time we'd admitted that to each other.

I kept to myself for the rest of the evening and went to sleep early. Somehow, I had to accept these new notions because I knew Alta Mae had no cause to lie to me about any of it.

Alta Mae—8

On a damp afternoon in late October, the air thick as soup, we arrived in St. Louis. Built of mostly wood and brick, the humble city saw much coming and going in the streets and shops, despite the wet weather. 'Twas the biggest rut in the road we'd seen, with few streets paved. Several partially paved roads, broader than many I'd known, were more difficult to navigate than the dirt ones.

The muck from the roads could not be avoided. We used the boot scrapes beside the entrance to a mercantile where we stopped for supplies, and still added mire to the patchwork of muddy bootprints on the floor inside.

Ivan had taken our belongings on a cart to the Planters Hotel two doors down. He meant to leave from there to find a place to stay nights on his own.

After our business in the mercantile, we went into a small office next door to speak with an agent who booked for a company running wagon trains out of Independence, Missouri. Following a lengthy discussion between Carla and the agent, we left for the hotel.

A girl about my age in a gray smicket and men's shoes way too big, followed us at a distance as we entered the foyer, cleaning up the worst of the mud we tracked in. She carried a bucket and a scraping tool. We walked a distance of about three blocks from the boat, and she was the first child I'd noticed in the city. I stood at the door and looked out along Main Street while Carla talked to the clerk about a room. His false teeth were loose, and his words came out funny.

Looking up and down the lane, I saw fewer people than I might have seen in the points, but also much fewer children on their own. Those I did see followed adult men and women or seemed to be working at some sort of labor. I watched a boy in the road shovel horse pies into a hand cart.

Where were all the urchins? Did the city have laws against

children being idle on the streets, or just fewer children with no parents?

What protected most of the orphans in the Points from ending up in orphanages or having to earn a crust in the service of others was the large numbers of us on the streets. A nuisance, yet the city seemed to have little desire to take charge of us all. Perhaps it also didn't have the means.

Come to think of it, I'd not seen many children on their own in any of the cities and towns we'd passed through.

I knew that the hardship of coming to America, finding work, and beginning a new life often left those without means homeless and took the lives of many men and women, some of them parents survived by one or more children. At the time, I had yet to understand that New York City saw immigrants in much greater numbers than other cities and towns in the United States.

I remembered Egan telling me, "Life on the streets may be hard for us, but at least we have the freedom of choices." As he'd said that, it had little meaning. Now, I worried that if Cedric and I became separated from Carla and stranded in some smaller city or town, we would have little chance of keeping our liberty.

Those thoughts wound up the spring in me, and I wanted to find Ivan right away. As steady as Carla had shown herself to be, I feared for our safety without his protection.

Standing in the entrance to the hotel, I saw a figure in shadows across the lane. Something peery about the man, I watched him for a time. Even if I could not see his blinkers, the stranger seemed to be looking in my direction, possibly watching me. When he turned and looked back toward the river, the silhouette of his mug seemed to be missing something from the left cheek. "The one on his face," I remembered Carla saying.

I hurried to the counter where she stood talking with the clerk and interrupted. "The rough missing part of his cheek is across the road, watching us."

Carla said to the clerk, "Please excuse my daughter's rudeness, but a man traveling on the boat with us touched her a few times and tried to get her alone for Heaven knows what obscene purpose."

The clerk looked me up and down, perhaps to fancy what sort of obscene purposes anyone might have for me. He seemed to come up short.

"Do you have a back door we may use? Once the threat has passed, I'll return and book a room. You have our belongings." Carla gestured to the trunks and bags Ivan had left stacked beside the counter.

The clerk set his ivories better in his bone box, said, "This way." He lifted a section of the counter, took us through a back office and into a hall that led to a side door of the establishment.

We found Ivan hiring loft sleeping space from the groom and proprietor of a livery stable, an old, stooped black man named Emile Voss. He was shiny with sweat, and so dark, he looked a bit blue. We drew Ivan away, and told him about the sighting.

"If it's him" he said, "and not just the fears of a child..." He glanced at me, a small apology in his manner. "...then I must hide you three away and find a way to fight him."

He returned to Mr. Voss, who seemed to foresee his request. "You can't have them up there with you."

"They will come down as soon as I return."

"Please, sir," Carla said. "There is a man after my girl. As soon as the threat is gone, we intend to take a room at the Planters Hotel."

He bowed his head as if in thought, then said, "You may go up." He gestured toward a ladder with a dark, claw-like hand.

Cedric started up the rungs.

I listened as I climbed.

"Is a white man you're chasing?" Mr. Voss asked Ivan.

"Yes."

"And are you a free man?"

"Yes,"

"You won't want to use a weapon. Not against a white man in these parts"

"No?"

"Not if you have a choice."

Ivan nodded and went out.

89

Once I stood in the loft, I turned to help Carla onto the platform. Looking about, I saw loose straw where those who hired spots to sleep made their beds, saw old, moldy tack, tools, and something large under an oilcloth. I didn't see Cedric.

"Where is he?" Carla asked.

I looked around, then behind the cloth-draped mound. "I don't see him."

"He's hiding," she said.

The scattering of straw on the floor was missing from a trap door almost hidden in shadows. I lifted it and saw a pile of hay directly beneath.

"No," I said, "he went back down. I must go after him."

She took me by the arm. "It's too dangerous."

I looked her in the eye. "Cedric and me ain't much if we ain't quick and shady. He's gone to watch what Ivan will do. I can be extra eyes and ears for them both. Let me go."

Carla watched me for a moment, perhaps deciding.

"There's no time to think about it," I said. "Trust me."

Another moment passed before she let go. I dropped into the hay below and dashed out of the livery stable into the street, headed back toward the Planters Hotel. Dusk had fallen.

I pulled my bonnet down to shade my mug as best I could, and kept to the shadows of porches as I went. Looking for signs of Cedric among those in the street, I walked briskly, but as casually as I could, pretending to be just a girl on an errand for her mum. Two blocks on, I saw Cedric ahead take a turn into a back lane. I believed that lane would take him to Main Street with a view of the Planters Hotel.

He was crouched down, watching around the corner when I reached him. He'd heard my footsteps and glanced up.

"What—" I began.

"Stubble your red rag," he whispered. I went quiet and crept closer to see what he saw.

Fletcher Carson came out of the office where we'd spoken with the wagon train agent.

A man and woman walked by the opening to the back lane,

90

staring at Cedric and me in a manner I feared might give us away to anyone watching.

Fletcher didn't seem to notice. Larger than what I'd seen of him in shadow, he stood a daunting six feet and more, twenty stones at least, his blinkers, conk, and bone box all set crooked, as if the grapeshot damage had broken most of the bones of his face and they'd healed up wrong. I recognized him as a cove I'd seen before in the Points and steered clear of. When he removed his plug hat to scratch his pale hair, I saw that the scar, which started at his cheek, climbed almost to the top of his head. The shoulders of his coat had ridges that suggested straps lay beneath the cloth, and that told me he carried hidden firearms. He looked to his right and headed back toward where I'd first seen him, the porch of the building across the street from the hotel.

"If Ivan comes along now, he won't see the man hidden in the shadows," I whispered.

"We must mark his position," Cedric said, slipping away from me. "Whistle if you see Ivan coming."

"Come back here, little nimenog." I whispered.

He didn't look back but moved swiftly and quietly along the edge of the building until he reached the long porch, then crawled underneath it. I didn't understand why.

I could not see the cove from where I hid. The business in the ground floor of the building had gone dark, closed for the night. People walked by in the street, paying me no mind, a young man and his sweetheart giggling in delight at their own quiet talk, what looked like a merchant in a hurry carrying several books, the boy I'd seen earlier with his dung cart.

In the alley directly across the street, I saw a shape that looked like Ivan walking toward me. If he came into the street, he might not know Fletcher hid in the shadows unless I warned him. Hoping the rough would not recognize me, I hurried across the street and into the alley before Ivan had got too close to Main Street. When I reached him, I knew we were far enough back that we could not be seen.

"What are you doing here?" he asked, his voice low and urgent.

"The rough is hidden on the porch across the street." I pointed toward a spot we could not see from our vantage. "Cedric is under that porch."

"Why?"

"I don't know!"

He stared at me for a moment, perhaps trying to make a decision.

"I'll go get him out of there." I said.

"No!" Ivan reached for me, but my blue-steel spring had wound tight, and I moved too fast for him. I entered the road, just one of several others, and crossed quickly to the porch, crouching low and calling, "Here, kitty, kitty, kitty."

I recalled the cove had stared at me for some time while I stood in the door to the hotel. Now, I could only hope he had no head for remembering children.

"Get away from here, child," I heard from the porch above. Sounded like a Britisher with a deep voice, full of sand.

I glanced toward the alley where Ivan hid, hoping he would not step out.

"No, sir," I said, "I must find my cat. Clarabelle is her name, a calico. Have you seen her?"

All at once, it came to me that Ivan could do nothing as long as I stood between him and his target. Cedric and I spoiled his effort to get Fletcher! Yet if I could draw the rough into the light....

"Please sir," I said, "Come help me find her." I didn't truly believe he would, but had to try.

"If you don't leave," came the deep voice again, "I *will* find your cat and *wring her neck!*"

I believed he didn't recognize me.

"Go," I heard Cedric whisper from beneath.

I could tell he crouched to my left, just beneath where the deep voice had come from. I moved in that direction and crouched down low. I did not want to leave Cedric there. Ivan might accidentally shoot him. I got down on my knees as if still searching for the cat.

Cedric whispered, "I can't see with you there."

Looking again toward the alley and seeing Ivan peeking around the corner, I remembered Cedric telling me to whistle, and I let out a note.

Heard a spunk flare to life, saw a brief glow under the porch that went out right away.

A scuffling of steps on the porch above, and the deep voice again. "That's it—I'm going to wring *your* neck if you don't go."

"Run," Ivan said, and then he appeared briefly in the road.

Swiftly, I backed away toward the corner of the back lane, saw Fletcher raise a pistol and fire toward Ivan.

Two men in Main Street dashed toward Chestnut Street to get out of danger, as I slipped back into the alley. I saw Ivan hiding around the corner. Couldn't see if he'd been shot.

Rapid, heavy footsteps sounded on the porch. I leaned out from the alley, and still could not see Fletcher within the thick shadows. I did see another sudden glow under the porch.

Cedric called out. "Ivan, he's directly above me!"

Ivan stepped out of the alley into the road and fired. A cry of pain came from the shadows, followed by the sound of a large body falling.

Cedric would later tell me he'd tried to stay right beneath Fletcher's footsteps.

Waiting for another shot, all grew still and quiet for a moment, the smell of burnt powder, like a great metal fart, heavy in the air until a wet breeze took it away. Then I heard voices, saw a few people gathering down the lane, perhaps to see the commotion. Two constables entered the road, moving fast. One, a plump cove in a tall bowler and a short woolen coat, had a lit lamp and a pistol. The other, a much smaller fellow in a flat cap and long coat, had a rifle. Both aimed their firearms at Ivan. "Cease," said the one with the rifle, "or we will fire."

Ivan had stepped toward the alley. He stopped and dropped his barker.

The constable with the pistol made pushing gestures toward those gathered in the street, said, "You folks stay back."

"There is a man, there—" Ivan began. He tried to point.

"Lower your arm," shouted the constable with the rifle.

Ivan did as told, said, "He fired a shot at me."

Stepping out of the alley into the street, I said, "'Tis true, a cove in the shadows."

Cedric crawled out from under the porch. "He shot at our servant," he added, as I helped him up.

Fletcher whindled and groaned loud enough to be heard by everyone.

The constable with the pistol, stepped onto the porch. In the dim light of his lamp, I saw Fletcher propped against the wall, a darkly gleaming wetness on his trousers below his right hip. He moved as if in agony, the pain twisting his horrible mug further.

"And you say this man is your slave?" The constable in the road asked, gesturing with his rifle toward Ivan.

"No, sir," I said, "he is in our service."

He chuckled at that.

"Clarence," said the constable on the porch, "take him to the jail, and send someone with a wagon to carry this big fellow. The way he's on about it, I think his leg's broke."

"Were self-defense," I said.

"His pistol has just been fired," the constable said, "but we'll let the sheriff decide what to do with these men. The jail is on Sixth, between Market and Chestnut."

Clearly, he knew we weren't from St. Louis.

Clarence took Ivan by the elbow and led him away into Chestnut Street.

I sent Cedric to tell Carla to meet us at the jail, while I followed Clarence and Ivan.

Cedric—9
Fall and winter of 1846, early spring of 1847

With little else to do but wait out the cold, wet weather in St. Louis, we talked often through the winter about what had happened on our first day in the city with the rough, Fletcher Carson. The constables had removed him to the hospital, and Ivan to the St. Louis jail.

Carla set to work trying to get Ivan out. In order to prove he was a free man, she presented his certificate of citizenship from the State of New York to Sheriff Maether, a cove with a long, sharp nose and a squiffy way about him.

"The man he shot," Maether said, "Fletcher Carson, may want to have charges brought against your man, and he did break several city ordinances. I shall hold him for now."

Carla became most vexed by all this. "That drunkard Sheriff is holding Ivan because he's a bigot or he fears bigots will lynch him." She wanted to hire a lawyer.

"Save your money," Ivan said. "They'll let me go sooner or later."

Visiting him in jail, I saw no one there up in arms about what he'd done. He seemed to be treated quite well. A mulatto woman named Tessa, slave to the household that drew the duty to feed prisoners that November, had delivered to him ham and cornbread on that day.

Watching them for a moment before he noticed me, I'd have said they got along too well. Truth is, I'd turned jealous. I'd grown quite fond of Ivan, and I'll allow now that I wanted him to pay heed to me over her.

Seeing me, Ivan gave me a big smile, much like the one he'd given the night I'd crawled out from under that porch after helping him with Fletcher.

"Were a nacky thing you done," he said, "lighting a spunk under that rough and calling out so I'd know where he were."

Bashful, I spoke of something else. "Alta Mae nearly ruined it."

"She were trying to protect you. She's a brave girl, willing to risk all to protect you."

I hadn't thought of it that way and had been cold to Alta Mae.

Felt good to hear him say those things. He had no need to puff up a little boy like me or to repair my feelings toward my sister. I decided then and there that he was a brave cove with a good heart beating in his chest.

And that left me troubled by the thought that Egan would not have tolerated my friendship with the black man. With the idea that Ivan might remain with us in California, I tried to think of things to say or do to make him more acceptable to my brother. Little came to mind but that Ivan taught me things and defended us against blackguards.

I could just hear Egan ask, "Were he also defending himself at the time?"

Never mind that Alta Mae almost spoiled my effort to help Ivan against Fletcher—what troubled me more was that she'd taken a shine to Mrs. Angelo. I worried about Alta Mae's judgment, and for the first time had doubts that she knew what would be best for us.

After a week at the Planters Hotel, in early November, we removed to lodgings in Fourth Street. Carla found plenty of Catholics in the city and a church to attend a couple blocks away in Walnut Street. She got Alta Mae to go with her to Mass one Sunday. I stayed in our lodgings, stewing about it.

Turned out I had little to fear—big sister returned complaining. "The Mass were like a theatre play with a bunch of people dressed in costume, saying all kinds of high-falutin things that made no sense. Then they swung around a big brass thing on a chain giving off smoke that stank and made me choke. Got so sick from it, I had to go outside and wait in the cold until it ended and Carla come out. I'll never do that again."

I was relieved she hadn't lost her head entirely, and warmed to Alta Mae again. I still fretted over her judgment.

Carla did use the church to good advantage, finding out what she could about Fletcher Carson.

"At church today," Carla told us, " I met a woman, Felistas Peregrino, who is a nurse at the hospital. She says Fletcher is going nowhere. He's bed ridden. The shot Ivan put in him broke his right leg near the hip. He's braced and done up in starched bandages, won't even be able to use crutches for four months and more. He won't be fit again until at least May. We join the wagon train in Independence April fifteenth."

Two weeks later, Sheriff Maether released Ivan.

"Surprised me to find out Fletcher Carson didn't want to have charges brought against me," Ivan told us that night. "That's an odd thing, unless he now has it in for me, and figures he can't get to me in the jail. The Sheriff kept me there as long as he did because he could. I were as pleasant as I could be while in his company, and after a time, I think he got tired of paying to have me fed. Never did hear what charges they had against me, what ordinances I'd violated."

Ivan also told us he had *redeemed* Tessa, the mulatto woman who had fed him in the jail.

"What does that mean?" Alta Mae asked.

"I bought Tessa from her master to give her freedom. I want to free her right away, but I can't unless we're wed. She doesn't have a certificate of citizenship from a U. S. state, so, once freed, she won't be allowed to abide in Missouri. The state would fine her ten dollars and force her to depart. If she fails to leave, she'll be given a jail term and twenty-five lashes in the public square. I would marry her, yet want to be certain she wants that too before we do it."

Carla agreed to have Tessa stay with us, since plenty of room remained in the bed she shared with Alta Mae. Ivan had got a job at the livery stable owned by Emile Voss. He'd also found lodgings in Mr. Voss's home.

A dimber woman, Tessa had pretty, blue blinkers, a wide mouth, square jaw, and head of wild, curly dark brown hair she usually had done up in a kerchief. She didn't smile for anyone but Ivan. I figured she wanted him to marry her. They were quite taken with each other. Of course, that meant I had a great dislike for her. The more I showed that, the more Ivan turned away from me, so I learned to hide it.

A long, boring winter. Early on, Alta Mae caught me in Second Street, buzzing a fellow plump in the pocket.

Once she got me alone, she smacked me on the back of the head, said, "We'll have no lay here, no buzzing, no partial at all. Do you hear me? You are well-fed, and have a warm place to sleep. There's no sense in taking risks with the law before we leave."

I showed her what I'd got, a silk handkerchief, black with a pattern of red posies.

She smiled, said, "A fine, squeeze billy, that," then eyed me stern again. "Promise me."

"I promise." I folded the sneezer and put it in my back pocket.

After that, seeing the rubes in the streets, their pockets ripe for the picking, I resisted temptation. She'd been right, especially about being well-fed and kept warm. Spoiled I'd become, having meals at regular hours, sometime three in a day. Even if I did find it rousing, there wasn't any need for thievery.

I learned to play the games children of the neighborhood had in the back lanes. December had come on cold and Carla had Alta Mae and me bundled in new warm rigging; coats, hats, and boots. No one knew of my humble beginnings. Playing hoop and stick, I was one of five boys kept a hoop rolling for nearly two hours. We played different types of kick the can, we tossed the Diablo, and got up to all sorts of hide and seek games.

In January, I got into a fight with a boy over a clasp knife he'd been given for Christmas. I'd won it from him fair and square playing mumblety-peg. He tried to take it back, and I gave him what for with my fist. He fled crying. Though a lot bigger than me, he'd no doubt grown up in some comfort. Feeling sorry for him, as if that would do the boy any good considering the life he'd had, I gave the knife back to him the next day.

When Ivan heard about it, he bought me a folding knife of my own, said, "You're reward for doing the right thing for yourself."

I thanked him, but I had to think about what he said for a long time before I could see past just feeling sorry for the boy.

—m—

Carla came home upset from church on a Sunday at the end of

March, said, "Fletcher Carson left the hospital. Felistas said he'd been hobbling about on crutches for about a month."

Ivan had joined us for supper that evening. "Try not to worry," he said. "He won't be dangerous until long after we've gone. I can easily defend us against a cove on crutches.

—⁂—

In April, Carla bought a wagon for our westward journey, one she said folks called a prairie schooner. The heavy conveyance had been to the Oregon Country to deliver emigrants, and then returned to St. Louis for resale. Came with a canvas bonnet the salesman bragged had been waterproofed with a mixture of beeswax and borax. The borax made it less flammable. To pull the wagon, she bought six oxen, oxbows, and the needed harness.

Ivan picked out a fine chestnut quarter horse to take with us as well.

Since we would not be riding much, Carla bought heavy boots for me, Alta Mae, Ivan, Tessa, and herself. She bought a small 32 calibre percussion cap pistol for each of us but Ivan, who had plenty of barkers already.

Illegal for a slave to have a firearm in Missouri, Tessa could not have her pistol until we were out of the state.

So excited to have my very own barking iron, I spoke of all sorts of wild fancies I had about how I'd use it to defend us against bandits and Indians. Like a pudding head, I held it at arms-length and waved it around, pretending to fire it. With that, Carla decided I shouldn't have it until we departed.

"It's not loaded!" I cried. "There's no cap on the nipple."

I grew as huffed and wrathy as I'd ever been once she'd taken it away. Tried to take Alta Mae's, and she clouted me good, raising a lump on my head the size of a mouse.

—⁂—

Numerous times, Ivan took me to an open field on Duncan's Island in the Mississippi where I practiced shooting my pistol. The chunk of land sat so close in places to the western bank of the river, I could have hit it throwing a rock.

On our last visit to the island, as we practiced, Ivan spoke of

Carla. "She gives you and Alta Mae pistols because she trusts you. Would be a good thing if you trusted her."

"She made me do a thing that put us in danger," I said. "She told me she held Alta Mae prisoner, and that I'd do her bidding or not see her again."

"Is that truly what happened? I ask while knowing Alta Mae were not ever held against her will."

"At the least, she made it out that way, and I saw I had little choice."

"She is strong-willed. Once she's set on a course, 'tis hard to turn her from it. She had need to get that booty from the privy since she'd lost everything when her house went down a sink hole."

"Alta Mae told me about that."

"But she has a good heart," Ivan said. "She would treat you like a son if you would give just a little."

I thought about that. I'd had something hollow in me for a few years, ever since reasoning that my parents could not be the Cow Bay and Old Brewery tenements. A good thing to cast off those foolish beliefs. Yet in the believing, even seeing them as dead, I'd at least had a sense of where I came from.

Now, I had Alta Mae, an untrustworthy Egan, and I'd begun to see Carla and Ivan as family, though I didn't want to believe it so, since they might be gone tomorrow. Still and all, I got from that some warmth in my heart.

Carla did provide for us well, and she *did* give me a pistol.

Again, Ivan taught me rules to follow with firearms to help prevent deadly mistakes. With Ivan's rifle, I'd already learned how to load the powder, patch, and shot into the barrel, place the percussion cap on the nipple, pull back the trigger, aim, and fire. With my pistol, I had to learn how to use the captured ramrod. Difficult at first because I had to turn it just right for the end to meet the barrel and go in. With some practice, I got to doing it swiftly enough.

On that last visit to Duncan's island, a white cove appeared at the edge of the field, watching us from about a hundred yards away. I waved at him. He didn't wave back and had a dour expression on his rather square mug, as if he didn't approve of what he saw.

"What do you suppose has him huffy?" I asked Ivan.

"Perhaps he doesn't like seeing a black man here with a pistol," he said. "This is where the abolitionist, Charles Brown, and three of his confederates were hanged five years ago. Been reading about it in a book. Could be the cove thinks I'm trying to get up a slave rebellion with my able young companion." Ivan clapped me lightly on the shoulder and laughed heartily.

Certain he'd heard, I turned to see how the cove took the laughter. He adjusted his cap, turned away, and became lost in the trees.

"You can read?" I asked Ivan

"Yes, Aunt Carla taught me. She'd teach you too, if you weren't such a cussed young imp to her."

I didn't want to think about that. "What's an abolitionist?"

"'Tis someone who wants to see slavery abolished."

"Why, don't slaves get a home and victuals in return for their work?"

"No, it's not like that. They have no contract such as an indentured servant might have, one that sets a date of release from service and is agreed to."

"Still, they get something for their labor."

"Weren't their choice. They were either stolen from a life of freedom or born into slavery."

I thought of Egan selling me into the factory room in the Old Brewery. Not fair, what he did. No one should be able to do that to another. I knew the contract had been for five years and even then found it intolerable. And of course, I was white. Carla got me out easily, maybe because my color helped her make an argument for fairness.

"What if someone come along right now," Ivan said, "clapped me in irons, and sold me down the river to someone wanted to buy a slave."

Listening to the nearby sounds of the river moving south, I wondered how anyone might come back from that. A frightful thought, but I considered his trick of making something like that up unfair.

"You have a white father and Carla," I complained. "You are

more than just a black man."

"Ain't everyone more than the skin they wear?"

Thinking back on the conversation, I can say that Ivan treated me kindly in that moment. He didn't show a short temper like I did.

I huffed and turned away. "That ain't gonna happen unless someone mistook you."

"That sort of thing does happen, free blacks taken and sold into slavery. I've kept a sharp lookout for such danger ever since we entered Missouri since it's a state that allows slavery."

Again, I thought of the time I'd spent in the factory room, and how it still haunted me. Tears gathered in my blinkers. Ashamed, I walked away.

Then I saw the scaffold where the abolitionists must have hanged. The gallows sat tucked in amongst the small budding trees toward the northernmost point of the island, overgrown some with brush and vine. The thought came to me that we were in a dangerous spot. I wiped away my tears and turned back to Ivan. He sat on a log, watching me.

I went to him, took his arm, said. "Let's go back."

—⁓—

That evening, Ivan dragged me to Carla, said, "Say the words, boy."

I hadn't been willing to ask. With him pushing me so, even giving me the words to use, I couldn't say no. "Mrs. Angelo, would you please teach me to read and write?"

"Yes," she said. "I'd be delighted to, if you'll take up the task in all seriousness."

I agreed and we began to have lessons in the evenings. Tessa wanted to learn too. Alta Mae joined in, though she'd had a big head start.

Had been a long winter, followed by a wet spring, but it was also a peaceful pause, right before the trials of journeying further west.

Alta Mae—9
April 1847

We gathered outside of Independence, Missouri with those who had signed up with the New Pacific Emigration Company to head west on April 15th. Our pilot was an older, white cove named Erick Hawker. He had a scout and guide named Tsula McBaird, a Cherokee cove. Both men hailed from Tennessee. Hawker, a large muscular fellow, had a bald, red pate, like a big scar with dents evenly placed across it. That started on his forehead, just below where his hairline might have been. He also had a crooked nose, a long scar on the right cheek, and the top of his right ear missing. He dressed in buckskins, and had two pistols in his belt, a long rifle, and a knife called an Arkansas toothpick—a long, fat blade, not quite a sword. The Indian was a dark brown fellow in trousers, shirt, and a vest that acted as harness to hold three pistols. His dark, waxed topcoat reached his knees. He also carried a long rifle.

Four out riders would also go with us, protection for the wagon train provided by the New Pacific Emigration Company. I didn't get a good look at those men at first, just that they looked lean and sharp-eyed. Their names: Sam Hoog, Niklas Gruber, and the brothers, Hiram and Wayne Southall.

Teamsters, a man and his three sons going by the name, Costello, drove four of the five supply wagons belonging to the staff. An Indian woman named Issa drove the fifth. Rumor had her as the pilot's daughter.

Eighty-nine wagons altogether—a very few drawn by mules, the rest with oxen—maybe five hundred people, about fifty horses, and around two hundred head of cattle. A reserve of fifty oxen would come with us to replace those that got worn out or injured during the journey. Plenty of firearms seen among the travelers.

The pilot and guide led us westward into more open, less wooded land. They didn't take us far before calling a halt for a meeting to elect officers. I didn't understand what it was all about except that those chosen would have to answer to the rest of us. No doubt Carla and Ivan weren't considered for such a role. Still, they might have done a better job than most of the party.

Perhaps seeing himself as a lawyer of sorts, a man named Ned Tollard did a lot of talking. He shouted everything he said, like he was the big bug on stage and wanted to make certain everyone could hear him. Except for his sturdy boots, he wore toff-togs, checked suit and satin waistcoat. The way he went on, I'd say the stout gold watch chain he sported looped to an empty pocket.

He nominated himself to be the general superintendent of the wagon train party but lost out to a man named Atimus Lucere who had a military background. Still needing to be the hog in armor, Tollard became a member of the board of trustees along with three other men, one being Olin Tipton, who owned all the cattle.

Not interested in the whole meeting, I moved on and gathered with some of the girls and made talk about this and that. We said where we'd come from, and what we hoped to find in California. Come my turn to say what I wanted there, I said simply, "My brother," although I wasn't certain I believed that. A few of the girls' gazes said they didn't know what to make of me. I tried not to fret about it and just let them stare.

Cedric had gone off with the boys. I know he'd wanted to show off his barker. Before leaving St. Louis, Carla had said, "You children are not to let anyone know you have the pistols."

He had not liked that, and had opened his bone box to say something scoffing when Ivan gave him the EYE. And if Ivan glared at you sideways, with the yellow-white of his eye showing all around the dark center, you knew he meant to have his way. Cedric backed down.

Now calling itself the Lucere Party, the wagon train set out again, and traveled for a few hours before stopping to make camp at sunset. The outriders came in and helped Mr. Hawker and Mr. McBaird organize us for the night. The animals foraged, while the wagons were drawn up into two circles. Women set up fires for cooking inside one of the circles.

I stood watching all this with a girl, a little older, named Tilsa Svensdotter, from Michigan. She had a heavy accent—maybe German—flaxen hair, blue eyes, and cheeks so red I thought at first they must be rouged. Truly quite dimber.

I told her I'd come from New York City, and knew little about the animals. Not a friendly girl, yet she did answer my questions well enough.

We watched Olin Tipton, a stout, bow-legged cove. He led one of his cows into the other circle of wagons, and all the rest of the cattle followed. He hobbled that animal, but not the rest.

"Is that cow a troublemaker?" I asked.

"No," she said, "all the cattle look to that one to know what to do. If it cannot go anywhere, they won't either."

The prancers were picketed amongst the cattle, and that circle was closed, two wagons filling the gap.

The mules got picketed outside the circles, and the oxen roamed free, except for two that were hobbled.

I opened my bone box to speak and Tilsa must have known what I'd ask. "The mules and oxen are outside the circle because they can defend themselves against danger," she said. "The oxen will not roam off as long as there are a couple that cannot go with them."

"What dangers do you think are out there tonight?" I asked.

She gave me a wary look, like perhaps I made fun of her.

"I never left the city until this August past," I said.

Her smile looked a bit mean. "There are wolves, big gray ones and smaller red ones. And there are lions and jaguars. There are also thieves, bandits, and absconder needing a meal or the means to flee faster. Then there are the Indians."

As she spoke, my hands slipped into the pockets of my skirt to touch my protection, the knife Carla had given me on the right, pistol on the left.

I nodded, and she seemed to know when I'd caught up with her. Tilsa was a farm girl, quicker than I would have thought, and that just showed me what I didn't know. Quick or not, I didn't know if I liked her.

Ivan had told us of much the same dangers as he'd found them in the reading given out by the emigration company.

"I must go help my mother," Tilsa said and walked away.

I found Carla and Tessa chopping vegetables inside the circle of wagons that surrounded the cook fires. They worked with several other women making a stew at the fire closest to our wagon. Iron rods formed a tripod over the fire set within a ring of stones. A pot hung from the tripod over the flames. Four dutch ovens were set in the embers around the edge of the fire, hot coals heaped on their lids. This set up was the same for all the fires. I counted ten of them within the circle of wagons.

Carla introduced me to the women I had not met, claiming me as her daughter. I didn't mind—indeed, felt proud that she would want to claim me. Some of the women had foreign accents. The others I thought to be American. A black woman, named Florence North, said her family had come from Indiana. Florence had a lazy left eye and a scar on her upper lip. She had a daughter with her, maybe eight years old, named Zeata, quite dimber, with big brown blinkers and a round mouth, most often smiling.

I told her my name, and she asked. "Is Mae you surname?"

"No, it's just added to my given."

"I wish I had two names. I could be Zeata Mae."

"That's very pretty."

She giggled and shyly covered her face.

Most of the men talked amongst themselves, some serious as lamp black, others making jokes and laughing. They smoked and drank, with plenty of fustian and bingo passed around in jug and bottle.

Of course, the loudest had to be the blunderbuss, Ned Tollard. He thought he was some pumpkins, always speaking as if what he had to say were most important. He got some leery looks from the other men.

Outside the ring of wagons, the growing gloom rang with the voices of children playing. The pilot had told us before we set out that we might be noisy for a couple of nights, but that the farther we traveled west, the quieter and more on the lookout everyone should be.

I suspected most of the laughter, the shouts, and shrieks belonged to boys, as they didn't have to help with the cooking. Seemed like they meant to get all their shouting done before they were asked to stop. Most of the girls had remained within the circle, fetching and toting for their mothers.

Carla said my part would be cleaning up after supper. She had me retrieve several comestibles from the smaller barrels among our supplies, and a bucket of water from one of the two larger barrels strapped to the sides of the wagon.

Returning with the water, I saw Ivan walking toward us with another black cove. He introduced the fellow as Aubrey North. "This is my cousin, Alta Mae, my aunt, Carlotta Angelo, and my wife, Tessa."

I wasn't certain I wanted to be cousin to a black man. Kept that to myself.

Tessa had not yet become his wife, but he and Carla had decided they should introduce her as such.

"This is my husband, Mrs. Angelo," Florence North said.

"Delighted to meet you, sir."

I had to admit to myself that I didn't like her saying "sir" to him. Didn't bother me that she'd said it to Emile Voss at the livery in St. Louis. Of course, she'd been wheedling him at the time. Did she want something from Mr. North? I couldn't say.

Why, I wondered, was I so begrudging toward the black cove whilst being comfortable with his wife and child? Tessa didn't trouble me either. I decided it could simply be that I saw myself in the female. Though I'd slowly warmed to Ivan because of Carla's feelings for him, I still looked with doubt upon black men I didn't know, just as Egan would have me do—just like he'd wanted me to do with Catholics.

Carla's character had put the lie to the picture he'd painted of Catholics. With plenty of treacherous and cruel people of all sorts, couldn't it also be true that there were some good ones among all types of people?

I watched Mr. North; his blinkers, his bone box, his gestures. His head, cheeks and chin had been shaved clean, and he had a pleasant enough mug; broad forehead, high cheeks, and square chin with a notch in the center. I considered his manner. Being from the streets, I'd got good at seeing a person's character, and knowing if something about them didn't sit right with me. I saw nothing in that cove that looked false, hid away, or half-truth.

At ten years of age, I found these notions stirring, not in small part because they felt particularly mine, stewed up in my idea pot, yet they also gave me the all-overish feeling that I betrayed Egan.

After supper, we had music; a couple of fiddles, a guitar, and a flutina. For a time, Ivan joined in, playing his penny whistle. With the sour notes given flight, one of the violinists must have had a bent ear. No one complained.

Tessa showed Ivan some steps, and they danced together. Showing much experience at dancing, she made circles around him as he kept to the simple steps she'd given him. Others joined in and soon the center of the circle had filled with dancing couples.

The boisterous commotion of children playing outside the circle of wagons became louder still. I'd have joined them but had to help Carla and the other women with the cleaning and stowing.

When the play outside began to sound like wild things circling, roaring, and scratching to get inside, a sharp, high whistle went up into the night, cutting through the noise. A silence fell upon the camp, and the deep voice of our pilot rang out, "Enough! To your work or your beds. We have an early day tomorrow."

No one argued. Voices dropped to a murmur.

Carla set out our bedrolls, and doused her lamp. A fine weariness came over me as I lay down, something like I'd known in the past on the occasions I'd had beer as my only supper. I was dimly aware of my three other companions returning to the wagon, and the sounds of their last preparations before sleep.

Through the spokes of a wheel, I saw the sky had cleared but for a few clouds to the East. Oliver rose behind them, a thin glowing crescent close to the horizon. Higher up, the stars gathered in a shimmering band that crossed the sky. I remember my sleepy thinking telling me they had to be powerful old to be so dusty and full of cobwebs.

Cedric—10

We had an easy first day on the trail and that night at our camp was, for me, the most fun of the whole journey. Before supper, I met other boys that would become good friends. I'd had enough experience in the back lanes of St. Louis to know some of the games we got up to. Also, I'd gained a sense of what children raised with parents had in common. Listening to what they had to say about their lives, saying little about my past, and pretending I'd been raised within a family, rather than on the streets, helped make me more acceptable to them.

I played mostly with boys twelve or younger. Older than that, and they were with the young men or chasing girls. One boy, Tommy Stilton, tow-headed, maybe thirteen years of age, tried to bully us into doing what he wanted. When he spoke, his words came out oddly because he had a cleft lip. His F's came out as P's, and his S-sounds were a hissing from the back of his mouth. Although he might have thought we'd done, no one laughed at him.

He hid the ball to ruin our game of catch. He tripped those running to catch others in a game of tag, then laughed at Jack Jacobson, who fell on his face and got a bloody nose.

I'd known a boy in the Points who wore a tall shoe since he had one leg much shorter than the other. He learned to box and if he thought a boy so much as looked at him sideways he'd give him a lumping. Maybe Tommy looked upon others in the same peery way.

We tried to put some distance between him and us, but he always got right in the thick of it. A big, strong fellow, he meant to have his way.

Aron Yarmanowitz said to him, "Why don't you go see what the older boys are doing?"

Tommy took Aron's arm and twisted it until he squealed. "I'll de-sss-ide what game-sss we play," Tommy said. His words broken up odd in his throat and growled some, it took a moment to understand him. "Unle-sss one of you want-sss to try and sss-top me."

I'm certain some of the boys would have returned to their families if they hadn't been afraid of looking weak. Instead we gathered around Tommy.

Even though he'd let go of Aron, I wanted to threaten him with my pistol. Of course that was the reason Ivan had persuaded me not to take it with me just anywhere.

No, I would have to find another way to teach Tommy a lesson.

Someone said, "What shall we play, then?"

"We're going to play blind man-sss bupp," Tommy said, his plooky mug a one-eyed challenge against anyone thinking of arguing with him.

"Blind man's buff?" Jack asked. He dodged as Tommy swung at him.

An idea came to me, and I spoke up quick. "I volunteer to be the first blind man." From my pocket, I pulled the silk billy I'd buzzed off that fellow in St. Louis. The silk was so fine, I knew I could see fairly clear through several folded layers held close to my eyes. Yet, to look at it, that didn't appear to be so because of the pattern: black with red posies.

"All right, then," Tommy growled, grinning like he knew just what sort of mischief he'd bring to the game.

I handed him the fine sneezer.

He looked at it and his brows went up. A rough b'hoy, he may well have never felt silk before. In the dim light of dusk, I'm certain he could not see much more than its dark pattern. Nodding, he said, "That-sss a pan-sss-y handkerchiep."

"Were my Grandmother's," I said quickly.

He told us the rules as he knew them. We could shove the blind man and knock him around, but if his hand touched anyone, that person became the next blind man.

He folded the billy, wrapped it around my mug, and tied it at the back on my head. I could hear the fabric tear a little as he cinched it way too tight. He was the sort of b'hoy that liked to hurt others whenever, however possible.

The boys all spun me around, doing their best to make me wobbly and dizzy, Tommy shoving me harder than the rest, and taking advantage of the confusion to punch me in the gut. I figured he'd try something like that, and had my muscles prepared. Through it all, I kept to my feet.

"Get ready," Tommy shouted, giving a smack to my head, "now, let him go!"

And they all stepped away from me.

I wanted to go straight at Tommy, make him the blind man, then teach him a lesson. That wouldn't work, though, since he'd be able to see through the blindfold just as easily.

Instead, I stumbled about with my arms outstretched. Laughing and jeering, the other boys kept coming for me, especially from behind; shoving me, buffing my legs, my arms. Tommy's blows were coming harder than those of the other boys, and getting harder still. Being taller than any of us, he made a show of smacking at my head. I made as if to grab some of the boys even as I meant to fail. Biding my time, I looked for my chance to thump Tommy's sweaty, bleb-spotted mug. I had to get him before he could mete out a cruel blow.

Finally, he appeared right there in front of me. He braced himself to deliver a punch to my mug. Seeing it coming, I blocked it, knocking his arm to the left so his fist missed me. Not expecting that, he perhaps leaned in farther than he'd wanted.

I took that chance to give him a nose ender with my fist, a blow hard enough to acquaint him with the floor. Tommy curled in a ball on the ground, blubbering and holding his bloody sniffer.

I pulled the billy off my mug and gathered with the rest of the boys around him.

"Serves you right," Jack said, and several of the others gave loud agreement.

Tommy got up off the ground and turned to me. I leaned in toward him with my fists clenched and gave him a steady gaze. I wasn't afraid of him, and I think he knew it.

"You'll regret that," he said, wiping blood from his nose onto his sleeves.

"That the first time someone stood up to you?" Aron asked.

Tommy lunged at him, but I shoved the bully boy and he fell again. He got up, glanced back at me with tears in his blinkers, and stumbled away toward the wagons.

"Maybe you'll think twice the next time you want to pick on someone," said a boy named Will Murman.

The boys rushed toward me, laughing and shouting, cheering my name.

Tommy slipped into the circle between wagons, and I lost sight of him.

Saw Zeata North standing just this side of the wagons watching, grinning wide, then covering her mouth with both hands. She looked rather dimber in that moment. I believed the smile was for me alone, a laughable notion. The thrill of my victory over Tommy and the praise of all the other boys had turned me into a Billy Noodle, I decided.

"For such a small kid, you're something," Jack said. "A bully trap is what you are!"

Jack, a dark-haired Jewish boy with brown eyes that slanted some, would become a good friend during the journey west.

"My grandfather came from Poland where his name was Yakovlevich," he'd said. "He changed it to Jacobson after he came to America."

The rest of the night, we had pure-fired fun. I learned many new games, some that I played well, and some that made me laugh at my own bumbling. Though hungry, I didn't want to stop when the call came for us to eat.

"You remember before we set out," I said, "the pilot said we'd soon be in parts where we'll have to be quiet at night and more watchful. I say we play as long as we can, for what nights we can, because soon we won't have the chance."

They all agreed, and we made plans to meet outside the circle of wagons as soon as supper ended.

Had a fine meal of stew and fresh-baked tommey, then returned to the games with my friends. We filled the night air with our joyous hullabaloo, pounding the prairie grass to pulp, and wearing ourselves out. Seems we'd just reached the end of our strength as the whistle and shout from the pilot called us in for the night.

—∽∽—

The next day, the wagon train moved on into more open prairie with fewer stands of trees.

Tommy Stilton traveled with his family two wagons ahead of ours. He eyed me a few times, nothing more. His nose had a new crook to it. Couldn't help thinking he would be ashamed that a smaller, younger boy had bested him. I might have been as old as nine years by then.

Keeping a distance, I saw a lot of Tommy Stilton and he saw a lot of me. Would the shame I fancied he had turn into something much worse with time? I thought I saw a change in his eyes, and believed he planned something cruel for me.

Alta Mae—10
May, 1847

The trail took us northwest along rivers that flowed in a southeasterly direction, the first being the Kaw River. We passed beyond the Missouri frontier and entered the wilderness of what would become the Kansas Territory in 1854, then the State of Kansas in 1861. Occasional rain and cane breaks slowed our progress. Mosquitos came for our blood in greater numbers.

From the supply wagon she drove, Issa handed out daily doses of something called quinine she said would help keep the bites from harming us.

The cane seemed to have been cleared from the trail by earlier travelers. New growth had sprung up in our path, especially in the low, marshy stretches. The larger stalks had to be razed and their stumps hammered down so as not to catch feet, hoof, or wheel.

"We could make syrup from that," Tessa told me.

I followed her. She got Florence, Zeata, and others, all women, to help her harvest stalks of the giant grass. As slow as the wagon train moved on that day, we had plenty of time. I had my knife. Several of the women used sickles. We cut eight inch lengths from the lower segments of the cane the men had cut down.

Carla saw the work and asked what we were doing.

"Is sorghum cane," Tessa said. "If we boil the stalks, we can make a sweet syrup."

I knew sorghum syrup, but had no notion until then where it came from.

Carla and Cedric lent a hand. We made a big pile of the cuttings and gathered all of it into our wagons before moving on.

Reaching the swampy land where the Kaw and the Great Blue Earth River came together, we were forced to a crawling pace. Headed in a more northerly direction along the Great Blue Earth, we lost our trail in a morass perhaps twenty miles wide. We spent a week going around it whilst the rains tried to make it bigger and the swampy ground tried to swallow our wagons. The experience of the teamsters, Costello and his sons, got us through. With ax and saw, and the help of our oxen to drag the larger encumbrances out of the way, we cut new trail. Plenty of times, one wagon caught in the bog forced all the others to stop for hours.

I thought of Olin Tipton hobbling two oxen each night because the others wouldn't leave them behind. The members of the wagon train also couldn't leave anyone behind. That was no doubt part of the contract. Still, they were all different sorts of people thrown together. Like most folks they would be used to sticking with their own. Now we had to work together to get somewhere. Without complaint, our fellow travelers freed our wagon from the quagmire more than once, and we did the same for them.

We had less hearty meals during our struggle with the morass since they had to be prepared on small camp stoves in the beds of the wagons to get above the wetness.

Our reading and writing lessons resumed at this time and would go on for at least an hour most nights during the rest of the journey. Cedric had become devoted to the learning.

While we had plenty of time to forage, a woman named Ezra Bissett, a French Canadian woman, and her daughters, Celeste and Amelie, asked Carla, Tessa, and me to help gather wild vegetables.

"I used to go west with my husband, a fur trapper," she said, "until Blackfoot Indians killed him in the Rocky Mountains. I was traveling with him at the time. We were far from our home in Montreal, and I had to make my way back there on my own. I had but a knife to defend myself."

Listening to her, I gripped the handle of the knife in my pocket and tried to imagine being alone in the wilderness with little else to help keep me alive.

"Frightening!" Carla said.

"Yes," Ezra said, "yet now I know much more about getting on in the wilderness. As for my husband, he wasn't a good man."

Carla nodded as if she understood just what the woman meant.

I wanted to ask Mrs. Bissett questions. With the task at hand, I didn't have a chance.

We found slightly higher ground to root around in, a place with giant trees Ezra called willow and cottonwood. Tessa knew some of what to look for. She helped us learn. Felt good to know something of what grew wild that could be eaten. We gathered miner's lettuce, violets, stinging nettles, wild onions, garlic, asparagus, and cat tail roots. We harvested twigs from the willows and peeled the bark for a tea used to dampen pain.

Cedric and I enjoyed the hard work with our new friends. The pilot and other men and women commanded, and we children did as we were told.

I didn't like the nights spent stuck in the swamp with wetness everywhere and having to sleep propped amongst the supplies in our wagon. The bloodsucking bugs tormented us something fierce.

A cove named Kloos, bitten by a snake, spent several days laid up in a wagon, folks fearing he'd die. Although he did live, he remained ill for some time and could not help much.

As some of our party began to fall ill with fever, the pilot passed along the line saying, "Speak up if you become ill. When we have room to maneuver off the trail, we'll move those with illness to the rear of the wagon train. Bunched up as we are now, that's not possible without aiding the spread of disease, so we must give some distance for any family that falls ill; at least ten feet for any wagon with disease. Keep the same distance from anyone that claims to be ill."

Fearing the shadow of sickness would find me, I stayed close to Carla and tried not to be disagreeable as she prayed for me. Cedric kept close to Ivan.

The fever's shadow took the lives of 33 people. Some entire families lost; husband, wife, and children.

I felt lucky that none with our wagon had fallen ill. Though the danger had passed, weeping and prayers of mourning reminded us of death for many days while our work to cut through the swamp went on. Troubled me greatly. At times, I wanted to scream for silence. I had enough sense not to.

I sought Tilsa. Catching up with her, I said "Miserable, I am, in my wet boots, and grum thoughts,"

She had no reply except to walk faster. I matched her pace.

"I got so frightened we'd *all* catch the fever," I said. "I'm glad our families were spared."

When Tilsa said nothing, I knew she pretended I was not there.

"Will you not speak to me?" I asked.

She stopped and turned her blue blinkers on me. Her cheeks had grown a hot red. "My mother said she saw your mother carries rosary beads, and that I should not speak to you because you're Catholic."

"I ain't Catholic."

"Then what are you?"

I'd never thought much about that. I didn't know what I believed of God, yet I knew better than to admit such. One of Egan's lies came to me, and I repeated it. "I am a Protestant."

In my ignorance, I didn't know that Protestants and Catholics both believe in much the same things. For a moment, I worried that Carla had somehow gummed me, and that Egan perhaps had more cause to hate Catholics than I knew.

"I would praise you for that," Tilsa said, "but Papa says your mother has amalgamated with a dangerous sort."

Suspecting I already knew the answer, I asked, "What's your meaning?"

"He says your black man isn't a servant."

"His name is Ivan."

"Your mother is the black man's aunt, and he's your cousin. I will have no more to do with you. Do not speak to me."

This silly girl and her family had no more good reason to hate than Egan did.

I wanted nothing more to do with Tilsa.

—⁂—

Beyond the morass, or in the middle of it—I'm not certain where and when exactly—we located the next stream we meant to follow, the Little Blue River, and with it, dry land and the trail we'd lost in the morass. By then, we'd most likely entered what would become in 1854 the Nebraska Territory, and the State of Nebraska in 1867.

117

We buried our dead. The two preachers we'd had having died of the fever, the ceremony was led by Lemuel Clanton, a cove calling himself a lay preacher. Seemed that all attended. I saw Tilsa gazing at me and whispering to other girls. They stared at me in a way meant to be cruel, I think. Little did they know what it took to hurt my feelings. Still I felt alone in a most all-overish way.

We followed the water upstream for many days before parting ways with the Little Blue River sometime before finding the next leg of our journey.

Now that we'd found dry land again, the men spent more time hunting. They brought in mostly fowl: Partridge, grouse, ducks, geese, and wild turkey.

The outriders brought in Antelope and mule deer. Those larger animals were butchered and shared among the Lucere Party, their meat cut into pieces and packed in the barrels that held salt pork. Since each wagon carried such barrels, and some of the salt pork had been eaten from each barrel, there was room for the venison and plenty of leftover salt to help preserve it.

Arriving at the Platte River, our trail took us along that water, again upstream, but more directly westward. We took a day for rest.

Tessa and Mrs. North began the making of sorghum syrup from the gathered cane. Carla and several of the women took part in it too. I helped as well. We smashed the stalks with hammers, then boiled the pulp in three large pots for hours, straining off a green foam that formed on the top. When the pulp had given all the sweetness it had to the water, and much of the liquid had been boiled off, we got a honey-like syrup.

I didn't feel good about Tilsa and her family being offered some of the syrup, and I told Carla about my words with the girl. "You should tell Tessa and Mrs. North about what I said," I told her.

"No, we will not be like them," she said.

As we sat the next morning, enjoying the sorghum on corn cakes and biscuits with our breakfast, the pilot addressed the members of the wagon train.

"We now commence the climb toward the Rocky Mountains. We'll be able to see farther here, farther still as we proceed. Keep an eye on the horizon. Look out for bandits and Indians. If you see anything suspicious, let me, Mr. McBaird, or any of the out riders know about it straight away."

He paused to take on a stern look. "We will be seeing herds of buffalo, and the powerful urge to shoot one will come over more than one of you gentleman. I know I said this back in Missouri before we set out, but I'm saying it again—*don't* do it. They get spooked, and sometimes they run away. Other times they run toward the hunter. We do not want a herd of buffalo stampeding through our wagon train. If that were to happen, many would be killed and there would be little left of our endeavor."

"What if we see one all on its own," someone asked.

"We cannot take the time to dress and butcher such a large beast, nor do we have the ability to carry all the meat. To leave a dead animal on the field will attract wolves and possibly anger the Indians."

The climb he'd mentioned began slow enough. We rose up out of the forested valleys and into rolling plains with tall grasses and colorful flowers.

Many of the girls and women picked flowers from the prairie to put in each others' hair. No one offered to put flowers in my hair until Tessa saw I didn't have any. She brought me white lilies. I helped put them in her hair instead, since, somehow, I had it that I was not meant to be dimber. I think Egan told me that once and it stuck.

Envious, I became, of Cedric walking with his friends. He did so most often with Jack Jacobson and Aron Yarmanowitz. They laughed and played as they went, Cedric often walking backwards for a time so he could face the others while in spirited talk.

Surprised to see Zeata North walking with Cedric a couple times. More surprised he didn't run her off when his friends caught up with them.

I stuck with Carla, Tessa, and Ivan until two girls came to talk to me, one my age, named Frances Adair, with red-hair and thousands of freckles, and the other, a giant, dark-haired girl from Illinois named Missouri Hughes.

"Tilsa has ugly things to say about you and your family," Missouri said, "so we thought we should make friends with you. We don't care much for Tilsa."

"She has turned some of the other girls against us," Frances said. "She has scorn for me because of this..." she held up her right hand to show it had suffered something crippling, "... and because of my peeling." Frances had suffered sun burn most everywhere she didn't have a freckle.

"And for me," Missouri said, "since I am so tall and rawboned." Twelve years old and ungainly, she had grown to nearly six feet in height. "Tilsa does not like people who are different. She's persuaded many of the other girls that we are marked in some way, so they mock us too."

"Very pleased to meet you," I said.

And just like that, I had new friends too! We stuck together and played games as we walked—a kind of follow-the-leader about having to remember a string of dance steps, and a hopscotch-like game Frances made up.

Without letting on that I'd lived in the street, I answered many of their questions about New York. I allowed them to continue thinking of Carla as my mum.

"My father is a blacksmith, my mother a midwife," Frances said. "Last place we lived was Chicago. Before that, Boston. I don't remember much before that because I was so little, but we were in Scotland. Da gets in trouble gambling, so we have to keep finding a new home."

"My mother passed away when I was very young," Missouri said, "I've spent most of my time on the Mississippi River with my father. We ran flatboats down to Natchez, where the cargo and the boats were sold. We'd ride keelboats much of the way back up to Illinois, and then walk the rest of the way. I grew such long legs so I could keep up with him. Otherwise, he'd have left me behind."

Though I wondered if she truly believed that, I didn't ask.

Missouri had great stories of river pirates, and a couple of brushes she and her father had had with them.

By and by, a plump g'hal named Meg Alberti, walking with Tilsa, threw ox dung at Missouri.

"The big target you are," Meg said. "you should expect that sort of thing." She laughed.

Quick, that spring inside me got wound tight. I picked up some of the dung and charged at her. I think she'd never seen such fierceness in a girl before. She and Tilsa hitched up their skirts and ran, all the while squealing.

Missouri, with her long legs, pounded after them too. She caught up and grabbed them each by the collar. They swung to hit Missouri and found most of her beyond their reach. They clawed at her arms instead.

By then I'd caught up. "Cowards! Stop fighting or I'll feed you the ox dung."

Tilsa grew still. The g'hal, Meg, kept struggling until I made as if to shove the dung in her mug.

Frances was behind us now, laughing. She held dung at the ready too. "Together, we are strong. You remember that, Tilsa, and hope we don't decide to turn on *you*."

Missouri let them go, and they staggered away looking cowed. I knew that would not last.

After that we called ourselves the Ugly Step Sisters, and were proud to be different from what Frances called "Tilsa and her gaggle of Cinderellas."

—◊—

We saw fewer and fewer woods, until just the broad grassland spread out treeless under the largest sky I'd ever seen. Unsettling how big until I got used to it.

For the first time, I asked myself, *where did all that blue come from?* I knew how Carla would answer the question so I took a moment to ask our pilot.

"Was like that when the first fur trappers came to this land," he said, "and we ain't put together the funds yet to have it repainted."

I thought he said that because he didn't have time for little girls and their foolish questions. Then he crouched down to look me in the eye. "What color should we paint it?"

"I like the blue," I said in all seriousness.

"Good thinking. Just a fresh coat, then. That'll save us some money."

I hadn't expected him to be so full of fancy.

"Still, it is a leaky ceiling. You've seen the colorful stains at sunset?"

Finally, I allowed a smile. "Yes. I like those too."

"You're very practical." He patted me on the head, stood, and walked away.

He'd treated me like a child. A moment passed before I knew he'd been right to do so. I decided I liked him.

Our party became quieter, more weary, and more watchful each day. The musicians didn't gather to play. Children were no longer allowed to make noise at night.

Two wagons, the Attleroys and the Coltranes, came down with Cholera and had to be set some distance in the rear. They were given laudanum and extra water and told not to approach the main body of the Lucere Party until the sickness had passed. Issa prepared pap-like food for them and left it in the trail for them to find.

Someone started a rumor that Tessa and Mrs. North had brewed up the disease in the sorghum and fed it to the families that grew ill.

The pilot spoke to the entire party that night. "Since we have a very short grapevine out here in the wilderness, I know who started the tale about cholera in the sorghum. I will not say who, but I warn that person that such mean-spirited tales will not be tolerated. You must cease your lies or suffer the consequences."

As he spoke, Hawker kept looking at a boy, may sixteen years of age, named Sven Svenson. Because of the difference in their surnames, I didn't learn until later that Tilsa was his sister. Once I understood that, I reckoned he shared his parents' beliefs about blacks and Catholics.

Within a day and a half, seven of the nine with cholera had died. The two that survived, Mrs. Coltrane and Mr. Attleroy, were too weak to handle the wagons. A fellow named Moffit volunteered to lead the oxen of one wagon with the two survivors riding in it. The pilot had the other wagon and much of the supplies of both wagons burned. When Mrs. Coltrane and Mr. Attleroy had mostly recovered, they bathed thoroughly and burned their togs.

The second wagon also had to be burned. Mrs. Coltrane then joined the Katz family. The pilot approached Ivan and asked, "Would you folks be so kind as to allow Mr. Attleroy to travel with you?"

Ivan consulted with Carla, and we agreed to have him join us.

"Should I be afraid I'll get cholera?" I asked Carla.

"I believe the danger had passed, darling," she said.

Mr. Attleroy—William his given name—was a young cove perhaps twenty-five or a bit younger, tall and lean, with a long mug and sandy hair. At first, tearful at times and downcast, he kept to himself.

Knowing he suffered so, I felt all-overish walking with him. I failed to think of anything to lift his spirits.

Tessa did him the most good. She gathered purple flowers she called lupin, and gave them to William, saying, "In remembrance of your departed family."

I'd not seen him smile until then. He carried them as he walked, and I grew more comfortable with him.

Not long after, he seemed to rise out of his grieving some. He showed Cedric and me a magic trick that made a small handkerchief disappear.

"I poke the handkerchief into my closed fist thusly, wave my hand over it and, voila! It's gone." He showed his empty hands.

Cedric got taken in by the jig. I'd seen how it worked, but I pretended to be astounded.

William spoke to us children before he became willing to talk to the other grown men and women, told us many things about his lost family members as we walked along behind our wagon.

"My brother, Harold, juggled." he said. He picked up rocks, juggled them poorly, and dropped them. "I was never any good at it. Harold would have astonished you with his skill. As boys, we earned performing in the streets of Chicago, my magic, his juggling. Had a little dog, Jasper, that could do tricks too. The Attleroy Circus truly never took in much, yet we were proud of what we did earn."

Though he said a great deal more about his brother, I cannot remember much else. Then he'd turn to speaking of one of the others he'd lost.

"Harold's wife, Mary, liked spoonerisms and puns. She was quick-witted and droll. Always had a clever thing to say."

"Where we come from," Cedric said, "we call those word-peckers."

"I'll have to remember that," William said. He tousled little brother's hair. "Since my knees pop when I walk sometimes, she called me Little Willie Rattle Boy. You know, 'cause it rhymes with *Attleroy*."

I didn't truly understand him at the time. We laughed with him all the same. Took me a while to see he tried to bring up only pleasant memories.

He also spoke of his brother's children, a son, Philip, about my age, who drew cartoons, and a girl, Eleanor. I remembered meeting her. She was little, maybe seven. I don't think I ever spoke to her.

"Tarnation, that boy could draw *anything*," William said, "right out of his head, no model."

That's the one and only time I heard him cuss.

"And little Nell, she wanted to be a ballet dancer. Most girls don't like bugs, but she loved them. She said insects were dancers with too many legs."

He went on telling about them for several days, every now and then remembering something fun and saying it. He gave all of what he offered of his family with a smile and good humor. I'd a sense he had to give it that way or not at all.

"Each one of them had a little bit of the *true* magic in the world," he said. "What I do is mere tricks."

That was the last thing I remember him saying about them.

After several days of that, he seemed a lot better and would easily speak to anyone.

A widower named Dreyer died one night, leaving his five children on their own, the oldest a girl named Sally, sixteen years. William Attleroy volunteered to travel with them, and we saw less of him thereafter.

At nine years of age, I'd seen my share of the dead and dying in New York. The way people acted around death could be as different as the people themselves. I'd known much wailing and weeping over the dead. And anger, especially with a person killed by another. Sometimes vows of revenge, followed by more violence.

Never had I known someone to so gracefully let their loved ones go as I saw with William Attleroy. I could only hope I would do as well saying goodbye to my loved ones.

One day, I saw William and Sally together in the distance among the grasses. He offered her a bouquet of Lupin.

Ivan might have seen that too. From time to time, I saw him collect different colors of flowers from the prairie and present them to Tessa. After one such offering, I saw her kiss him.

Those gifts of flowers were a good thing to have come from all that death.

—⁂—

Word went around that the pilot spoke to Mr. Sven Anderson and his wife, Agnes Eriksdotter, about their children, Tilsa and Sven, speaking out against members of the party. We had no notion as to how that talk went.

Not understanding why all their surnames were different if they belonged to the same family, I got the notion that perhaps the father and mother had their children out of wedlock. I thought to hold that against them. Remembering Carla's words, I let that go.

—⁂—

On occasion, we saw Indians on foot or horseback, watching us from the horizon. They kept their distance.

The night after some on horseback followed us for a disagreeable time, I dreamt that my giant Ma and Papa met with a colossal Indian, sitting amidst the open plains we'd recently entered. The Indian was part rock, part forest, with brooks and springs running along his arms and legs. When he opened his mouth to speak, a beautiful waterfall spilled from the rocky cleft of his mouth, splashed down his chin, and fell into a sparkling pond in his lap.

Ma offered him a stripey blanket, slightly stained. Papa gave him whiskey.

Unaccountably troubled by their gifts, I turned away and sought other dreams. I found none, and lay awake for a time, hearing others among the wagon train restless in their sleep. In the distance, an infant born within the last week cried for a short time. Some moaning and a few muted cries reached my ears. I heard someone say, possibly to a troubled family member, "You've had a nightmare, is all." From a different direction, I heard, "Just a bad dream. Go back to sleep." What might we have had in common that disturbed our sleep, something already past or fears of the coming days?

The world didn't have enough flowers to keep all of us happy. Much of the good will at the beginning of our travels would be lost with time.

Cedric—11
June, 1847

I'd done some walking with Zeata North. Had to wonder what allowed me to so easily accept this black girl as a friend. I decided that my friendship with Ivan had somehow changed me. Yet it wasn't just that some of my bigotry had fallen off. Until I met Zeata, I'd looked upon most other girls but Alta Mae as silly. Something about the way Zeata gazed at me squarely when she spoke caught me up and made me look back at her the same way, something that felt good, like we truly saw one another. Otherwise, I couldn't have said why I liked her.

I told her something of my life in New York, leaving out most of the hard parts. I'm certain she continued to believe the lies we'd all told about being Carla's children.

"We come from Indiana where Daddy was a sharecropper," she told me. "Mostly corn and pigs. Before he met Mama and I was born, he escaped slavery in Tennessee, got up through Kentucky without being caught, and crossed the Ohio. He said he lay low for ten years, working for others on farms in Indiana till he believed his old master give up on him and it'd be safe to take his own contract. Mama grew up working the Ohio River with her family. Her father piloted flatboats and become boss of his own crew of fisherman."

"I might like to be a fisherman," I said. "Caught some fish in Indiana once with Ivan."

"What kind of fish?"

"I don't know. He didn't say. They tasted good."

"My favorite is catfish. Grandaddy and his crew catch many kinds of good fish. They also gather river mussels."

"What's a sharecropper?"

"Someone who farms a landlord's property and gives a share to him as rent. We did well enough with that till the landlord passed away. His son inherited, bought the mercantile in town, and raised prices for all his sharecroppers. Then we was tied to the land with debt. Daddy grew angry and talked about it with other sharecroppers working that man's land. They tried to do something 'bout it, going to meet with the landlord. He returned from that meeting bloodied, and with a broke arm, said they were set upon by angry men beholden to the landlord. Daddy couldn't work for the longest time and we got in worse debt. Mama and me, we did all what we could, and done all right, but Daddy said he would not be a slave again, so we all went to work for Grandaddy, saved enough to go west. I think Daddy left Indiana without paying all his debt. We just ran."

She covered her mouth and giggled.

Something shy and endearing about her when she did that. I smiled every time.

—⁓—

Found out Jack Jacobson could read. His father had been a printer and hoped to open a book shop when they got to California.

"My favorite books are adventures," Jack said, "like *The Swiss Family Robinson*, *The Count of Monte Cristo*, and *The Hunchback of Notre-Dame*. My most favorite is *The Last of the Mohicans* by James Fenimore Cooper. It's a fine tale of Indians and war. I'll loan you my copy."

During our evening lessons, Alta Mae, Tessa, and I practiced with the book. We took turns reading it aloud until we'd had the whole tale. The day I returned it, Jack, all smiles, asked. "Did you enjoy it?"

"Yes," I said. "Though some of the story, I couldn't quite picture."

He looked disappointed, then offered me another book, *Oliver Twist* by Charles Dickens. Once we were done with that tale, Jack asked what I thought of it. "Yes, I could well picture that one."

We talked about the story for some time. He seemed surprised I had so much to say about Oliver's plight, and the ways of the child thieves in the tale.

"There are thieves of all sorts," I said. "Lots of them have a specialty. A mutcher robs drunks. A snoozer breaks into hotel rooms where people are sleeping. A bludget is a woman who lures someone into a quiet place where they are easily robbed. When someone is beaten up and robbed, that's called rolling. All kinds of different ways to roll people, and each way is a specialty for some thief."

"What about the pickpockets?"

"There are names for the different types. Wipe haulers are buggsman that steal handkerchiefs. A fine tooler goes after more valuable things, like watches. Autumn Divers pick pockets in church."

"How do you know so much about all that?"

"It's common knowing in New York City, where I come from," I lied.

He looked at me like he thought I was *something*. Almost told him about my life on the streets of New York so he'd understand that I knew those things because I'd been *nothing*. I set aside the temptation.

—⁂—

While we camped near Chimney Rock, a tall, thin peak of stone, trouble found us.

Seems that Florence North was alone, fetching water from the river, when one of the out riders, Hiram Southall, tried to get under her skirts. They fought, and though battered, she got away and he chased her. Her screams alerted her husband, Aubrey, and he came to her aid.

I heard the shot from Southall's barking iron that put a hole in Aubrey's shoulder. I think everyone heard it. Carla, Ivan, and I headed toward the commotion with numerous others, Alta Mae and Tessa not far behind.

We discovered Aubrey and Southall in a tussle on the ground, Florence trying to find a way to help her husband.

The men were pulled apart and held so they couldn't hurt each other. Two big men, Chaim Beile and Herman Franz, had Southall by the arms. Ned Tollard grabbed Aubrey and roughed him up, striking him in the mug and gut.

The pilot, arriving on horseback, shouted, "Stop hitting him!"

When Tollard didn't stop, Hawker pushed his mount forward, grabbed him by the collar, and pull him backwards away from Aubrey. He let go and Tollard fell on his arse. Then the blunderbuss scrambled to rise and get away from the prancer's moving hooves.

The pilot dismounted and addressed the growing crowd while walking in a widening circle. "Folks, please calm down." He had to shout to be heard over the many voices. "Please be quiet. What has happened here?"

Out of breath and gulping for air, Florence said, "Mr. Southall tried to have his way with me at the river, sir. My husband was trying to help me." She bled from a gash on her forehead and one on her left cheek.

"She made advances toward me," Southall said.

"You are a liar, sir," Aubrey said. He coughed, stumbled back a pace, and someone steadied him.

"Then, her husband comes running at me," Southall went on, "murder in his eyes, and I defended myself. You know how these boys are, Mr. Hawker—like animals when they're stoked up."

Zeata North came running for her mother. Florence stopped her, saying, "No, girl, you go stand with Mrs. Angelo."

Zeata, her tears making lines through the dust on her face, joined us. *She* is *one of us* us, I found myself thinking. I took her hand, wanting to protect her. That seemed an odd thing that came over me.

"Do you have a firearm with you, Mr. North," the pilot asked.

"No, sir."

"How did you get those wounds to your face, Mrs. North?"

"*He* done it to me at the river, sir." Florence pointed at Southall. Hawker nodded.

"You're going to believe her?" Southall asked.

I feared that with a white cove speaking against them, the black couple would surely lose to bigotry. Thinking back on my mistrust of Ivan in New York, I believe that then I would have sided with Southall.

"You seem none the worse for wear, Mr. Southall," Hawker said.

Hiram's brother, Wayne, rode up and dismounted, wanting to know what was going on.

Hawker ignored him. "Get Mr. North some care," he said. "Mrs. North, you, your husband, and daughter go with Issa and she'll help clean and bandage your wounds."

Zeata looked at me kindly before letting go my hand. Issa led the North family away, back toward the camp.

"Let go my brother," Wayne Southall said to Beile and Franz.

"No, sir," Hawker said.

His words raised sounds of surprise from the growing crowd of onlookers.

"You two hold on to that man." He turned to Wayne Southall, the older of the two brothers. "I'd heard a few whisperings about Hiram, but I liked you, Wayne, and we would have been shorthanded if I hadn't taken you both on this season."

His purpose clear, the pilot kept walking the edge of the center circle, getting too close to the onlookers so that they had to stepped back, keeping about twenty feet open. Being so near the action, though we moved back a few times, we still stood at the edge of that open circle. By now, most of the Lucere Party had arrived to join us on the gravel downslope to the river. Finding myself in a crowd, surrounded by hundreds of people sorely tempted me to reach into a few pockets.

Some folks elbowed their way to a better vantage, others craned their necks to look over the shoulders of those in front of them. Their voices became a constant murmur behind us, most of it making no sense. I did clearly hear someone say, "The black man and his wife tried to rob the out rider." Was a man, yet sounded something like the girl, Tilsa, that Alta Mae had befriended for a time. I'd heard that Tilsa's whole family helped start the rumor about the sorghum being tainted. I had been steering clear of them.

Some parents told their children to go back to camp, while others allowed their children to stand behind them. Alta Mae seemed to think it best to do as the other children did—she pulled me back behind Carla's and Tessa's skirts.

"If my brother says he didn't do anything wrong—" Wayne began.

"I *didn't* do anything," Hiram said. "Man alive!"

"Since you're the only one unharmed, common sense says you did," Hawker said.

Someone called out as if surprised, "He trusts the blacks,"

followed by further grumbling from some.

The out rider, Niklas Gruber, arrived and stood across the center circle from us.

"Now, hold on, sir," Wayne Southall said. "Land sakes, you can't take the word of those people over Hiram's."

"I can and I will." The pilot placed a hand on the hilt of his Arkansas toothpick.

Again, sounds of surprise from the crowd.

"I shouldn't have to remind you that I am in command here," Hawker said. "Your brother will be relieved of his duties and he'll be restrained."

"In what way, sir?" Wayne asked.

Undaunted, the pilot looked him in the eyes. "He shall be shackled, tethered to a wagon, and walk as we continue. At night, he will sleep chained to a wheel."

An outraged voice from the crowd, asked, "A white man?" I looked toward the voice and saw Sven Anderson.

"No," Wayne said, his hands out and away from the weapons at his belt, as if he knew to take care with Hawker. "There's got to be a better way to handle this."

The out rider, Sam Hoog, arrived and stood with Gruber.

A cove name Terrance Otter stepped forward to speak to the pilot. "I'll allow it looks bad for Mr. Southall, but ain't there a better way than taking his liberty?"

"Was his liberty that afforded him the opportunity to do what he did," Hawker said.

Wayne Southall paced angrily within the circle. He looked to be trying to make a decision.

Artimous Lucere, approached the pilot. "Sir, we need his protection. He's been guarding our left flank, and he's brought in plenty of venison."

"No, sir," Hawker replied. "You are bargaining to replace a danger from without with a danger from within."

"She is *just* a darky," Otter said.

I could see the muscles in Ivan's jaw stand out, and he took a step toward Otter.

132

A simpkin through and through, the man glanced at Ivan, said, "No disrespect to you."

"Everyone has paid for the same guidance on this journey, and the same protection," Hawker said. "The North family is as important as any other in the wagon train."

"Seems to me, you think they are more important," someone shouted, "the way you turn on anyone who stands up to them." The voice belonged to Tollard. He stepped into the central circle with a barker drawn. "Wayne, draw your pistol and take charge. This man—" he gestured toward Hawker, "—doesn't see the world for what it is. We can't have him leading us."

Wayne Southall's hand had hardly touched his pistol grip when he discovered Ivan aiming a pistol at him.

Just as swiftly, the pilot used his left hand to grip Tollard's pistol, the flesh between Hawker's thumb and forefinger slipping in between the hammer and the percussion cap. Quick, his right fist found Tollard's jaw with a sound like a cleaver striking a butcher's block. He went down. The pistol remained in the pilot's hand.

The out riders, Gruber and Hoog, had drawn revolvers.

Hawker drew his long knife, then turned to say to Ivan, "Thank you. You are welcome to keep that pistol pointed at him."

"I will, sir," Ivan said, "until you say otherwise."

The pilot faced his men, said, "Niklas, get over here and help me with these makers of mischief. Sam, fetch three sets of shackles."

Tollard's family—I believe twelve of them altogether—beseeched the pilot for mercy, their voices a meaningless jumble.

"Go on, now," the pilot said, making a shooing gesture. "You folks all go back to the camp."

The crowd was in no hurry to leave.

"I mean all of you," he shouted, still waving his free hand at them. "Go! We need room to do what has to be done."

I saw a blood blister on his left hand where the hammer of Tollard's pistol must have come down on it.

Wayne Southall got loose as the out rider, Gruber, tried to disarm him. He broke away and ran. At least ten men of the party went after him. Once they got him down, it took six of them to keep him there.

He hollered and lashed out, drew blood from more than one mug.

I'd begun to fear there might be enough hatred of blacks among the Lucere Party that Ivan and Tessa would be under threat too. Seeing so many willing to help capture Wayne Southall helped ease my worries.

Now, they had him hogtied on the ground. The pilot kept an eye on him.

Gruber sat on Tollard. Addled from Hawker's blow to his chin, he wasn't much trouble.

People were moving away toward the camp. I suspected those who stayed behind believed Hiram Southall had been maltreated.

Hoog, carrying a jangling sack wrapped around the horn of his prancer's saddle, passed us as we headed back toward the camp.

Though glad to see the Norths would not be blamed in any way by the pilot, I remained fearful the anger we'd seen in our party might grow and spread.

—⁓—

The next day, The pilot spoke to the entire Lucere Party.

"We've had hard feelings from yesterday's events, and I've had to think long and hard about how to address it. I've spoken to General Superintendent Lucere, our board of trustees, including Mr. Ned Tollard, who will be giving up his role on the board, and numerous others showing concern about our troubles. The Southalls are indeed part of the protection for our party, and among those who provide much needed meat to supplement our supplies. Yet, I cannot just forgive and forget. Hiram has committed a crime. Mr. Tollard and Wayne have acted against my command with an attempted mutiny. They are acting in some part on their hatred of blacks. Whilst I can do nothing about what grows in a man's heart, I will not tolerate such bigotry expressed openly. Some have asked that, since we will soon arrive at Fort Laramie, I should hand Mr. Tollard, and the Southalls over to authorities there. The fort is a trading post, not a military outpost. There is no law in this wilderness but what we brought with us. I am in charge and represent the highest authority within our party."

For Ivan's, Tessa's, and the North's sake, I was glad to hear

Hawker's words.

"And that brings me to the persistent rumor of the poisoning of the sorghum syrup. I have heard several versions of this bunkum. All of them pretend that Mrs. Tessa Angelo and Mrs. North somehow gave cholera to those who became ill. One story has them dancing by moonlight to call faeries to do the work for them. Let me assure you that they could not have done anything of the sort without getting the disease themselves. The only purpose of these cock and bull stories is to besmirch the character of these women, who have done nothing wrong. Indeed, they have done as much or more than any of you to help make our endeavor a success. From this moment forward, anyone who aids the spread of the cruel falsehood will suffer severe consequences."

The pilot looked directly at Sven Anderson and his family. "Some among you have said that if the three men in question are treated as prisoners my authority will be compromised. I don't have a lick of spit for those who question my command. The Southall brothers and Mr. Tollard are still a danger. They cannot abide among us without being restrained."

Anderson spat upon the ground to show his disgust, and a clamor of voices rose up among the party.

The pilot paused, holding his hands out to ask for calm and giving time for the voices to die down.

"With all that, some have declared the reasonable concern that we'll suffer the loss of security should the Southalls be restrained. I spoke with the brothers and Mr. Tollard this morning, and we have come to an agreement. They will take one of the supply wagons and follow us at a distance no closer that half a mile. Mr. Tollard, his family, and two wagons will join them. Wayne Southall will continue to protect our rear—his original duty—with his brother's assistance. Ivan Romano has agreed to take the position protecting our left flank."

Again, he paused to allow the hubbub to die down.

"I know from my discussions that there are those among us with such hard feelings that they might wish to join the Southalls and Tollards."

Again, he looked at Anderson and his family. "I do not recommend that. Still, if you feel you cannot be civil among the Lucere Party, please consider going with them. We will be marking dangers, such as the quicksand pits near where we ford the Platte River a few days hence. The Southalls will recognize the markers and help you get through safely. Those interested, meet me at the western flank of Chimney Rock at dawn tomorrow.

"Finally, within four days, we will arrive at Fort Laramie where we can take a day to rest, and resupply to a limited amount. Those who don't want to go with the Lucere Party or the Southall Party will have the opportunity to wait there and perhaps join a later emigrant party."

—⁂—

As the Lucere Party moved on the next day, we had eighty wagons and four hundred and five people.

Four wagons with twenty five people had split off to join the Southall Party, now seven wagons and thirty-nine people altogether, Anderson and his family among them.

Good riddance.

Yet I knew that many with scorn for blacks remained hidden among us.

I retrieved my pistol, a few paper cartridges, and percussion caps from the trunk where they were kept. After loading the barker, I placed some caps and cartridges in my pockets. I tucked the weapon into the waist band of my trousers and hid it beneath my shirt. There it would stay until such time I might need it.

Alta Mae—11
July, 1847

The agreement with the Southall Party took some trust since it required them to halt and wait if they got close enough to see the Lucere Party.

The pilot asked a fellow named Argus Leventis, a short, black-haired fellow who wore a hat with a long bill, to take his wagon and three brothers to the rear position and keep a watch on what might be seen of the Southall Party.

"What skills do you suppose they have that make them right for the job?" I asked Cedric.

"I don't know about his brothers," he said, "but Argus Leventus is known to sight his Sharps rifle on game very far away and bring them down. He's made many kills without leaving the wagon train, and the outriders bring them in to us. His rifle takes percussion caps on a tape roll housed in the gun, and—"

"How does that make him a good choice for our rear?"

"Yes, well, Leventis has good eyes. He doesn't miss much. He'll tell the pilot if the Southall Party gets too close."

A moment later, he added, "Is a bene rifle, is all. Wish I had one like it."

The Lucere Party voted to replace Ned Tollard on the board of trustees with Argus Leventis.

As we set out again, rain found us on and off. The weather warm, the wetness made little difference.

Fort Laramie had not even come into sight when Mr. McBaird rode back with word about it. Cedric's friend, Jack Jacobson, came running back along the line of wagons shouting the news, "The fort flies the yellow flag!" He was soaking wet from the downpour up ahead. Within moments the rain had reached us.

I looked to Carla for answers. "That means the fort is under quarantine. We won't be able to stop there."

We gave Fort Laramie a wide berth. Thin smoke rose from the pale brown castle made of logs smoothed over with mud. The walls stood maybe twenty feet tall. Overhanging houses squatted at two corners, and one perched over the entrance gate. The yellow flag flew from a pole fifty feet tall. Heard it snapping in the high wind until another sudden downpour drowned it out.

The prairie surrounding the fort was spotted with the stone rings of campfires, and worn trails from recent foot traffic. That told me that there had been many people camped there, possibly hundreds. Maybe a hundred and fifty yards from the entrance, two burnt heaps stood out on the field, one giving off lazy wisps of smoke. When Jack Jacobson headed back up along the line, he said he'd been told those heaps were burnt teepees, perhaps where the disease had been discovered.

We moved on a couple more miles westward before making camp for the night. From there, I saw in the far distance the dim outlines of great mountain peaks.

We took the following day for rest.

—w—

The trail took us through a few difficult crossings of the Platte River. Where we found the river as shallow as three feet, the water wound crazily within its path, leaving sandbars and trapped water that reeked of rot and death. Mr. McBaird located a path across each time. He and the out riders placed willow stakes in the ground every five to ten feet to mark the way through the firmest sand and shallowest water.

"Stay well within the rows of stakes," the pilot told us at the first crossing. "Quicksand lies just beyond."

Each time, Olin Tipton led his lead cow across first, and the other cattle followed.

One cow got too close to the edge during the second crossing. The sandbar beneath its hooves crumbled, and it fell with a bellow into water only a few inches deep. I thought it would get up. As it struggled to do so, the sand beneath it open up and swallowed the animal within moments.

Shocked, I stood on the bank and said nothing, did nothing but watch bubbles rise from the hungry sand where the beast had gone down. I believe most everyone else, Mr. Tipton too, had greeted the disaster with much the same dazed silence.

The pilot said loudly, "And there's our lesson for the day."

The wagons, with oxen harnessed at both ends crossed after the horses. Then the members of the Lucere Party crossed while holding onto a rope anchored to each bank. We got plenty wet and the current did its best to drag us downstream.

We'd come to land where the grass wasn't as tall. Instead, much of the growth knitted itself together tightly, as if to hold the ground down. Indeed, there looked to be little soil covering rock that appeared close to the top. In places, that rock poked up out of the ground in odd shapes hundreds of feet tall. The big ones had been given names; Chimney Rock, the Courthouse and Jail, and Scott's Bluff. That last one, because of its name, I kept wondering how it might be part of some trickery by a cove named Scott. I asked Carla about it. "It's not at all the same, unless both mean face. Hmm..., rock face and gammoning face. I can see that."

I didn't know what she meant.

The long, hot summer days wore us all down. The birth of three infants within two weeks and their crying at night made sleep more difficult. Folks had become weary enough to argue over foolish things, with now and then fisticuffs among the men. The pilot ended most of those. When the women fought, insults and bitterness flew, although one woman put a serving fork through her sister's hand.

I saw a fight between two men over a rock. One was John Stilton, father of the b'hoy that failed to bully Cedric. He and his family traveled two wagons ahead of ours. The other man, a cove named Claud Marco, traveled with his family in the one just ahead of ours.

The fight happened some distance beyond a giant stone—more like a hill—named Independence. We'd begun a steep climb that went on for many miles. In a long stretch of sand, one of the wagons far ahead of us began to suffer and we had to stop for the repair of a wheel. Folks were placing chocks behind the wheels of their wagons to keep them from rolling back the way we'd come. That also relieved the oxen of the burden of holding them in place.

"One of my chocks is missing." Mr. Stilton said. He set the chock he had behind a rear wheel of his wagon. Then he and his family started looking around.

Mr. Marco had set a chock behind one of the rear wheels of his wagon.

Stilton said to him, "I seem to recall you complaining you'd left both of yours behind after that commotion at Chimney Rock."

Lifting a rock to place behind the other rear wheel, Mr. Marco said nothing. The stone appeared to be the only one of any size within sight upon the slope.

Stilton approached and shoved Marco, knocking him off his feet and forcing him to drop the rock.

"Mine," Stilton said, "since you stole one of my chocks." He picked up the rock and moved to place it as his second chock.

His son, Tommy, laughed at Marco. Mrs. Stilton hid her mug and turned her back to her husband.

"I did no such thing," Marco said. He rose and bowled into Stilton, knocking him down behind his wagon. The rock rolled away.

Marco grabbed the chock Stilton had already set.

Stilton's wagon lurched back. The oxen, slow to take up the slack, allowed the wagon to run into Marco, knocking him off his feet. The men fell to wrestling with one another, scratching and gouging mostly because they couldn't get away from each other enough to swing a punch.

Tommy cheered his father on.

Stilton managed to garble out, "The brake, Tommy."

The addle-cove had forgot to set his wagon's brake! Not that it would have held on such a steepness, but it would have helped.

Tommy jumped up into the driver's seat to do his father's bidding.

By then, several men had arrived to break up the fight. As the wagon still heaved backwards a time or two, they weren't in a hurry.

"Can't, Pop-sss," Tommy cried, "the sss-trap broke.

One fellow ran forward to take control of the oxen. What that cove did was no doubt the opposite of what he meant to do. The wagon rolled back further, rolling over the fingers of Marco's left hand. He screamed.

The Wagon stopped rolling, became still as Tommy hauled on the brake.

The men who came to break up the fight helped the two men up. They hurried Marco away to have Issa tend his wounds.

Chocks and rocks got sorted, Issa splinted the broken fingers, and that evening at our camp, the two men got drunk together and laughed about what had happened.

"I thought they hated each other," Cedric said to me. "Why would they be laughing together?"

I shrugged. "What better have they got to do?" I said for amusement.

When he nodded as if understanding, I knew I was on to something.

Cedric—12
August, 1847

Following a couple of days of steady uphill climb, we enjoyed a downslope into a shallow valley, or basin, as the pilot called it.

Evening of the second day, he spoke to the Lucere Party. "We are nearing South Pass at the Continental Divide."

"Where the mountains cut the land in two," my friend Jack Jacobson shouted.

Hawker turned a stern gaze on Jack, said, "Truly, it divides the flow of water. If rain falls to the west of the divide, it flows toward the Pacific Ocean. On the eastern side, it flows toward the Atlantic."

"Sorry to interrupt," Jack said, looking chastened and a bit foolish.

"South Pass is close to the mid-point in our journey." Hawker said.

A man named Albert Loffler hooted loudly, shouted, "Cause to celebrate." He and several other men hollered and carried on as if they'd start the celebration right then.

The pilot waited for them to become quiet. "Other emigrant parties have celebrated there. I see no harm in it, as long as folks are careful and keep in mind that we have far to go before our travails are done."

Loffler and others took up their hooting and hollering again.

As if not wanting to encourage them further, Hawker turned away and left the meeting.

The brush in the basin was scrubby, except along the water where trees grew. What looked to be broad stream beds were far from full. We had filled our water barrels at a place called Sweetwater, knowing we would not have an easy supply again for several days.

Our first evening in the valley, Argus Leventis alerted the pilot that he'd spotted someone approaching from the Southall Party.

I did not hear what they said. Had it from Ivan when he told Carla.

"Hawker told Leventis to fetch me to lead that person in," Ivan said. "Turned out to be Wayne Southall. He were none too glad to see me holding a pistol on him again. I think it pleased Hawker to have me do it." I thought Ivan would smile at that. Instead, he shook his head, saddened, before going on.

"Southall tells the pilot. 'We lost our supply wagon to the river. Second crossing, that fool Tollard got too close to a fallen willow stake, and the wagon went over. Quicksand almost took him, but we got him out. The wagon was hopeless. Most of our supplies floated away down river. We spent a day and more going after what we could.'

"I remembered the cow that fell in had knocked that willow stake over," Ivan said, "and it come to rest some ten feet out amidst the quicksand. No doubt I weren't the only one meaning to place another stake, and then forgetting to do so, yet that troubles me a great deal." He shook his head sadly again.

"'You'll have to make do with what's left in the other wagons,' says Hawker.

"'See, that's where we're in a fix,' Southall says. 'Tollard's women gave him hell for the part he played in the split. They demanded to ride. He urged me and Hiram to let them do it until their anger died down. We agreed and their supplies went into the supply wagon to make room. Well, then the other women of the party had to have the same. To keep the peace, we let them and just shifted more supplies. Of course, whilst everyone got across the river on the rope, most of our supplies were in the wagon that fell in.'

"All business, the pilot says, 'You knew better than to allow that, Wayne.'

"Wayne seems to be working hard at holding himself together. 'Take pity on us, sir,' says he. 'We still have some flour and salt pork, and we're doing our best to hunt, but we lost most of the barley and oats the oxen will need when we cross the desert.'

"The pilot ain't having any of it. 'Wayne,' he says, 'you and your brother are lucky to have your liberty, Tollard too. The rest of your party had a choice and they made it. The company contract clearly states that those who willingly split from the wagon train forfeit any rights to our protection. I am beholden to the people who did not leave, and to give you more supplies would threaten their endeavor. Now, use that liberty you are fortunate to have and take your party back to Missouri. That's all you folks have left. Better that than go forward toward winter with too little.'

"Southall stares at Hawker for a long while, even though he's got to see early on that the cove is hard as stone. I don't like seeing it. Then he gets up and walks away. I take him back the way he come in and watch him move off into the growing dark."

Ivan shook his head and rubbed his forehead. "That damned willow stake! Hawker said it were a lesson. Little did he know how big that lesson would be."

"You are not to blame," Carla said, placing a hand on his cheek. "You didn't mean to leave that stake out there. Like you said, you wouldn't have been the only one meaning to replace it."

"Still and all, with my anger at those people, how easily did it slip my mind?"

I was grown before I fully understood that he simply regretted his anger toward them because it *might* have played a part in his forgetting.

Ever the mothering aunt, Carla said, "We can take comfort that no one died."

"Not yet," Ivan said, his tone giving me a chill. "You didn't see the look in Wayne Southall's eyes. We may not have seen the last of him."

Alta Mae—12

We took a day of rest at South Pass. The night before we'd made camp as usual, with two circles of the wagons, a western one for the livestock and an eastern one for our cook fires, the two separated by about thirty feet.

In and around the eastern one, the celebration to mark the half-way point in our travel went on all day and into the night. Within the circle, we had plenty of good food, drink, dancing, and music. Someone dragged a small harpsichord down from a wagon and sat to play.

In dutch ovens, Tessa baked cobblers with fruit preserves inside. Mrs. North broke eggs that had been sealed with bees wax for the long trip. She prepared batter from corn meal and flour, a little fresh milk, egg yolks, and sugar. Then she whipped the whites stiff, folded it into the batter, and baked all that in dutch ovens to make delicious, fluffy spoonbread. Had mine with a bit of honey. The best thing that ever touched my red rag.

Outside the circle, courts were laid for horseshoes and skittles for the grown men. The children split into groups to play their own games. I played with the girls, Cedric with some of the boys, while another group of boys with Tommy Stilton played some distance away.

The men got up to some foolish drinking games, and their wives stood by to show disapproval or to haul them off to their bedrolls if need be.

Carla and I left the celebration and returned to the wagon to get some rest despite knowing that no one would be silencing the revelers. I would not be getting to sleep easily.

Tessa had not returned from the celebration where I'd seen her talking and laughing with Issa.

Carla rummaged through a trunk in the wagon until she located a box and offered it to me. The box was pink and green and held shut by a pink and green striped ribbon.

"We'll save the dobbin for your hair," she said.

I smiled and nodded, struggling not to turn my nose up at the notion.

A beautiful green linen bodice and matching top skirt lay within, nestled in pale green paper.

"I were saving it to give you once we got to California," Carla said. "But I thought you'd like to see it now."

The bodice had a darker green ribbon sewn along the bust and a small bit of lace at the collar and cuffs—very pretty for the right sort of girl. Though I thought I'd look silly in it, I thanked her with feigned delight that seemed to have been persuasive.

I still didn't see myself as a proper girl. More like something scraped up out of a Five Points gutter and molded into female form.

"I think of you as my own," Carla said. "I can't help it. Please don't allow that to trouble you. You are not my servant and should not feel beholden to me. I give my affection freely. We didn't get off to a good start, me fighting with you and the demands I made. Please accept my apology."

I nodded and turned away some so she would not see the mist gathering in my blinkers.

For the first time in my life, I felt like I had someone to look out for me, some one—unlike Egan—that was dependable. I had gained a mother!

"I know I did the same to your brother," she said, "and I am truly sorry for that. I have tried to treat him right since, with the hope that he'll forgive me one day."

"You might apologize to him too," I said, wiping away my tears.

Carla remained quiet for a long time. She bowed her head, and I feared she'd become angry and didn't want me to see it. I couldn't have been more wrong.

"I never knew what to do with boys," she said. "Lost one in childbirth and could not help thinking he must not have wanted me for his mum. I were very young and foolish, but I have never shaken the idea."

I knew how such notions could be hard to shed.

Surprised to find myself giving her a hug.

When I pulled away, she mopped at her cheeks. "I will find a moment to apologize to your Cedric."

I clasped her hands. "He's changed. You'll see once you speak to him. He might not admit it easily, but he's your Cedric too, now."

Cedric—13

During the celebration, two drunk men, Albert Loffler and Sabin Hendrix, made a miniature continental divide. Jack Jacobson and I heard their loud voices and left our games to go have a look at what they were doing. They'd set up a couple of washboards to make a mountain with an eastern side and western side. Over that, they draped one of the waxed canvas bonnets off a wagon. They shaped the folds so that liquid poured at the summit would flow to a small outlet on either side. Other drunken revelers took an interest in the goings-on and gathered round.

"We drink to the Continental Divide!" Loffler said.

He and Hendrix positioned themselves at the outlets and asked Claud Marco to pour red wine over the summit so it flowed on each side. The wine spilled down the eastern side and leaped into Hendrix's gullet. He swallowed heartily to the cheers of the onlookers, then said, "I am the Atlantic Ocean." He belched loudly, and seemed to swoon a bit before catching himself. "That's my last drink of the night. I'm off to bed." He stumbled away, looking like he might hash.

"And I am our future, the Pacific Ocean!" Loffler cried. He took the western position and began to drink. When Hendrix ceased pouring, Loffler raised a hand and gestured in a circle to encourage him to send more down the slope. While the loud cheers of the crowd goaded him on, he drank the entire bottle that way.

A commotion came from someone elbowing through the crowd toward us. "Let me through!" the pilot said. The gathering parted to let him approach the miniature Continental Divide. "What goes on?"

"We're jus' hav'na drink," Loffler said.

The crowd had become quiet quick, like children thinking they'd done something wrong. And it looked like they had done.

"Why is this bonnet doused in wine?"

"Show 'em, Sabin," Loffler said, and he placed his mouth to receive more wine.

Sabin began to pour from a fresh bottle.

"Stop!" cried the pilot.

Sabin ceased pouring. Loffler kept his bone box where it would receive the wine.

Hawker shoved him out of the way and the wine spilled onto the ground. "If that's one of the bonnets treated with borax, then you have poisoned yourself, sir."

"'Tis off my wagon," Loffler said. "I'll do's I please."

"Sir, was your bonnet treated with Borax?"

"No, sir, s'far's I know."

"If you don't know, you need to give up the drink you swallowed."

"What? Puke out all that good wine?"

"Yes," the pilot grabbed Loffler by the arm, twisted it behind his back.

Loffler struggled mightily, dislocating the shoulder of the arm Hawker held. He cried out and the pilot let go. Loffler dashed into the crowd. Hawker tried to follow. Claud Marco got in his way.

"We're just having some fun, sir."

"Out of my way!" The pilot shoved him aside, but the crowd had closed in behind to get a better look at the struggle.

Hawker sent several men to search for Loffler, and had the miniature Continental Divide taken apart.

The searchers returned after half an hour to say they had not found him.

"Keep trying," the pilot said.

Weary from the long day of rest, I said goodnight to friends and headed back to the camp Carla and Tessa had set up at our wagon. Zeata walked with me since her camp lay near ours.

"I seen you rubbing your root today," she said.

I turned to her, hoping I'd misheard. The briefest glimpse of her face told me I'd heard correctly, and I wanted to hide. I bowed my head, my face hot. Though I kept walking, I'd fallen into a deep wallow of shame, something like that quicksand that swallowed the cow. Sudden and final-seeming, it gulped me down.

I'd been fetching stores for Carla and thinking of Zeata when my knob got big. Not knowing I was going to do it, I reached to make it go down, as I'd done all my life. At least I didn't have it out.

Still, she'd seen me touching it. Like as not, she'd have no more to do with me.

And that would be best, because I couldn't face her.

For all that, a loneliness came over me that said, *Find a way to make it right.*

I turned back to her, expecting to see her disgust, but she looked at me as squarely as ever.

"Seen you do that a time or two now. Some people are cruel and might make more of it than you mean for them to. If you did that sort of thing in private, that wouldn't happen."

And with that, she'd lifted me out of the quicksand. Her even gaze put me at ease.

"Yes," I said. "I'll be more careful."

She gave me a mow on the cheek, and walked away toward her family's camp.

What swelled then was my heart. Grew inside me with such feeling for her that I worried there might not be any room left for the rest of me.

Standing there, trying to put myself back together so I could walk away, I heard the sound of a barking iron in the direction she'd taken.

Whole again in an instant, I ran toward her family's camp. Heard screams and a scuffling in the brush as I neared their wagon. In the gloom, I could not tell who were the three dark shapes I saw; one moving toward the wagon, a smaller one backing away, a third with a lamp.

As the lamp turned with the one holding it, light fell on Ned Tollard. He moved toward the one with the lamp. Now, I could see that that one wore skirts—Mrs. North, I figured.

Had my barker out as he raised a pistol to fire on her. My shot found him first; tore a hole in his neck.

Once he was down, and not moving, I hurried to Mrs. North. She took me in a great hug, but released me quick. "Aubrey, Zeata!"

she said.

She led us in a search around their wagon. On the far side, we discovered Zeata crouched beside her father. Aubrey lay dead upon the ground, shot through the chest. Zeata wept, her head on his left shoulder.

"That skinny one that hurt Mama," she said. "He done it and run off." She pointed eastward.

I decided she meant Hiram Southall.

Heard those from a neighboring wagon approaching. One among them, a woman seeing Aubrey on the ground shouted "murder!" Several times.

More shots to my right, toward our wagon.

I looked at Mrs. North.

"Don't," she said.

I left her and ran toward our wagon.

Alta Mae—13

"Carlotta Angelo…," came a Britisher's voice from behind Carla. I looked up to see Fletcher Carson appear out of the night, a single shot barker in each hand.

"…you'll fetch me Lowell's darby," he said, "or I'll kill you here and *now*."

In the dim light, the shadows beneath his scarred left cheek and the twisted, bulging brow above it gave him the look of an angry, snarling cur. He had sacks on his feet, tied at the ankles. I didn't know what to make of that.

The spring in me wound up so fast, I became dizzy.

Carla stood slowly and turned, moving away from me. "I spent all of the funds on this wagon and accoutrements for our travels."

"Mostly hard cole, that darby should easily buy twenty or more of those."

"You do know I were the bookkeeper," Carla said, still moving away from me.

I had to do something and made to get up and follow.

"Stay where you are, darling," she said, showing me a hand.

"We spent much of it just keeping ourselves housed and fed through the winter in St. Louis," she told Fletcher.

"Were a deep hole you put Lowell in," he said. "so you'd have plenty left." He quickly craned his neck as if looking out into the night toward the west for something. "Find me that darby, now!"

Though he said "now" he didn't seem to be in a big hurry. I had it that he waited for something.

"Lowell must have told a great, tall tale of this fortune for you to stick to such a fool's errand. How long has he wanted to be rid of you?"

Did his twisted features show a shade of doubt at those words? Flashed across his face so fast, I couldn't be certain.

"Do you know how far you are from the Points?" Carla asked.

"Yes, I do," he said. "For months now, I've eaten little but the scraps your party left on the trail. Do you see my determination in that?"

Again, he glanced out into the night toward the west, and I quickly slipped my hand into the pocket of my skirt that held my pistol.

I heard a barker fire toward the west, not too distant, and Fletcher glanced again.

Carla made a quick move to draw the pistol she carried. Fletch saw, and fired one of his barkers at her. The shot backed her up against the wagon, and she dropped her pistol.

He aimed the other one at me.

I struggled to draw my pistol.

The hammer on his weapon snapped down and my heart leapt, expecting a shot that didn't come. He lifted the barker to see what had gone wrong and it went off harmlessly into the air over our wagon.

The blue-steel coil in me wound fit to break, I was shaking and unable to aim my pistol. I couldn't pull the trigger, could but wave the weapon in his direction. Threat enough, he turned and ran eastward.

Shadows quickly had him hid. I could only hope he kept running.

Heard a second shot from the same direction as before.

Carla still stood up against the wagon, her breath coming in a hitching manner. In the dim light, I could not see if she'd been shot. I went to her and held her.

Ivan appeared out of the night from the South, running.

"Fletcher Carson," Carla said, pointing east.

Ivan ran after him.

I heard a woman shouting, "murder," the sound coming from the direction of the earlier gunfire.

Carla wrapped her arms around me, said. "Just hold me." She trembled and quaked in my arms.

With that, I feared the worst.

153

Almost lost my barker trying to reload it as I ran. I dropped the cartridge I'd pulled from my pocket.

Heard someone running off toward the East, but I couldn't see who in the dark.

I arrived at our wagon to find Alta Mae holding Carla. They stood up against the side of the wagon. I thought they were unharmed, though Alta Mae wept and Carla looked pale, even in the dim light from the one lit lamp.

My sister pulled away from Mrs. Angelo enough to turn to me. "Help," she said.

Then, Tessa was there, clearing a spot for Carla to sit, as I aided Alta Mae in lowering her. Carla sat with her back against a wheel. She'd been shot through the left side of her chest.

Tessa placed a rag over the bloody hole and held it there. Carla looked like she might swoon from the pain that gave her, her eyes closing for a moment.

"No, no, no!" Alta Mae said.

"What's that, child?" Carla said. Now, she had a wide-eyed look of surprise and pain.

That's when she seemed to see me for the first time. She grabbed my hands, said all in a rush, "Please forgive me for treating you poorly."

That frightened me so bad, I couldn't think what to say.

I heard others gathering behind me. With them came more light, more voices.

"What can we do to help you?" Alta Mae asked, her words a mess of spittle and tears.

Carla turned back to her. "Trust Ivan to protect you."

"Where is he?" I asked.

Her blinkers awash in bitterness, Alta Mae said quietly, "Chasing after Fletcher Carson!"

I had questions, but then the pilot and Issa were shouldering us aside and lifting Carla. They lay her down on one of the bedrolls. Hawker took someone's lamp and held it close to Carla so Issa could inspect the wound.

In that moment, Mrs. Carlotta Angelo seemed to let go her last breath.

I knew that to be true since Issa didn't try to keep Alta Mae away from Carla. My sister fell upon Mrs. Angelo, hugging her and weeping into her neck and shoulder.

"Did you see who shot her," Hawker asked.

Alta Mae shook her head.

"Too dark," I said.

We did not want to have to explain why Carla's killer had followed us all the way from New York.

Issa and the pilot stood and stepped away.

I grabbed at Hawker's hand. "Aubrey North were shot."

"Yes," he said, "we came from there. Mrs. North said you shot Ned Tollard."

The way shadows fell across his features in the darkness, I could not read his mug. Not wanting to allow what I'd done, I shrugged, a clumsy gestured as I quaked with the fear still racing in my blood, my head feeling like it wobbled on tilting wooden shoulders.

I'd a dread of his next words.

He held up the lamp so we could see each other clearly, looked at me closely, his eyes troubled. "A good thing you did. Saved her life. Hiram Southall shot Mr. North. Mr. Gruber and Mr. Hoog are out after him right now. You take care, now."

He put his big hand on my shoulder for a moment before turning away to talk with others, to give commands. Then he was gone.

Though relieved to think I would not suffer for killing Tollard, I found myself thinking of little else. Might I have shot him in the leg? Might I have drawn him away from Mrs. North somehow?

I could not gather my thoughts, and stood there unable to decide what to do, torn between wanting to comfort Alta Mae and making certain Zeata and Florence North were unharmed. Reasoning that the pilot would have done for the Norths, I turned to Alta Mae and held her as she wept. Instead of pushing me away, she held me tight.

I became a stiffened rag in her grip. No tears of my own. I'd killed a man, and for that, I could not know my feelings.

That would come later.

A new commotion commenced at the far side of the circle of wagons. I heard shouting, saw the swing and shift of light from carried lamps.

I tried to step away from Alta Mae, to go look into the new trouble. I could not get loose. She held on so fiercely, she hurt me.

"No," she said, now with tears of anger, "I will not lose you too."

"Please," I said, "I won't leave you. I just need to load my barker. If there be more trouble, it may find us here. I should be ready."

Alta Mae let go.

As I loaded my pistol, Hawker's voice, bellowing orders in the distance, reached us. I couldn't make out his words.

I thought to make a dash for it, but Alta Mae needed me.

Alta Mae—14

Waiting with Cedric to find out what more had happened, I saw lamps held by running figures making a jumble of light and shadow beyond the cook fires.

We crawled under our wagon and watched through the spokes of a wheel. Carla remained with us in a way, lying beside the wheel. While her hand did not grip mine, it still felt warm as I grasped it for comfort.

I'd lost the one true mother I'd ever have. I'd let her into my heart just in time to be heartbroken over her loss.

I felt so foolish, and didn't know why. Perhaps because I should have seen the calamity coming. Carla had brought the danger upon all of us, as Cedric had warned. I'd chosen to forget all about Fletcher Carson.

I could not have stopped him, but if I'd made a break with Carla....

No—No matter how much the loss hurt, I would not trade the time I'd had with Carla for one in which Cedric and I were on our own, unloved and with no one to care for us.

She'd made a terrible mistake, betraying her partner in a criminal scheme, and paid for that with her life. We still had the darby, stolen ill-gotten gains. Ivan would know where it had been hidden. I thought of speaking with him to ask if we should give it to Fletcher if he came for it again.

Would that be going against Carla's wishes? Would that somehow mean we rejected what she'd done for us? In that moment, I could not properly sort my feelings on the matter without condemning my own criminal behavior. With all I had suffered just trying to get on in life, I could not do that yet.

I could but hold Carla's hand and allow time to pass.

Cedric reached to hold my other hand. Through his, I felt him quaking. I, too, shuddered inside. When finally we became still, he slept.

Issa and two men came. "The danger is past," she said.

They had come to fetch Carla. I didn't mind as the warmth had left her. Cedric remained, asleep beneath the wagon, as I followed Issa, the men, and their burden.

Carla was wrapped in a waxed canvas, and placed in one of the supply wagons. Plenty of room there since supplies had gone missing from it. I asked about that, and Issa told me that the last commotion of the evening had been a raid on the supply wagons during the shootings.

"Some of our stores were taken," she said, "barley and oats that we'll need for the livestock as we cross the desert." She gestured toward empty barrels lying upon the ground.

I would later learn that though some heard the raid happening, and went to see about it, no one had seen much in the dark, merely shapes running away into the night carrying sacks of goods pulled from the barrels. Since lives had been taken by gunfire, no one risked giving chase. The outriders might have, but they'd gone off searching for Hiram Southall. Mr. McBaird only arrived after taking several men with him to put out a large fire that had been set several hundred yards to the west of our camp.

McBaird was there going over the ground near the raid. I heard him tell the pilot, "There's no sign of boot prints in the soil. Might have been Arapaho that made the raid, taking advantage of the distraction of the shootings."

As I thought about that, something occurred to me that I said aloud. "The man that shot Carla were wearing sacks tied to his feet. Wouldn't that hide his bootprints?"

Although McBaird looked as if he might like to dismiss my words, he just stared at me for a moment before nodding his head and saying, "Yes, it would."

"Mr. Tollard also had sacks on his feet," Hawker said in a ruminating fashion.

"Perhaps they wanted us to think Indians brought all the trouble tonight," McBaird said. "The raid, the shootings, and the fire to the west were likely all the work of the Southall Party."

"We'll pay them a visit," Hawker said.

He turned to me. "You and your brother have suffered a great loss. Please accept my condolences."

Not knowing what condolences were, I thought he would hand me something. Like a goosecap, I just stood there looking at him, waiting.

A moment later, he said, "We will hold a funeral for your mother, Mr. North, and the fool that attacked his family tomorrow."

He walked away with McBaird.

I thanked Issa, and returned to Cedric.

He still slept.

I wanted to take my bedroll and sleep under the wagon that held Carla, but my brother would need me.

Thinking of her, I lay awake beside him. I had taken all that Carla had to offer, and given what in return? Not much. I could not help wishing I'd done more. Had I given her back the daughter she lost? Had I merely stood in Hetty's place?

Those and other questions about my words and actions with Carla threatened to spoil the memories of the short life I'd had with her.

I decided to take a lesson from William Attleroy, and think of the good; the way she called me "darling," her knowing smile and allowing me my secrets when I clearly hid the truth from her, her stubborn push for something better, and her unspoken willingness to share that with Cedric and me....

———✕———

By the time I awoke mid-morning the next day, Ivan had returned. He'd gone to sleep as he'd been up much of the night. I learned from Cedric that Ivan had not caught Fletcher Carson. I could only wonder what had happened to the rough and if he would be back for another try at the darby.

Albert Loffler had been found dead about a half mile from our camp, possibly poisoned by borax. Sabin Hendrix had fallen ill.

The pilot gave us another day to rest, in part so we could bury the dead—four altogether— and hold what services we could.

I felt the spring in me winding up as I spoke to Catholics among the Lucere Party, trying to find help giving Carla a Catholic funeral. The first few either didn't have time for a girl like me, or perhaps they didn't believe a woman who amalgamated with blacks, as Tilsa had put it, deserved such respect. The blue steel had got awful tight in my chest by the time I spoke to Ezra Bissett. "I have a last rites kit I brought along for our journey," she said. "I'll speak with the lay preacher, Lemuel Clanton, who did a fine job with the burials before. He is a Protestant Christian, but he believes much the same as Carlotta did. Perhaps he will be willing to help us."

"Thank you," I said, and felt an easing in my breast.

Hawker, Gruber, and Hoog went to confront the Southall Party over suspicions that all of the calamity from the night before had been their doings in the service of robbing the Lucere Party. The outriders returned leading a chastened group of people and their wagons; most of the Southall party. The Southalls had fled. The staff kept the splitters isolated from the rest of us, under the guard of Gruber and Hoog.

That evening the pilot addressed the Lucere Party.

"I am satisfied that most in the Southall Party did not know that some among them intended murder last night. It seems that a stranger, who went by the name Brown, approached the party several days ago, and spent some time encouraging those among them with grudges to help him rob us. A plan was laid to distract us during our celebration so that members of the Southall Party could steal into our camp and make off with supplies. I'm satisfied that those who volunteered to participate in the raid did not know of Hiram Southall's and Ned Tollard's intentions to commit murder, nor that Mrs. Angelo would lose her life in the fray. I truly don't understand what this fellow, Brown, thought he'd get out of it. He appears to be the one who killed Mrs. Angelo. She had a pistol, and challenged him when he appeared at her wagon, and that decision proved fatal. Thankfully, Alta Mae Angelo, with her at the time, was unharmed. Mr. Brown fled and we have not been able to find him."

He paused to allow us to swallow what he'd said, and talk amongst ourselves.

Of course, I reckoned this Brown would have been Fletcher Carson.

After a time, the pilot raised his hands and asked for quiet.

"The violent among the Southall party are dead or have fled. We've brought the others to our camp. They have all expressed regret for what has happened, for their role in it, and a willingness to join us again in a spirit of good will. My question to you is, can we make an effort in good faith to forgive them?"

Again, he allowed a moment before continuing. Numerous arguments arose within the crowd and some time passed before calm returned. "Speak with your board of trustees members. They will speak with our General Superintendent, and he will speak to me in the morning. Then I will announce our decision concerning whether the Southall Party will rejoin the Lucere Party."

We buried our dead at dusk. Seems everyone attended the services, including those of the Southall party. Lemuel Clanton did perform a Catholic last rites ceremony for Carla. Few walked away during his words. Surprised me to see that Sven Anderson and his family remained. Saw Tilsa watching me but could not have said what she had stewing in her idea pot.

Afterward, some Catholics said Clanton's effort had been false or incomplete.

"His intentions and ours were good," Ezra said, "and that is what matters in God's eyes."

I was out of tears. The spring inside me had gone slack.

Cedric—15

The two parties became one again, not without some hard feelings. I certainly had my own anger. I would not have anything to do with any of those who went with the Southalls and Ned Tollard.

Most of the stolen supplies came back to us in the wagons of the Southall party. Our next chance to resupply would be at Fort Hall, about a month's journey away.

Licking our wounds, we took on water at a place called Pacific Springs and moved on westward. As we traveled, the mountains to the north, south, and directly behind us, a great stone wall, slowly came into better view. On clear days, the peaks, streaked with pure white snow, gleamed clean and bright against the bluest sky. In sunset light, they were cast in orange and pink against that blue. I had never seen anything as beautiful.

I stuck close to Alta Mae, because I could see she still hurt badly from the loss of Carla. Though the North wagon had been moved to travel in a position just ahead of ours, and we had the sense that we traveled together as one now, Zeata North, grieving for the loss of her father, stuck with her grieving mum, so I didn't see as much of her as I'd have liked.

Truth is, I hurt too. Told myself I had any number of reasons for it, other than the loss of Carla. I had Ivan, Alta Mae, and Tessa behind me, but I did feel the loss of Mrs. Angelo, as if what held us all together had gone missing.

Within a week, we'd moved down into lower lands again, passing between shorter mountains along a trail through scrub with a few streams here and there, trees growing in the dips leading down to them.

Tommy Stilton came ambling back toward Alta Mae and me one day. Having my weapons in my pockets, I remained at ease.

Tommy took up walking beside me, said, "I hap a que-sss-tion."

"If I can, I'll answer it," I said.

"You've taken up with sss-ome that are *dipperent* from you. Why?"

"Do you mean, Ivan and Tessa..." I then thought to include, "...and the Norths?"

Alta Mae glanced at me, eyebrows raised, but said nothing.

"Ye-sss."

Now I could feel myself growing huffy, yet I tried to hide it. "They are fine folks. Do you have something against them?"

"No. I had a black pal in Pitt-sss-burg. We used to go looking por pight-sss together." He pounded his hand with his fist to make certain I knew he meant "fights."

"Why'd you do that?"

"Make other-sss have re-sss-pect for u-sss they wouldn't have otherwi-sss-e."

The gangs in Five Points always made the same point in deadly street battles. "That doesn't get you respect," I said, "They're just afraid of you."

Tommy kept quiet for a time.

"The other-sss treat you with re-sss-pect because of what you did to me."

"You started it."

"That, I did..."

Again, he became quiet for some moments. He glanced at Alta Mae, and she seemed to understand he wanted to talk to me alone. She wandered off a bit and walked about thirty yards away from us.

"I'm dipperent," he said, gesturing toward his lip. "Can't tell you how many time-sss I've been beaten up por the way I sss-ound when I talk."

"I'm sorry to hear it," I said, looking him in the eye.

He held my gaze for a time, then said, "Ip you'll have me por a priend, I'll be your-sss."

A jig, I wondered, one to put me at ease, making his next cruelty easier to get away with?

No, I didn't think so.

"I always need friends," I said, "but I won't help you mistreat others."

He waved my words away. "Mom gave me a hiding por that, said it wa-sss time I grew up and let people think what they want op me. You have courage I lack, sss-o I figured I might sss-pend time with you."

"I'd be glad to have you," I said, yet I felt less at ease with the idea of him as a friend than I did as one I'd have to best in a fight. Kept that to myself.

We walked together for the rest of the day, and on into the days to follow.

He told me of his life in Pittsburg, and I told him about mine in Five Points. Found myself not holding back. Told him Carla wasn't our mum, and that Alta Mae and I grew up on the streets.

"I had no notion what I wa-sss going up again-sss-t when I de-sss-ided to pick on you," he said. "I'm sss-orry for being such an a-sss."

He laughed, and I did too.

———

Zeata started walking with me again. "Thank you for saving Mama," she said, and gave me another mow upon the cheek. I allowed myself to like that a lot.

Once Aron, Jack, Will, and several other boys saw that Tommy was no longer a threat, they walked with us too.

Alta Mae's friends, Frances and Missouri joined us.

Soon after, we'd all become fast friends.

Jack and Aron talked about what they'd do in California. Aron spoke of the farm his father would start, and Jack about the bookshop his father wanted to open in Yerba Buena, the town that would later be named San Francisco.

"I'll be making sss-hoe-sss with Pop-sss," Tommy said, pointing at his shoes to make certain we understood.

"Sardines," Missouri said. "Papa has some plans for putting them in tins that I don't understand."

Frances didn't speak of a future, and I thought she had little hope hers would be good. Alta Mae had said her father did much gambling.

"I don't know what we'll do without Daddy," Zeata said. "Mama won't talk about it yet."

"Perhaps you can stay with us," I said.

She nodded with a smile.

Since I had no plans but to find Egan, I had little to say about the future. That's when I knew I should think on it. If Egan remained much the same as he'd been, he wouldn't have much. I'd got used to the feeling that Alta Mae and I could make something of ourselves, much as Carla had done for herself and those she considered her own.

I choked upon thinking of that, a powerful sadness coming up. "Excuse me," I said. "Must let out some water." I stepped off the trail into scrub and pretended to piss, while I tried to understand why I'd started crying over that damned woman, Carlotta Angelo.

Took some time to see and accept that she had done for us what no one else had. Though she'd done it with stolen funds, I knew that all I had now was owing to her kindness. She'd been hard on me at first. Of course, I'd been little better than a hungry animal when I met her, no gratitude, not a kind thought for anyone but my sister and maybe Egan.

Now I felt grateful, and had no way to tell Carla how much what she'd done meant to me. Too late!

I sat in the gravel and wept for the loss of her. Must have been there longer than I knew because Zeata came back for me.

Odd that I had no shame for her to see me cry.

Alta Mae—15
September, 1847

About a month passed before we arrived at Fort Hall, a trading post along the Snake River in the Oregon Country. We camped nearby.

General Superintendent Lucere and members of the Board of Trustees went into the fort to trade for supplies. They replaced much of what had been lost to the river by the Southall Party.

"The fort is too small for everyone to enter at once," our pilot said at the camp. "The soldiers will allow you inside in groups. Be very careful in considering trade with both the whites and Indians outside the fort. Much of what the two gentlemen with the carts have to offer is of no account. The victuals the women offer may not sit well in your gut. They do have some fine possibles bags, moccasins, and other garment pieces for sale. Their bead and porcupine quill work is quite good."

Approaching the fort, I reckoned he meant the old Indian women seated against the log pilings that formed its palisades, and the white fellows dressed in skins, standing beside rickety folding barrows. One woman had odds and ends spread out before her on skins, some the products of animals, some from plants, and others a mystery. A couple of others offered the crafted items the pilot had mentioned. The barrows were laden with old, worn flintlocks, corroding blades, ratty skins and furs, and again, more mysteries.

"What's that?" Cedric asked Ivan, pointing at hoops with cords and rotten canvas.

"Worn out snow shoes," he said.

He had to explain to us their purpose, and how they worked.

Cedric wanted to look at everything, but Ivan and Tessa drew him away.

We headed toward the gate that led inside the fort and stood in a queue with Indians. I tried not to let them see me staring. Their clothing, skin, and hair looked so different from my own. Both the men and women had hair like black silk threads, dark and yet shining in the sunlight. Both men and women had colorful decorations on their buckskin moccasins and rigging, some made of beads, others with shells, or added pieces of trimmed and shaped hide. Both also wore beaded necklaces, bracelets, and earrings. Some had a mix of Indian and white types of togs. Saw one woman with a man's waistcoat on over her buckskins

One man I could not easily turn away from wore beneath his buckskin jacket a white shirt that had turned an unwashed gray. The cuffs of the shirt, poking out of the jacket's sleeves, were held together with silver cufflinks.

That fellow was perhaps the most beautiful person I'd ever seen. The perch of his straight nose and full lips between the high bones of his cheeks, the arch of his black brows over dark jewels of eyes, all drew my gaze as none had ever done before. Though my description is lacking, it's all I have to give. So fine to look upon, and I truly could not have said why, even then, with him directly before me. I fought with myself to keep from approaching him, because I knew I'd have had nothing to say, would have merely stood and gawped at his dark features and slim, proud figure. He didn't deserve that.

By some effort of will, I turned away to consider other things.

A treaty with Great Britain the year before had allowed the Oregon Country to be included in United States territory. A few soldiers of our army stood guard outside the gate.

"I wonder how Egan looks in a uniform," I said to Cedric.

"I were thinking the same," he said with an eagerness that surprised me. "Might the army have sent him here?"

I'd noted that he'd grown fidgety as we waited our turn to go inside the fort.

"He went to the fight in California," I said. "That's far from here."

"Yes, but so long ago now, well over a year."

As we entered, his blinkers began searching.

"You're looking for Egan," I said, surprised.

"Wouldn't you like to find him here?"

Since I had to think about that, I didn't answer.

With all that had happened on our journey, I had not thought much about big brother. While I had lost Carla, I had Tessa, Mrs. North, and Ivan now. Egan would not like that.

The spring inside me might have had me going with big brother, even as my thinking told me not to have anything more to do with him. I'd have to think carefully about the choice ahead concerning him.

At a small chapel inside the fort, Ivan hired a preacher to perform a wedding. He and Tessa were wed with Mrs. North and Mr. Hawker standing as witnesses.

The ceremony seemed a bit of play-acting. I found it touching all the same, especially to see them kissing at the end.

Cedric made noises during the ceremony, humming a tune, talking aloud to himself, and rapping his knuckles on the arm of a chair. He'd been disappointed when he hadn't found Egan, and was doubly so now to see Ivan wed. The preacher eyed little brother a time or two. The rest of us paid him no mind.

After the ceremony, Tessa tried to speak to Cedric and me. "Would you two—"

Cedric interrupted. "I will look around a bit more before going back to camp." Then he was out the door of the chapel, no doubt searching again.

Seeing Cedric's eagerness to find Egan, I knew he would be unhappy if I decided to abandon our big brother.

"Would you two stay with us once we get to California," Tessa asked, "as family?"

I choked back a lump in my throat, and blinked a few times to discourage the tears that threatened.

"I would very much like that," I said. "I'll speak to Cedric."

Ivan smiled and gripped my shoulder as he might have done to a boy.

Tessa gave me a hug, something I most often didn't like. Somehow, she made it tolerable.

Then and there, I made my decision concerning Egan.

Cedric—16

Some miles on from Fort Hall, the California Trail split off from the Oregon Trail, and we headed southwest. Within a few days, the land had gained a sameness that wore on me.

"We're traveling through high desert," the pilot said. "We'll have about a month and a half in these conditions. Sources for water are fewer now. In a few weeks, we will enter parts where the water is not fit to drink, some of it quite poisonous, so we must depend on our guide to point out what's potable. Conserve your water, both in your barrels and your person. Though you may become hot, wear sleeves and a hat. For those who don't know how to wash pots, pans, and dishes with sand, Issa can show you."

Not long—a couple weeks—before my bone box felt dry most of the time. My boots, having lost much of their fit, did a poor job protecting me from the stony ground. My feet ached, and I had grown stubbornly irritable, contrary, and foolish.

After Ivan and Tessa's wedding, Alta Mae had said "They would like us to stay with them as family once we get to California."

I had not offered an answer at the time. She brought it up again as we walked the desert.

Like a bottle head, I said, "I already have a family."

Her silence told me she didn't like my answer.

Soon, everyone had grown miserable. Hours passed while we walked with no one saying a word. Then someone would start up and there would be words for a time, a few voices maybe. Yet the sound would die out quick, as if keeping talk alive had become a bother.

One of those times, Alta Mae said, "Egan will not like our new family."

I thought she'd grown as irritable as I had, and just wanted to cause trouble for me. At least she'd waited to say it until Zeata was riding with her mum.

"I will show him he's wrong about blacks," I said.

With a sneering curl in her lip, she asked, "You truly believe that?"

My anger quickened. "Yes, he thinks enough of me to listen."

Missouri, walking with us, said, "If he's like your sister says, you'll not change his mind with talk. I've known a lot of bigots, and I'd say they rarely change."

I ignored her. After all, *I* had changed.

Tommy, walking with Aaron and Jack a distance away, had overheard. "Sss-he sss-peak-sss the truth," he called out, pointing at Missouri.

"How do you think he will treat Ivan?" Alta Mae asked.

I had thought about that a lot during the journey. I knew Egan would never like Ivan, but then Ivan had married Tessa and had little to do with me now, despite what Alta Mae had said of his wishes. Maybe I didn't need him.

I shrugged, as if unconcerned.

"Egan is a liar and a thief," she said with no anger in her voice. "He stole our freedom."

"He *gave* us our freedom, *kept* us free for the longest time! *You* are a liar and a thief."

"Not like him."

Her calm was maddening!

I kept my distance from Alta Mae for several days.

Alta Mae—16

Cedric had not spoken to me or looked at me in four days. Though he returned to his bedroll at our wagon at night, he had little to do with the rest of us.

In that time, I reassured Zeata that he wasn't angry with her. I answered a lot of questions from those who overheard my last words with Cedric. I did that while Zeata rode with her mum, since telling her about it would be Cedric's decision.

Wanting to know more about Carla's past, I found time to speak with Ivan about her.

"Her parents came to New York from Italy," he said. "My grandmother, Marion Romano, were a singer, my grandfather, Gastone Romano, her manager."

"I heard Carla jabber in what might have been Italian once."

Ivan nodded. "My father, Paul, were born in Italy, Carla in America. They spoke Italian with their father."

"A celebrated singer, her mum?"

"For a time. They did well until grippe took Marion in their second year in New York. Gastone went to work for Coulter's Brewery. When old enough, Carla worked for the brewery too. As the Points changed she changed with it."

"And she married once?"

"Yes. Thought she'd be a spinster, but she married late to an Italian man whose name I will not repeat. A violent man. Carla had a girl, Mehetabel, she called Hetty. Her husband died at home from drink, a mystery that she were suspected of having a hand in. Hetty died in childhood."

I wondered if Carla had done her husband in to save herself. As the property of a cruel husband, she would have had little remedy for what may have been a frightening and painful life. I could understand a woman coming to that.

"Somehow," I said, "I'd had it that she'd led an uncommon life."

"My father had all the adventure. He went to sea as a boy, and has seen the world."

"You too are a sea crab, yes?"

Ivan nodded again, yet offered no more about his past. "A woman with a child, Carla bettered herself with learning. She taught a lot of girls in the Points to read, write, and cypher. When I went to live with Papa in the Points, I were one of the few boys she taught. Perhaps as I do, you think of her as uncommon because you loved her."

Even though difficult to say aloud, I had to admit, "Yes, I did."

—⁓—

Late in the fourth day of his silence, Cedric came to me and said, "I'm sorry I become so cross with you, but you needn't tell everyone about our lives in New York. I don't want Zeata and Mrs. North to know."

I could see he remained angry with me.

Keeping my calm, I said, "Mine to tell. I told Missouri, Frances, Jack, Aron, and Tommy. I also told them Carla weren't truly our mum. Tommy said you had told him some already. If you don't want them to leak it, you should tell them so. I'm tired of hiding."

"What's your meaning?"

"When we lived on the streets, we had to rob, steal, and hide to make our way. I'm so weary of it. I don't want to keep Fletcher Carson a secret, yet to save us all a lot of pain, I will."

"Good!"

"We're still hiding! In New York we believed no one would help us without using us cruelly, and maybe that were true enough, yet now we are part of something better, if we want it enough."

"You mean the Angelos and Norths?"

"Yes, and that means giving up Egan. After all we been through and the sides we took on this journey, I cannot abide your eagerness to be with Egan."

"I will find a way!" he said, his mug screwed up in an angry scowl.

"No, you won't. If you try, you may lose what you've gained."

This time, he left me for almost a week.

When Ivan, Tessa, and Zeata asked why he'd been so grum, I said he was merely weary of the travel.

—⁂—

Tilsa found me at a time I had no friends nearby. I fancied she'd come to cause more trouble, but decided I didn't know that. The pilot had asked us to forgive the members of the Southall Party for the good of the Lucere Party.

"I'm sorry you lost your mother," she said.

"That's kind of you to say."

A moment later she said, "I made a friend of a girl. You chased her. Meg Alberti is her name."

"Yes," I said, "I remember her, a baconning, fleshy girl."

Tilsa smiled. "Yes, she *is* a bit. You scared her so bad, she *pissed* herself." She covered her mouth as if the worst word ever invented had slipped out.

Tilsa had led a life much different from my own, a more protected one. Because of that, I thought of her as younger, though she must have been a couple years older than me.

I smiled, said, "Good. She were *bloody* mean to throw ox dung at us."

Tilsa's blinkers got big at my "bloody," and she laughed. No one nearby to hear, I taught her a few more oaths. "Well, I swan, girl, do you know swow, snore, ding, dang, dad burn, and Gol?"

She giggled. "No! Some just sound like ordinary words."

"They are, while standing in for *much* worse.

Her smile lingered, and I'd become at ease with her.

"What tarnal words do you know?" I asked.

"I do know tarnation." She looked around to make certain no one heard, and added. "Also blame, bull, cussed, and blazes."

"Those are good ones. Some of them also stand in for worse. Do you know, quim, tackle, cat heads, and boat-licker?"

"No, I haven't heard those either. What do they mean?"

I had to think about whether I should tell her. None of the ones she used were about hogmagundy, except maybe "bull." If she repeated the ones I said and folks discovered I gave them, trouble might find me.

"I just made those up for fun," I said.

Walking, we remained quiet for a time.

Then she spoke up as if she'd forgot something. "She's also a Catholic."

"Meg?"

"Yes, but I didn't know that until I got to be her friend. She's the best friend I've ever had. I was surprised to find she believes much the same as I do. Mama and Papa didn't like your mother for her being Catholic, so I didn't tell them about Meg. I figure if they're wrong about Catholics, they might be wrong about blacks too."

I nodded.

Her smiles fell off, her good humor got tucked away, and I grew uneasy again.

"I'm sorry I was so mean to you," she said in a hurry. "I'm sorry for trying to turn Meg against you by saying things about your black cousin. I know Mr. Tollard and them already had the hate in them, yet I fear my part in it made things worse. I helped my brother spread the rumor about the sorghum. Then people got killed. Please forgive me."

Her dimber face became pinched and the red of her cheeks spread over her mug as she held back tears.

I took her hand and held it as we walked.

With time, we spoke of other things and we were both at ease again.

Cedric—17

I'd kept away from Alta Mae for about a week, trying to sort my feelings before speaking with her again.

I took up walking beside her and not a word had escaped me when she said, "You know I speak the truth. It's him or us."

I wasn't having it, but tried to stay calm. I'd spent much of my time away from her trying to reason out how to talk to Egan.

"What if I tell him about the good in them?" I said.

"What would you say?" Alta Mae asked.

"Ivan is a smart and loyal friend. He's good at hunting and fishing, and taught me things. He's good in a fight, and defending his own. He can play a penny whistle better than anybody."

"What else?"

"Tessa is a good cook. She can sing and dance since she were once part of a traveling minstrelsy. She can tell a good ghost story too."

"And…"

"Mrs. North loves her daughter. Always willing to do whatever needs done, she works hard without whinging. I've known her to butcher mule deer, clean and gut fish, and sew up wounds her husband had got—"

"And now, I'll be Egan, asking 'How'd he get those wounds?'"

"A man shot him."

"What kind of man?" She must have seen I didn't know how to answer, and answered for me. "A bigot."

As if I didn't hear her, I said quick, "I have one more—she shaved her husband every day."

Alta Mae said, "I'm still Egan, asking, 'Until what happened?'"

I didn't want to answer.

She just kept staring at me.

Grudging, I said, "He were killed."

"By what *kind* of man?"

"A bigot," I allowed, now struggling with my calm. "I can't say that to Egan."

"Why not?"

"That'd be like a slap in the mug."

I wanted to slap Alta Mae for being right about Egan. Even as I said the words about Ivan, Tessa, and Mrs. North, I knew big brother wouldn't care about those sorts of things.

"What about Zeata?" she asked.

I knew Egan would be less upset about Zeata since she was a child, and because maybe she was my girl. I knew he'd had friends that got up to horizontal refreshment with black women. I'd a notion that he would see what I had with Zeata with such forgiveness.

Yet I could not say such a thing—should never have thought it!

How could I allow that blacks were good enough for hogmagundy, but little else? I found that notion so cruel, I turned on Alta Mae, and did strike her in the face.

She backed away, her left hand over the cheek I'd struck. The look in her eyes—I cannot describe it. Hurt to look upon her.

I didn't understand why I'd done it, except that somehow I blamed Alta Mae for my own cruelty.

I ran.

Alta Mae—17

This time Cedric stayed away for some weeks. He'd gathered a blanket and a bag of his belongings from the wagon, and took off toward the Southeast. As huffy as he'd been, no one tried to stop him.

When he didn't come back the next morning, we got worried and alerted the pilot. Hawker halted the wagon train and commenced a search that went on for the rest of the daylight hours. I couldn't understand how Cedric kept himself hidden out on that rocky land with just the lowly sagebrush and rocks to hide behind.

Ivan spoke to Hawker on the second day of the halt and the searching ceased.

As the wagon train prepared to move on, I grew alarmed. Seeing that, Ivan hurried to speak to me. "I seen him out there. He's to the southeast of us, and he's good at hiding. He may have chosen that position since I am out there on our left most of the time. I tried not to let on I know he's there. I'll keep an eye on him as we continue, make certain he follows and doesn't stray too far."

"He's been angry with me over a disagreement about our brother, Egan, in California."

Too ashamed of my own past bigotry, I couldn't begin to tell Ivan about Egan's, so I told a half-truth instead: "Big brother sold us to the factory rooms in the Old Brewery. I cannot forgive him for that. Cedric wants to."

Ivan nodded.

"Cedric is hurting from the loss of Carla," he said. "Something hard for him to allow. Whatever your older brother is, he's the only father the boy had. Cedric is feeling weak and under threat without him, now that Carla is gone."

I was surprised Ivan could see so clearly.

"He were looking to you for the longest time," I said, "When you took up with Tessa, he felt cast aside."

He nodded. "Did you tell him what Tessa and me want with you two?"

"Yes. He didn't say what he wanted."

"You both have plenty of time to decide, but I won't have you living on the streets in California the way you did in the Points."

"How is he getting on out there? He's got to be out of food and water by now."

"He took a canteen with him. At night, he sneaks into camp and steals food and water from our wagon."

"He's thieving again!"

"Ain't you surprised we haven't caught him doing it?"

"No, he's a shady little mouse when he wants to be."

Ivan placed a hand on my shoulder for calm. "Try not to be upset with him. It's just victuals and water that he'd have from us anyway. We've told the pilot about it so he won't be surprised if he sees him sneaking about. He's kindly disposed toward Cedric. Tessa and I will start leaving a few biscuits and johnnycakes out for him."

"What if animals get him? What if Indians find him? What if Fletcher Carson catches him?"

"As you say, he's a shady little fellow. I shouldn't worry too much. If Fletcher Carson is out there, he can only follow us. He doesn't know the land and must feed on our scraps. He won't stray for fear of losing us. Cedric is far enough off our trail, he won't be found. He's got his clasp knife and pistol. I'll keep an eye out to make certain he keeps up with us, but maybe we let him be for a while. He has a lot to think about."

Despite my worries about Cedric, I thought that sage advice.

Cedric—18

I woke up surrounded by sleeping snakes, let out a yelp, and choked back a scream. The sound and my flinching had awakened them. Wrapped in my blanket with folds over my head, I saw only one at first, its head near mine. Looked like one of the rattlers the out rider, Sam Hoog, had rounded up to show the party what to steer clear of. The thing moved slow, like it had little life. I tried to back away, and came up against another snake—I could feel it moving against my back—then another one down around my feet. They lay snug up against me in the cold morning.

I tossed the blanket off to either side so it fell over the ones beside me. Drawing my feet away from the other one, I rose slowly, and stepped away.

I could see the one that had been at my feet had no rattle on its tail. Small, it was, so maybe too young. Quickly snatching the blanket off the others, I jumped back to avoid a possible bite. The largest had been the one I'd faced. None had rattles. Hoog had said some other snakes had near-like markings, weren't poisonous, but could give a mean bite. Although moving faster, the snakes remained sluggish. The pilot had called them "cold-blooded" and said they needed warmth to give them life.

Hoog called snakes "good eating," so I killed them. That night, when I stole into camp for food and water from our wagon, I left the snakes for Ivan and Tessa to discover. Hopefully, they would make a good meal or two of them.

A few days later, I had a visit in the night from three coyotes. I would not know that name until Ivan said it later. I thought of them as small wolves. One, sniffing around my feet, awoke me. I sat up quick, and it began to snarl.

My heart beating fast enough I could feel it in my neck, I got my pistol out, aimed poorly, and fired. The shot tore along the dog's side and it yelped, much like I'd done at the snakes. The beast took off running and another went with it, but one lingered about ten feet away.

I stood, drawing up my blanket with me. Seeing the creature cower a bit as I rose, I held the blanket out to make me look bigger still, and yelled at it. The animal chased after its brothers.

I walked southwesterly for a while, and located a new rock to fetch up against.

In the morning, I found Ivan, waiting for me to awaken.

"You safe enough out here all alone?" he asked. "Heard your barker."

I shrugged, not wanting to give him anything. "Little wolves come for me in the night. My barker is louder than theirs."

He smiled, and I shrugged again.

"Thanks for the snakes. Tessa made a delicious soup we shared with the Norths and some of the labor."

By that last, perhaps he meant the pilot, Issa, and the outriders.

Trying to sound brave, I said, "I lured them in, cuddled with them through the night, and killed them in the morning."

He nodded, smiling. "Coyotes—that's what those small wolves are called. You're a stinker with grit, scaring them off."

Again, I shrugged.

"I'm proud to call you friend," he said, then stood and walked away.

—⟩⟨⟨—

October, 1847

I stole into the Lucere Party camp for more water and dried meat. Moving silently among the sleeping families without getting caught gave me a sense of pride. Just to look around, I'd climbed into numerous wagons over the course of several nights. I would open trunks, chests, and cabinets and rifle through their contents. Still, I had not taken anything because I remembered Alta Mae's anger when I buzzed the squeeze Billy off that fellow in St. Louis, and my promise not to steal again.

That night, I discovered a gold watch in a small cabinet resting in the bed of the wagon belonging to Sabin Hendrix, the man that got so sick from drinking wine off the borax-treated bonnet.

Told myself that no one would know I took it. Must have been some clever words rattling through my head to persuade me of that. I slipped it in my pocket, gathered what I came for form our wagon, and passed silently back out into the night.

I haven't the words to say how good that theft made me feel. Egan had given those skills to me. I was a sneaksman, a buggsman, a cross-squeaker, and what Ivan had taught about how to mouse while hunting had added to my skill.

The gold watch had been set fairly well, since the hands reached for twelve just as the sun reached the top of the sky. I wound it daily, and looked at it often at first.

With time, though, it didn't feel right. As good as I'd felt about using my thieving skills, I found I could not keep pretending the watch belonged to me. When I looked to see it shining golden in the sun, it had lost some of its luster. Feeling all-overish about the thing, I left it in my pocket and forgot about it.

Had I also done much the same with my feelings for Zeata? I'd made an ugly notion about her I didn't want to face. Too young for sexual congress then, I had no intention of using her like Eagan's friends had done with their black bedmates. But I'd become so needful of a way to present her value to Egan, I'd been willing to make less of her in my own mind to satisfy that end.

Yes, having tarnished my feelings for Zeata, I had put them away, much like I'd put away that damned watch.

Yet I couldn't forget about her. And once I'd thought of her a little, I began to think of her often. I would give her an apology if I didn't have to explain to her why. Even so, I would have to make some gesture to remove the tarnish of my ugly thought.

Brooding over such matters, feeling very much alone, I walked for many days. The constant wind whipped up dust from time to time and formed what looked at a distance like dancing figures. I'd have found them amusing if I'd been myself.

Tiresome trying to keep the Lucere Party just over the horizon to the northwest, and Ivan on his prancer just over the horizon to the west. Then I noted that we'd changed course and now traveled southwest, and that I had to keep track of Ivan in the southeast. I grew troubled by the notion that we headed the wrong way, but finally reasoned that our course had never been a straight line because mountains stood in our way, heights that had few passages through them. That's when I noticed a dim wall of mountains with white peaks to my right.

Seemed we came little nearer to them over the following week. Closer rocky heights, not as tall, were appearing in the same direction, blocking my view of the farther mountains except for their snowy peaks, which often disappeared in the dusty sky.

The sameness of the days wore on me more and more. I got an uneasy feeling the walk would never end; that the gray land, the sameness of scrubby growth, the wideness of sky, the rocky heights in the distance to the southeast and the west had become a dream I had been, and would be, returned to time and again.

While thinking of returning to the Lucere Party, I started to find things. Carried a coffee grinder for about half a mile before deciding it wasn't worth it—too heavy. Found a hat box with a fancy bonnet in it, a small safe, a dress dummy, and crates that held sets of broken dishes in excelsior. Saw some bones, big ones, then carcass parts with big birds plucking at them. The smell of that death got in my nose and wouldn't leave.

Saw a large carcass, probably an ox, in the distance with more birds.

More of someone's belongings left on the stony ground: A table and chairs set up as if awaiting supper and those that would eat it, a small loom, empty water barrels of the sort we had strapped to our wagon.

I worried a family of our party had lost some of their belongings and their water barrels. Yet, I knew I was too far southeast of them to be walking in their trail.

In the distance, I saw something like a big box. Getting closer, I could see it had wheels. One of the wheels, set at an odd angle, looked broken. The wreck of a wagon! Tatters of its bonnet hung from the bows and flapped in the wind. When almost upon it, I heard a tapping, and a sound like a voice, humming. Might have been the wind singing through the exposed bows, but it also could have been someone there. I hurried forward to see if help were needed. Some of the torn bonnet, sagged into the empty wagon bed, keeping me from seeing the driver's seat. The cloth there moved as if someone pushed against it.

Not certain why I didn't call out. Perhaps my years of creeping about cautiously had become too much habit.

I swung around toward the driver's seat. The flutter came again and then a startled cry, just as my sight lit upon a dead man somehow still alive. He had birds on him. He jerked, quivered, and rattled.

I screamed and backed away.

The birds scattered, one squawking as it came directly at me before turning away and flying off.

My blood pounded through me. Something like tiny white lights flashed in my sight. Unable to see well, I cowered down, expecting him to make a strike at me.

Stillness, but for the wind through the bonnet.

Full vision returned and I saw that the dead man had not moved. I'd thought he made the startled cry, but now understood that had been the voice of a bird. They had made him move while trying to tear away what remained of his flesh.

No, not a man, a boy. I could tell by the togs, though they had all been torn open, the tatters blowing with the wind.

Close to my age perhaps, he was mostly skeleton, nearly picked clean. I faced his back. An arrow had pinned him at the hip to the front of the wagon, as if he'd been climbing down. Another arrow hung from his ribs. His head, truly a skull, rested on his bony right shoulder.

I had the strangest feeling he was me. Moving to get a look at his mug, I heard my name from behind and let out another scream.

Spinning on my heels, I found myself facing Ivan upon his prancer. I'd not heard his approach for the flapping of the bonnet.

"We must leave here now," he said, and held out his hand to help me onto his mount.

—⁓—

"Paiute Indians, no doubt," Mr. McBaird said. "The wagon

probably got quarantined from the main body of a wagon train, and fell too far behind. The Paiute are known to take advantage of easy pickings. They may have paid a dear price, becoming ill themselves."

We were walking behind the supply wagon Issa drove.

"We should set more watch at night," The pilot said to Ivan. "eight is a good number. The outriders should halve the distance they normally keep from the party, both in the day and night. Go tell Hoog, Gruber, and Leventis. Have Gruber fetch that boy from the wagon so we can give him a burial."

"Yes, sir." Ivan mounted his prancer and left. I turned to go to Alta Mae and Tessa.

The pilot caught my arm. "A word, master Cedric."

I flinched, thinking I knew what was coming.

"I'm glad you're back and hope you'll consider staying with us, for your own safety."

Not trusting my voice, I merely nodded.

"I don't know much about you except that you and your sister come from New York City. I do recognize the canny, wary look of children that grow up on the streets, and I know that to get on in life they often must break the law just to keep themselves fed. Ivan confirmed my suspicions about you two, and told me more. You and your sister must have been good at surviving there, but there's no need for thieving here. I understand you needed to be on your own, yet from what Ivan said, you weren't as independent as you would have us believe."

I had a hard time looking at him. "Ivan said he told you I took victuals from our wagon."

"We handled that his way, as you are in his and Tessa's care."

"I'm sorry to have caused a problem." I gave him a smile stiffer than I meant to. "I must go to my sister now."

I turned to leave, and again he caught my arm.

"Mr. Hendrix says his watch is missing."

I gave him my most innocent, level gaze.

"I like you, Cedric. You are a good boy most often. This time you've failed me. Even so, If you will give me the watch, I'll forgive you. That doesn't mean you won't make restitution to Mr. Hendrix."

I felt like I'd been knapped by a copper, something that had never happened to me. I'd never even been touched by one before. *Too* quick, I was, *too* smart, I'd thought. Now I had to question just *how* smart.

"If I did such a thing, how would I make up for it?" I felt shame to hear my voice tremble.

"First, I would return the gold watch to him and say I found it."

"How could you have found it now if it were lost over a week ago, miles away?"

"He's very ill, and will not likely question me. Your reparation to him would be to check on him every day for the rest of the journey to make certain he has what he needs. You would ask if there is anything you might do to help him, and if he makes a request, to do as he asks. He's alone on this journey and still suffers from borax poisoning."

That seemed a lot to ask. I shifted from foot to foot, looking for an argument against his judgment. Terribly cross, I quickly knew I'd truly become angry with myself. I stood looking up at Hawker, wanting to say something mean. A plumb fellow, he didn't deserve that, so I reached into my pocket, palmed the watch and placed it in his open hand. Thankfully, he closed his fingers around it quick to hide it.

"Thank you, Cedric."

"Thank you, sir," I said, then turned and ran toward our wagon.

Alta Mae—18

Cedric busied himself working off his criminal debt through service to Mr. Hendrix, even as we rose out of the desert into the Sierra Nevada Mountains of California.

He apologized for hitting me, taking off like he did, and making me worry.

"Please know that I'm finished with Egan," I said. "What you do with him is up to you, but if he tries to get between me and mine, he'll regret it."

He seemed to accept that.

The trail was some of the worst we'd seen, with jagged switch backs that took us to rocky heights where the trees were squat and looked tortured. Many large patches of solid stone prevented anything from growing. The trail passed over much of that stone, and we could see where previous travelers had done their best to fill in the deepest crevices and pits, and to shore up drop-off edges with stone and wood to help even it out and make the passage wide enough for wagons. Higher up, we discovered more forest with beautiful weathered trees, a welcomed sight after so much desert.

The pilot had warned us of the difficulties of this trail in a meeting on our last night in the desert.

"We've done well," Hawker told us, "putting behind us much of the strife and hard feeling of the early journey. Now, perhaps more than ever, we must see our way through the trail ahead together, much as we did in the morass in May. We will suffer long days and much hard work, yet if we all pull together, we should win our way through and weather it well. Try to think of the success of the entire party, and guard against petty personal concerns."

He seemed to pause to collect his thoughts. The longer his silence went on, the louder came the murmur, then hubbub from the party gathered in a circle of the wagons to listen. The horror the

Donner Party suffered in these mountains just the year before had been on the minds of many among us. Fear that we might suffer the same fate had been met mostly with silence, as if to speak about it would give it life.

"Many of you asked about the dangers of these mountains at our first meeting in Independence, and brought up the tragedy of the Donner Party."

Having become bored with the meeting in Independence, I had missed that part. I'd learned of the Donner Party's misfortunes from Missouri and Frances during our own journey.

"Now, those good folks—"

"Good folks?" Someone shouted from the rear.

"They killed their own and ate them," came another voice, a speaker I didn't see.

More outraged murmurs about the evils of cannibalism.

Hawker held up his hands to call for silence before beginning anew.

"Now, *those good folks* suffered much bad luck along the earlier trail, and arrived too late in the season to escape the heavy snows. We are fortunate to have avoided many of the problems they encountered, and if we make it through, as I am confident we will, consider thanking providence that *you* reached the end of your journey without having to decide which one of your family members had to die so the rest might live. Though their most severe suffering and worst losses may have occurred last year, they endure pain still. Those among them who lived must not only bear the ravages of regret upon the conscience, but also the scorn of a great multitude who will never be faced with such onerous choices."

Thusly chided, those with uncharitable opinions about the Donner Party had gone silent. The rest went quiet as well, many perhaps thoughtful as they looked to their own future in the Sierra Nevada Mountains.

"I want you to know that we have arrived at a good time to cross the mountains. Mr. McBaird has taken the route we'll pursue. He and others have marked trees along it high enough that, should we find ourselves in deep snow, we will still find our way. We will not suffer the fate of the Donner Party."

For myself, I had scrounged and scraped to get by. I'd eaten much worse than what I fancied human flesh might be like. I did fear what the pilot had spoken of concerning having to make choices about who among family would live and who would die, yet as one good at surviving, that seemed a far off possibility.

My fears were of Fletcher Carson. We'd had word that he had returned to the Southall Party after killing Carla. He'd stolen blankets, firearms and supplies before striking out again alone on horseback. He'd come too far to go back. Ivan said he lived off the Lucere Party's scraps, so he might be unable to go back, even if he wanted to.

Cedric—19

"Why do you owe me an apology?" Zeata asked.

I hemmed and hawed, unable to explain fully out of shame. "In my idea pot, I didn't treat you with the regard you deserve."

"You are an odd one, Cedric," she said, giggling and covering her left eye with a hand.

She always laughed when I called my head a pot.

Since she didn't know what made me apologize, I'd risked nothing to give it. That didn't seem like a true apology. One day, I told myself, I would explain to her how I had shamefully likened her to the black women Egan's bigoted friends slept with.

As we entered the Sierra Nevada Mountains, happily, I saw more of Zeata.

I enjoyed the hard work of the uphill trail. Working with my friends and family, I welcomed the hardship.

Yes, I'd begun to think of Ivan and Tessa as family.

I looked in on Mr. Hendrix each day, but he often had little for me to do. Seeing that, the pilot found other ways to occupy my time with chores. He had me gathering wood for fires, feeding the oxen, digging privy holes and filling them, and gathering rocks for the fire pits.

Heavy downpours had washed dead trees down through the rocks, blocking the trail in places with a tangle of dead wood. Again, with ax and saw, we cut our way through, employing our oxen to haul the largest fallen tree trunks and limbs out of our path.

A couple of places, with the overhanging rock on one side, drop-offs on the other, we had to remove bonnets, hoops, and anything hung from the sides of the wagons so we could get past. In one spot, just to get by a rock face, we had to tilt each wagon to keep them from falling off the trail and tumbling downhill on the other side. As in the morass in May, we could not have made it through without the experience and hard work of the teamsters, Costello and his sons. Slow going, even so.

We had six days of climbing into the mountains. Unable to circle the wagons in the evening, we merely left two wide gaps along the trail between thirds of the wagon train. The cook fires were built in one gap, the cattle and prancers went into the other. We slept with the watch walking up and down the line in shifts through the night. The first night, when all had become quiet, Zeata and I spoke to each other across the trail that separated her family's wagon from ours. Mrs. North allowed that for a while before shushing us.

Each day we moved forward in fits and starts. By the sixth day, we'd neared the heights that would allow us passage to the other side of the mountain range, "the wet side" as Hawker called it.

Late in the afternoon when we stopped to make camp, our wagon sat next to a giant boulder just upslope off the trail. That felt too close. I had the thought it might roll over on top of us in the night, a troubling notion I couldn't shake.

After an early supper, Alta Mae took pity on me and went with me to do my work for Mr. Tipton—another chore the pilot had given me. "Mr. Tipton has strained his back," Hawker had said. "Be a good boy and feed his cattle tonight."

We fed them one at a time from buckets of barley and oats. Oliver's glowing crescent had not cleared the horizon when we started. By the time we finished, he rode high in the night sky.

Heading back to our wagon, we saw a shadowy figure darting among the brush and rocks above the trail.

"A mountain lion?" Alta Mae asked. "A bear?"

Clouds moved off Oliver's face, and I saw more clearly. "I believe it's Fletcher Carson."

He headed for the boulder beside our wagon.

"We should alert the watch," Alta Mae said.

"No, if he's caught, we'd have too much to explain," I said.

Her look told me she didn't like keeping silent about it. Still, she nodded.

"I'll warn Ivan," I told her. "You stay here, out of sight."

"No, he'll see you."

"I'll go below the trail and come up at the front of our wagon where Fletcher cannot see."

Then I was gone, too fast for her to stop me.

Alta Mae—19

I moved along the downslope side of the trail, while trying to keep an eye on the figure. Difficult, as I could only see him when there wasn't a wagon bonnet between us. I couldn't see him well enough in the dark to name him.

Because we had been unable to make camp off the trail, the oxen, six to a wagon, remained in their traces, putting some distance between families. I hurried past a couple of the oxen that were lying down, but most of the beasts stood, which helped me stay hidden from the figure's sight. Most of the party were bedded down for the night under their wagons, and the others would be busy with small tasks before sleep. No doubt, none were aware of the creeping figure in our midst.

Told myself that one of the watch would be along any moment to either know the person or rout the rough. If it were truly Fletcher, they wouldn't catch him if they just happened upon him. He'd flee before they could do that. Hopefully no one would challenge him with a weapon. If they did, they might well be killed.

The figure climbed a boulder just off the trail to the right, on the upslope side, to get above our wagon.

Drawing nearer, I heard Ivan clear his throat, and say quietly. "Fletcher Carson."

The figure crouched down atop the boulder, as if startled.

"Could be," he said after a moment, also keeping his voice low, "if that's Ivan Romano speaking."

I recognized Fletcher's voice right away.

"'Tis indeed. You should know that the watch will catch sight of you any moment, and then you'll have the whole wagon train down on you."

They spoke too quietly to catch anyone's interest.

"The watch looked so weary," the rough said. "One at a time,

I bid them sleep, and hauled them off the trail. Four of them. Your outriders are at the head and foot. I believe the pilot is sleeping, as he usually takes an early watch."

Fletcher seemed to know a lot about us, had no doubt watched us for some time. He moved down along the edge of the boulder closer to the trail. To see him, I crawled onto the trail and looked up between the legs of the oxen belonging to the neighbors behind us. For the most part the beasts remained calm around people. Even so, I did fear a misplaced hoof.

"And you think I'll be just as easy?" Ivan asked. "Like killing my aunt?"

Following that, I heard Ivan whispering to someone. Couldn't understand what he said. Thought I heard Mrs. North's voice, yet again, I didn't make out the words.

"No," Fletcher said, "I made certain not to start this while you had the watch." Before speaking the rough had cupped his hand next to his bone box so his words would be aimed back the way he'd come, perhaps to throw his voice so Ivan wouldn't know where he was. "Were Carlotta what stunned Lowell out of his regulars. You know that couldn't go unanswered. I've got nothing against the rest of your family, but if they stand in the way…."

"Go!" I heard Ivan whisper, possibly to Cedric and Tessa, then a scampering, as of persons fleeing.

"And what do you expect to happen, now that I know where you are?"

"I'm thinking you know I'll just keep coming back. Maybe you're willing to see reason and make a deal."

Fletcher had moved down to the trail, and I didn't want to move lest he hear and find me. I could feel the spring in me wind quick.

He crouched behind the right, rear wheel of our wagon, leaned down to look underneath. I'd already seen there was little there but empty bedrolls. I hoped he didn't turn to look beneath the oxen behind him, since I lay upon the trail there.

"Go on," Ivan said. "What did you have in mind?"

"We might split the darby, and I take my half and go."

Fletcher stood no more than twenty feet away from me. Reaching slowly for my pistol, recollection of the shot that killed Carla came to me; the sound, the smell, the fear. With that, I doubted I could aim the pistol and send shot into him. Still, I had to try. My breath came in hitches, and I struggled to keep silent.

"Where would you go?" Ivan asked.

"Why, back to New York, of course."

"You must think me a fool. You are no more going back to New York than I am. You depend on this wagon train to get by. Without our scraps, you would starve. You must follow us or perish in the wilderness."

As Ivan spoke, Fletcher had been moving slowly up along the side of the wagon.

"Why ain't you alerting others that I'm here?"

I got up carefully and followed the rough to be in a good position to fire upon him if need be. While I remained uncertain I could do that, I had good reason to.

"Because I don't want to answer questions about the darby, and about dragging a dangerous man after us, as we've done for so long."

"Then how about that deal? Otherwise, perhaps I should approach your pilot and tell him you robbed me?"

"I don't think that ship would sail far—we have a witness to your killing of my aunt."

I'd got out in front of the team of oxen when I stepped on something that snapped under foot.

Fletcher turned, saw me, and was almost upon me before I got my barker free. The pistol shook in my unsteady hand. Yet the blue steel inside had become so taut, everything seemed to move slowly.

He raised a pistol toward me.

Still shuddering in fear, I chose the moment my wobbling aim looked most true. I got my shot off first, striking him in the middle and spoiling his aim. His shot missed me.

I'd hit him in the bread bag, but he kept coming. I backed away swiftly and ran into the head of an ox. The creature complained, shoved me with its snout, and I stumbled back toward Fletcher. He dropped his pistol, and scooped me up in his great, muscled arms. I tried to strike him with my pistol. He knocked it from my grasp, pinned my arms, and crouched over me, pressing his broken cheek against my forehead. I screamed.

Ivan appeared on one side of the wagon, Cedric on the other, each about fifteen feet away. Both had pistols aimed at us. The rough had another pistol out by then, aimed at my breast.

I heard voices close by and others getting nearer, the curious from nearby wagons, possibly.

"Quick, now, Ivan," Fletcher said. "You get me that darby before I send shot into this one."

Cedric, standing beside the left, rear wheel of our wagon, sighted along the barrel of his pistol. He had a grim look, angry, yet determined. I saw little of the rest of his mug as he held his pistol out before him with both hands. I couldn't help thinking he aimed it at me.

"Be still and I *will* get the darby," Ivan said in a hurry. He turned toward the rear of the wagon, having to move closer to us to get to it.

Fletcher backed us toward the downslope side of the trail, the side where Cedric stood, now not ten feet away. The rough grunted and shifted. The shot I put in his gut giving him grief, I expect.

"Hurry!" he said, choking on the word a bit and coughing. "If I have to run, this girl will die first."

Ivan climbed into the wagon.

I heard others moving about nearby, some moving away, and the murmuring of those keeping a safe distance. No one approached.

Fletcher dragged me still closer to the downhill edge of the trail, no doubt to make easier his flight. Turning, Cedric kept his pistol aimed at us.

"Get back," Fletcher told him.

"No, sir. You harm my sister and I *will* kill you."

"Leave him be, Cedric," Ivan said, as he rummaged in a trunk. "Do as he says."

"He's only got the one shot," little brother said. "If he uses it, he'll die."

Fletcher adjusted his pistol, possibly to appear more ready to fire, perhaps because he was hurting. We'll never know.

Cedric fired.

The rough jerked backwards.

I felt a warm spatter against my face.

The oxen bellowed and stamped their feet, as I pulled away from Fletcher and he fell. I moved onto the downslope to get away from them. The rough lay upon the trail, his head too close to the danger of those great hooves. That mattered little, since he had a bloody hole above his right eye.

Little brother hurried to me with a most welcomed hug.

I heard frightened voices and the movements of more people nearby, no doubt getting away from our wagon and the bloody goings-on. A distant shouting might have been the staff looking to find where the commotion had come from and then trying to decide if they might safely approach.

Cedric helped me back onto the trail, and steadied me. I closed my eyes and tried to find a moment of peace. Under powerful strain, the spring inside me quivered and sang. My ears rang with the memory of the barkers firing. My idea pot pictured the hole in Fletcher's mug. I could not let it go until I opened my eyes.

Now, I saw deep into shadows I could not have pierced moments before. Even in the dark, I saw the pilot and Issa coming from eight wagons away, saw everyone in between and knew I'd remember all their names if I'd a mind to.

Ivan, beside us, called out to Niklas Gruber, and the man came forward. He spoke with Gruber and told folks coming close to step back and keep away.

Florence came for me. "We should allow these men to clean up their mess," she said. I thought it an odd thing to say.

Cedric let go of me. Florence took me to the bedrolls under her wagon. Tessa and Zeata were there. I lay down with them and began to shake. My frenzied thoughts about what had happened to Fletcher Carson circled about in my head; what I had done, what I might have done wrong, what I might have done better, and what I still might do and say. I didn't want to entertain any of it. Zeata cuddled up to me, held my hand. I wasn't certain I'd like that, yet it did stay some of my quivering.

Florence gently wiped at my face with a damp rag. When she

pulled away to rinse it, I could see in the lamp light that the cloth had cleaned blood from my cheek. She began to sing a song that made no sense to me, in some language I'd never heard before. Surprised me to hear Tessa join in. Whatever the jabber, she knew it too. I found Zeata's breath on my neck soothing. The cleaning ended, but the song went on, calming my shakes. I let go the world and slept.

Cedric—20
October, 1847

I didn't feel good about killing Fletcher Carson, since I knew too late I'd possibly killed him when I didn't have to. Like me, he was just another thief trying to get by in the world. Even so, I'd had little sympathy for him from the moment he threatened Alta Mae.

The pilot had a long talk with me about why I'd shot the man.

"Sir, perhaps mistakenly, I believed he were about to shoot Alta Mae as he took a firmer grip on his pistol. He'd already killed Carla."

"That, he did. Alta Mae confirmed it."

We stood out of the rain under the overhanging bonnet of our wagon. He'd taken off his fur cap, and I couldn't help staring at his bald, pink pate.

He seemed to consider for a moment before asking, "Should I presume you've killed only two men?"

"Yes, sir."

"Everyone who undertakes a journey like this faces a trial. I suppose you just got more than your share." He paused again, became thoughtful. "There is a breed of men that like to duel, and they are growing more common out here in the lawless wilderness. They thrill to best another by killing. As young as you are, I'd hate to think you'd be attracted to that sort of thrill, now that you've had a taste."

I shook my head. "No, sir. I would never go looking for a fight. Too much of that where I come from, and it don't settle much."

"I suggest you think long and hard before you ever tell anyone about killing those two men."

"Yes, sir, I promise I will."

He went quiet again for a moment, looking at me. I knew he'd noticed me staring at his pate.

"Ask me," he said. "I'm not shy about it."

"You were scalped, weren't you, sir?"

Hawker smiled. "Yes, but not the way you mean, I think. When I was a boy, I worked in a cotton spinning mill in North Carolina. My hair got caught in the machinery and I lost my scalp, broke my nose, and got most of these other scars too."

He bent toward me so I could see the top of his head.

"What are the dents in it?" I asked.

"The doctor who treated me drilled many little holes just through the top layer of my skull. Over time, new skin of sorts grew from the holes and joined together with my regular skin."

I just stared at him, dumb-struck. With a smile, he reached for my chin and gently shut my bonebox. What he'd endured to heal up made up for the less exciting way he'd lost his scalp.

Hawker smiled, said, "Makes me look like a great fighter, don't it. It's helped me considerable while traveling in the West, since I look like a mean cuss no one would want to tangle with. I'll thank you to keep that tale to yourself."

Said I would and only reveal it here because the man has surely retired or passed away by now.

Later Ivan told us about his conversation with the man. "The pilot says, 'the four men of the watch are well enough, except for a few bruises.'

"I tell him, 'The man, Brown, who approached the Southall Party, was a man named Fletcher Carson, the brother of a business partner Carla had in New York. Once I saw him, I knew him right away. He'd somehow learned of her savings and followed us west in the hopes of taking our stake. Carson must have kept at it because the funds amounted to a considerable sum, something we don't want others to know.'

"Listening to that, Hawker has a havey cavey look."

"If he doubts your story, what do you think he'll do?" Alta Mae asked.

"Don't get ahead of me. I think he wanted to believe it. So I tell him what happened in St. Louis, and that I'd thought we'd left him behind there, healing up in the hospital. He still has that look, so I says, "I reckon me shooting him just made Fletcher angrier, and more willing to chase after us. Maybe he also had a desire to go west.'

"'There's something missing from that story,' says Hawker, 'but I know you to be a good man, so I'll let my curiosity about the matter go. If anyone asks, I'll tell them I'm satisfied the children acted purely in self-defense.'"

Looking at Alta Mae, I could tell she thought, as I did, that we'd been fortunate to gain Hawker's good will.

—◊◊◊—

Within a few days of gaining the wet side, we began to see more and more signs of previous travelers just off the trail; felled trees, soil disturbed for privy and rubbish holes, broken parts of different sorts of equipage, hastily made cabins.

When the pilot had called it the wet side, he'd meant that the western side of the mountain range had more rain than the eastern side. Much bare rock here too, somehow giving the views a stern, majestic quality.

I have not seen a land more beautiful than we found on the western side of the Sierra Nevada Mountains. I'd seen large trees in the East—oaks in the forests of Indiana, and cottonwoods along the rivers west of Missouri—yet I'd never fancied they could grow to the sizes we saw in California. The further we went, the greater they became, some types being hundreds of feet tall, their trunks as thick around as a small house might be wide, their tops so high above us we often could not see where they stopped and the sky began. While the forests in the East may have had more green, the shade was much the same. Here there were many different shades of green.

For the steepest slopes, the teamsters had the oxen in their harnesses backwards and we drove our wagons downhill rear end first.

My knees got sore from all the downslope walking. Felt like the bones banged into each other more than when walking uphill or on flat ground. Some of my friends complained of the same. Missouri had to ride for a time, she got so sore.

As we'd walked through the mountains, Jack had been giving me queer looks. One afternoon, I'd had enough, and asked him about it while no one else could hear me. We slowed to allow our friends to move on some.

"Been thinking about you and Alta Mae growing up without a home in New York, and that maybe that's why you knew so much about Oliver Twist that I didn't see in the story. Then I reckoned that would be the reason you know so much about dipping and thievery, and not just from hearing about it." He had a big smile, so I knew he didn't look upon me with scorn. "You bested Tommy. Knocked him into a cocked hat, you did. You shot Ned Tollard, and that man that killed your Carla. Somehow you survived being in the desert for weeks on your own. You're like a true-life hero."

That was his love of adventures talking.

"My life ain't some thrilling tale to tell," I said. "Yes, it's had exciting parts, some of them good, some bad. Like everybody. Maybe that's what makes stories fun, the good and the bad. The middling stuff is left out. You know, the dull and unflattering parts."

He started to speak, yet stopped as if having trouble finding the right words. His breath puffed white in the chill air. Then he smiled again, said, "Still, you've done some daring things."

I shook my head, tried to think of a way to take the shine out of his eyes. "Did you ever skip a stone on water?"

"Yeah, what of it?"

"Stories are like that, the hero's derring-do is like the stone skipping off the water, staying above it, and not falling in. We like the ones that skip a lot. If that's all you ever see, that's a good story. The middling parts all lie on the bottom, the ones that skip once and go down, the ones that don't fly at all. But you've got to know that in the end the stones all go under."

"Not the ones that skip up onto the far bank."

"That don't enter into it!" I'd got annoyed because I'd also thought of my thieving as daring less than two weeks earlier. "Gol darn it, Jack, I had no parents to look out for me, had no home, suffered the weather and the cruelty of the streets. I *had* to pick pockets and steal just so I could eat."

I stopped walking and he did too. "Since I have a family now, get to eat regular, and have warm clothes, I've given up thievery. I wouldn't think of trading the life I have now for what I had then. You are lucky to have parents, a home, and all that."

He forced a smile, said. "Yeah, I reckon I can see that."

"Please don't tell anyone what I said about dipping and stealing. I'm ashamed of it."

And I knew that to be the truth, no matter that I'd once been so proud of those skills.

Jack nodded, and pulled me off the trail to make room for the team and wagon coming up behind us. He punched me lightly on the shoulder. "You're still a daring fellow, and I'm glad you're my friend, but I suppose stories ain't truly life, are they?"

"No."

His smile reminded me of the ones William Buckets gave in the factory room. I hoped Billy had got out of there.

Alta Mae—20

In the foothills of the western side of the Sierra Nevada Mountains, we found small, rough settlements and logging camps. Along rivers, we saw where trees had been felled in great numbers and the land left in a muddle, with broken trunks and cracked limbs in piles between innumerable stumps. We took as much of that fuel as we could carry.

Farther down, the river had been clogged with logs. Surprised to see men walking on the floating tree trunks and prying them apart with pikes and hooks.

"They untangle them so the logs will move downstream," Tessa told me. "They use the water to carry them to market."

Even knowing that people needed wood to build and to burn for fuel, I was appalled to see how much the logging marred the beauty of the land.

At that point in our journey, we followed more than just trail. We'd entered roads, wider and easier to manage, though muddy and deeply rutted.

As we walked, Cedric began talking about Egan again. At first I became vexed to hear it, after how huffed and wrathy he'd got while we were in the desert. Yet, I listened.

"I want to find him. He's family. I need to know where he is and that he's faring well. I will not allow him to get near our family."

"How will he take that? Don't you think he'll be curious about where you live, who's taking care of you? You are nine years old."

"I might be ten by now."

"That doesn't matter!" I didn't mean to show my anger, but I'd had enough of Egan. The less I thought of him, the better.

"I know…" Cedric remained quiet for a time. "I'll make certain he knows why he cannot see our family. I will tell him they're black and that we care for them a great deal. I'll tell him that if he cannot accept that, then I won't see him anymore."

"Are you certain you can tell him about them, and stand up to him?"

"Yes."

He said that with such confidence, I believed him. I understood he had the need to find Egan and I knew that need would not go away.

"I'll help you."

"Truly?"

"Yes. He won't be able to argue us both down."

—⚬⚬⚬—

November, 1847

New Helvetia, the first large settlement we reached, would be the end of the journey for the wagon train. The town had grown up on a hill above the Sacramento River. In a few years it would become the city of Sacramento. At its center stood a big brown mud castle, something like Fort Laramie, named Sutter's Fort. Surrounding that were a few cabins, orchards, and many head of cattle grazing in the fields. We replenished some of our depleted supplies at shops in the fort, and added cheese and fresh fruit to our stores. I have never again eaten an apple that tasted as good as the one I ate the day we arrive in New Helvetia.

That evening, we all assembled to hear the pilot give farewell. He stood with Issa, Niklas Gruber, Sam Hoog, and Costello and his sons. "You will make your own way in smaller groups from here, depending on where you're going," the pilot said. "Be wary and yet considerate of the Indians, be kind to those who are already settled as they may become your neighbors. The hostilities with Mexico appear to be ending, but you should likewise be considerate, and careful among the Spanish speaking population. If you have strong opinions about the conflict, consider keeping them to yourself."

He paused before drawing out a piece of paper from which he read, "On behalf of the New Pacific Emigration Company, I give you our thanks. As you correspond with family and acquaintances in the East, please consider telling them of the many good experiences of the journey, and mention our company as the reliable agent that saw you safely into west."

He looked up, smiled, and said, "I must read that to you, though you deserve so much more. We suffered difficulty and loss. We also worked together well, a few bad patches not withstanding. You are a fine group of people. Whatever you do in the future, I hope you find good fortune."

All of the Lucere party gathered around them. More than an hour passed before all hands had been shaken and everyone had given their thanks.

—⁂—

We had reached our destination, and still I had no sense that our travels neared their end. We camped for two days in New Helvetia, giving us a chance to say goodbye to those we had befriended on the journey. What addresses folks had of their destinations were exchanged. I had the address Ivan's father, Paul Romano, had sent to Carla in his last letter. Cedric and I offered it to all our friends, even the ones that would be continuing with us toward San Jose.

Frances Adair said her mother had put her foot down. "No more gambling, she told my father or she would take me and leave him. We will stay in New Helvetia, where Momma expects Poppa will take on hard, honest work. She spoke to the Sutter orchard manager, a man who is willing to take Poppa on. He once worked orchards in Scotland when a young man. I can only hope."

"I wish you good fortune for the future," I said.

She laughed. "As long as it's not gained by gambling."

Tilsa Svensdotter and her family also remained in New Helvetia, their intended destination.

The Jacobsons, Yarmanowitzes, Hughes, and Stiltons were among the families also headed southward. We traveled as a group of nine wagons.

The North family had firmly decided to stick with us, as Mrs. North had few prospects without her husband. We welcomed them, Ivan and Tessa pledging to help all they could. This especially pleased Cedric.

Took us a month and a half to get to the city of San Jose. Rain fell during most of that time. We spent weeks skirting flooded parts of the delta formed by the Sacramento and San Joaquin Rivers, and had to pay ferrymen to carry our wagons across swollen waters numerous times. As ever, to stay together, we had to help each other. Wagons ran into trouble, getting stuck in the mud or running off the road. The ferrying meant much waiting as the small barges took only one wagon at a time. If rain didn't fall, we had heavy fog.

Before reaching San Jose, we met a crossroads where the Yarmanowitz, Jacobson, and Stilton families would leave us to head to Yerba Buena.

"You won't be far away," Cedric reminded his friends.

"We'll see each other again soon," I told them.

I did not envy Cedric the hugs he had to endure.

Cedric—21
December, 1847

Miserable from the cold and damp, we arrived in San Jose in late December. The town wasn't much to look at, a cluster of rough houses at odd angles along deeply rutted curving streets, a market, a livery, a tavern, a church, and a square around which larger buildings were being built.

Seeing the sun slanting down out of the western sky on the day we arrived, I wished Carla had been there to see it. She'd once said that such spreading fingers of light coming through the clouds were the hand of God.

Missouri Hughes and her father said their goodbyes there. With three other families, they headed further south to the capital of Alta California, as the Mexicans called California, a small city named Monterey in a bay facing the Pacific Ocean.

An old woman greeted us shortly after we arrived at Paul Romano's address.

"Mr. Ivan Romano?" she called out as she approached.

"Yes."

"Your father bid me to meet you when you arrived, and to give you this key," she said.

She had come out of the building next door with her feet bare, wearing a night shirt, her white hair a tangle covering half her wrinkled mug. A drop of liquid clung to the end of her nose until she wiped it away with her sleeve. I'd thought Carla old. This woman looked to have risen from the grave to greet us.

"You *are* black, *aren't* you?" she asked. "He said you would be, but still I had my doubts."

"I am indeed part black."

"Mrs. Sanchez says, 'One drop of black blood makes the whole person black.' We share a room and a bed in the boarding house."

She pointed at the house next door. "She goes on about the evils of amalgamation. This world abounds with coots like her. You take care."

Ivan smiled at that.

"There's an old barn on the left," she said, pointing a frail, thick-veined claw. "Your wagon might fit, should you remove the bonnet. I don't know what to suggest for your oxen. The rent is paid until the 18th of January."

Ivan said, "Thank you, uh...?

"Miss Milleston."

"Yes, thank you. Can you tell me where my father has gone?"

"Oh, yes, I forgot that part. He had an opportunity come up in Yerba Buena, something with a fishing crew. He removed there last week." Reaching into a pocket of her night shirt, she pulled out a handful of gullyfluff and a note folded up small. "His address," she said, dropping all but the note, which she handed to Ivan. "Now, I must go. Hamish is going to read to us."

"Thank you again, Miss Milleston." Ivan said. "I shall write to him straight away."

She waved a bony hand in the air as she ambled stiffly back the way she'd come.

—ɯ—

The house had one room with two curtained windows in opposite walls, a bed, an iron stove, with oven and range, and a table and four chairs. Ivan insisted that Tessa and Mrs. North share the bed. The rest of us bedded down on the floor in our bedrolls.

Over the following weeks, all of us bought new boots. Ivan sold the oxen and the prairie schooner. He bought a buckboard, two mules, and two chairs. I went with him to fetch the new wagon back to our lodgings. As we rode home, it occurred to me, as if for the first time, that we had arrived at our destination, and that I should have some added sense of pride for the task completed.

Too much remained undecided for that. We had yet to choose to stay in San Jose or set a new destination. Listening to Ivan and Tessa, our goal would be to find a place to settle where he and possibly she might find work. Ivan's father had gone to Yerba Buena, so we would likely end up there.

That evening we sat to a proper meal that Florence had cooked after going to market; a roasted chicken, beans, and fresh-baked corn bread.

"I thought I'd go exploring the town some tomorrow," I told Ivan, "unless you need my help."

He looked at me funny, said, "I don't think that's a good idea until we know just what sort of people live here. This ain't New York where there are so many people of different sorts in the streets."

I'm not truly your child who has to obey you, I thought, yet didn't voice the words.

"I can get around without being seen," I said.

"No," Alta Mae said, taking my hand. "We'll have no more of that unless it's truly needed."

"Sneaking around would be worse than walking about proudly," Florence said, and Tessa nodded agreement.

"Stay with one of us for a while, just until we know." Ivan said.

"Know what?"

"Whether the town is full of bigots," he said, giving me that odd look again. "A small number are one thing. If there are many, we need to take care."

I turned to Alta Mae. She shrugged and said, "Just do as he says."

I looked to Zeata. "You know we have to be careful," she said. "Mama, tell him about how you lost Filby when he was my age."

Florence nodded with a sad look. "Charlestown, Indiana had long been a stop we made hauling goods along the Ohio," she said. "While there one day, my brother, Filby, went off on his own. He got accused of stealing firewood. Before my father could get to him, they had the poor boy hanged from a tree, dead. The local sheriff done nothing about it. We never went back there."

"Yes," Alta Mae said, "But Cedric is white."

Ivan, Tessa, Florence, and even Zeata gave Alta Mae a queer look.

"Not white enough for some," Ivan said.

"I don't understand," I said.

"For a black boy," Zeata said, "you don't have much experience with these things."

Alta Mae and I looked at each other. "I'm not black," I said. My sister shook her head.

"Sure enough, you'd easily pass for a member of my family," Tessa said.

Ivan nodded.

"You believe he's part black?" Alta Mae asked.

All four nodded.

"You too…" Ivan began, his voice trailing off like he might have said something wrong.

Then all four looked at each other, each with his or her own look of confusion. Yet, something about those looks made me think they'd never discuss this amongst themselves. That in itself told me they were right, something that could not stand in my mind.

"How could you not know?" Tessa asked.

Thoroughly bustled, I didn't know what to say.

I looked again to Alta Mae. She would fix this.

Her right hand hid her face except for the deep frown of her forehead. Then the hand fell away and her eyes got big. She turned to me, said, "Egan's lies!"

Looking her in the blinkers, I saw that new understanding had brewed up in her idea pot.

I grew frightened. Unable to face it, I got up from the table and ran from the lodgings.

Alta Mae—21

Dusk had fallen. I lit a lamp to take with me to look for Cedric. I found him in the crude barn beside the lodging house, hiding in the corner of a stall that held one of the mules.

With some persuasion, I got him up. We sat on the dusty floor outside the stall, the lit lamp between us. He didn't speak for a while.

As I waited, rain began to sound against the roof shakes, just as tears wet his cheeks. His bone box drew back and his blinkers clinched with a look of sadness deeper than any I'd seen him bear before. As if voicing his pain, the wind moaned a bit in the rafters, and the shakes on the roof rattled as he shuddered with sobs. I reached to take his hand, and he pulled it away.

"I ain't black," he said.

"It don't matter, Cedric. I don't care what color you are."

"You ain't black either," he said bitterly. Then he looked up, like he had to see the truth of that for himself.

I let him gaze at me for a time. His sad look lifted some, became more of a frown.

"They didn't mean us any harm saying those things. They were as surprised we didn't see what they saw as we were to hear them say it. We are dear to them. Zeata is in there now crying over your hurt feelings. They asked me to come out and tell you they're sorry, and that they must be wrong."

Cedric was still looking me over in the lamp light. His blinkers scrunched up and he said, "We've both got those tight, little curls."

"That must have been how they made the mistake."

"I've hardly ever looked at myself in a mirror," he said slowly.

"And I'm not much to look at," I said.

Cedric looked bustled. "What do you mean?"

"Well, I'm not a dimber girl."

"Of course you're pretty. You don't hold yourself well, and you're

211

always so *dirty*."

"You too!" I said in mock outrage.

I saw the shade of a smile, and took his hand.

He drew it away.

"Will you come in with me?" I asked. "Zeata's heart is fit to break over this."

He didn't answer, just sat there.

I reached for his hand again, and he didn't take it away this time. I stood and drew him up.

Through a light drizzle, we walked back to the lodgings.

Zeata waited at the door. "I'm sorry we hurt your feelings, Cedric."

"*Please* don't say that," he said. He covered his mug with his hands and tried to turn away.

I stood in his way.

Zeata took him by the hand and led him back to the dining table, where everyone remained seated before the uneaten supper.

"We waited for you, Cedric," Florence said. "I can warm up the supper if you're ready to join us."

Seemed he couldn't look at them or sit. Keeping his head down, he said. "I am at fault for the hurt feelings. I made out that being black is less than being white." He paused to wipe the mist from his blinkers. "I never been *anything* my whole life, never had much of anything."

Tessa made as if to say something. Ivan stayed her with a hand upon her arm.

"A time or two," Cedric said, "like a gold idiot, I'd think to myself, at least I were born white. I thought that give me *something*. The coppers in New York were awful cruel to the homeless black children. Yet, many a times, they'd turned a blind eye to me and Alta Mae. I thought they did that out of sympathy, like they believed we had a chance to be good or something, and ought to be treated fairly. We had an advantage over the black children. With what you said about me being black, I become scared to lose that advantage, like it were all I had in the world."

Cedric sat down in his chair, and I sat in mine.

"You don't lose anything," Ivan said. "Did anyone among the Lucere party treat you any different?"

"How would I know?"

"You'd know," Tessa said. "People like to make it plain, *especially* if they dislike you for no good reason."

Thinking about that, I said, "Cedric, when Tilsa turned on me, she had words of scorn for me being Catholic and having a black cousin, but that's not the same as saying I'm black."

Cedric shrugged. "We don't know who our parents were. Our brother, Egan, raised us. He hates blacks, so we believed, well...you know."

"Egan lied to us a lot," I said, "sometimes just to see what we'd believe."

Cedric nodded. At last, he looked up at the faces around the table. "I'm awful sorry. Please forgive me. I believe you're right about us."

"We may never know the truth," Ivan said, "and I think I'm not alone saying it don't matter."

We welcomed the nods and smiles from around the table.

Florence got up and heated the beans and corn bread. We decided to eat the roasted chicken cold, though she did heat the dripping for us to dip our cornbread in.

The solemn conversation turned to one with some good humor to it.

I felt like I had a home at last. Seeing the smile on Cedric's mug, I suspected he felt the same.

Cedric—22

We remained in San Jose until January 12th, then loaded up the buckboard and headed for Yerba Buena, a two-day trip.

On the way, we took the time to have a look at the Pacific Ocean. We climbed a low peak to find a vantage, and stood in a powerful wind, looking out at the endless water under a cloudy sky. Having a gray, somber beauty to it, that great flatness of water and giant dome of sky also seemed a terrible, lonely place. Still, I wondered what great fishes might be pulled from those waters.

The sun dipped behind the clouds. The chill deepened. Miserably cold, we backed off the peak and returned to our buckboard and the road north.

We arrived in Yerba Buena in the early evening of the second day, and found our way to the abode of Paul Romano, a two room cabin near Mission cove.

Paul received us at his lodgings in Kearny Street like we'd always been family. He didn't look much like Carla. While her mug had been round, and I couldn't help remembering it scowling at me, he had a long face that smiled readily, the stubble of graying hair, and long side whiskers. Stood maybe six feet tall, had thick arms, a broad chest, and hands that looked powerful.

He greeted Ivan with a hug, then asked to be introduced to Mrs. Angelo.

"Such a beautiful young woman," he said. "May I call you Tessa?"

"Yes, you may," she said, a bit shy. Tessa smiled, something she rarely offered people new to her.

"I am delighted to meet you," Paul said. "Ivan told me something about you in each of his letters."

We were all introduced. Paul had many questions, and most got answered. To a couple of them concerning Carla, Ivan said, "That's a long story, best left for later."

"She'd be gladdened to see us all together," Paul said with a sad smile.

Following a supper of fish stew, I asked Paul about the tattoo I saw peeking out above his buttoned shirt, a snout and beastly eye.

"Ah, that's the head of the dragon I got in Japan." He unbuttoned his shirt to show the rest of the serpent. The fanciful beast wrapped around his torso. Paul spent an hour showing us the art on his arms, legs, back, and shoulders, and telling where he'd got them in his travels at sea. Alta Mae, Zeata, and I could have listen to such tales for hours, but Tessa and Florence put us in our bedrolls in the corner and told us to sleep. The adults went on visiting, their voices becoming merely a warm murmur. I did hear Ivan say, "I hope to find lodgings where all of us might live together comfortably. I have thought to find a house to purchase."

In the days that followed, Tessa began tutoring; she taught reading, writing, and English to Spanish-speaking children. Alta Mae, Zeata, and I went to school in the new schoolhouse in Portsmouth Square. Alta Mae took to it readily. I didn't much like it, wanting instead to be outside. Then Aron Yarmanowitz showed up at school one day, and a few days later Jack Jacobson did too. Well, having friends there made all the difference.

The school days done, we would explore the town together. Nothing too ambitious, as I'd been cautioned by Alta Mae not to get into trouble. I taught my friends how to move about in a manner less likely to draw attention. Even so, we found ourselves running from peery shopkeepers thinking we'd come to their establishments for hoisting, and from those plump in the pocket who thought we might be dipping.

We discovered Tommy Stilton and his family working out of a small shed attached to a lodging house.

"We're repairing sss-hoe-sss por now," Tommy said, "ju-sss-t until we get sss-ettled in and pind a place to open a cobbler sss-hop. Bu-sss-ine-sss i-sss good. A lot op worn out sss-hoe-sss here, and more will arrive with each wagon train."

He looked at our feet. "I sss-ee you all have new boot-sss. But ip you have sss-ome needing repair, bring them to u-sss, and I'll do it por nothing."

"You could not have repaired mine after our long walk," I told him. "They had no hope."

Perhaps thinking of their own ragged boots, Jack and Aron

nodded.

Tommy would explore with us some, but he spent most of his time working for his father.

Nobody expected that gold would be discovered at Sutter's Mill less than two weeks after we arrived in Yerba Buena. Shortly thereafter the United States and Mexico signed a treaty that handed over much of the West to the Americans. The town began to change and grow almost immediately with more Americans flooding in during the gold rush. The name was changed to San Francisco. Rents went up. Many of the Spanish-speaking people were pushed out. Shanty towns began to form in less desirable parts, along the edges of the marshes leading to the bay.

Just before the market for dwellings grew difficult, Ivan had located a wood frame house for us in Sutter Street. He bought it with some of Carla's ill-gotten gains.

I believe the owner had started repairs before deciding to sell. The roof had been made whole, yet the place needed a lot of work. Doors and windows were drafty, and some of the clapboards needed to be replaced. Paul, who had once been a Carpenter's Mate Assistant, went to work on it, and the rest of us helped wherever we could. Within three weeks, we had the house strong enough to keep the weather out. Better looking repairs would come later.

We spent more of Carla's dodgy darby on furnishings for our new home. I slept in a room with Paul, Alta Mae slept in another with Florence and Zeata, and of course Ivan and Tessa had a room. The largest chamber, which had a cookstove, became the parlor and dining room.

The teachers at school got the gold fever and went to try their hands at mining. Tessa took over our education at home. She gathered the books we needed, and, along with our reading, taught us cyphering and history. I saw less of Jack and Aron until she agreed to have them attend our lessons.

On the advice of his father, Ivan also bought a fishing business from an elderly Mexican fellow named Garcia, Paul's employer who was retiring after running a fishing crew from his own dock in Mission Cove for many years. The purchase would take nearly all that remained of the darby. Florence had a hand in persuading Ivan that our newly mixed family could do well with a fishing crew endeavor, and promised to help with all she'd learned of the business from her father. The purchase included a shack and docking pier in Mission Cove and two forty foot catboats. Ivan, Paul, and Florence took over Garcia's business and kept the fishing crew on the job. They called the new business Romano Fishers. We fished the bay for sturgeon, herring, salmon, and the fish Missouri had mentioned, sardines. We also harvested shell fish; clams, mussels, and abalone. Turned out, I truly did want to be a fisherman. I worked with them whenever I could, but Tessa, strict about me attending lessons, kept me busy.

Alta Mae and I went to the U. S. Army garrison to talk with members of Colonel Stevenson's Regiment of New York Volunteers. We spoke to a Second Lieutenant about Egan. He spoke with another officer, then came back to us and said. "Private Egan Brewer is in the town of Los Angeles, about four hundred miles south. Shall I find you the address of where he's billeted so you can write to him?"

I looked at Alta Mae. She shrugged.

"My understanding is that his company will be returning here in August," the Second Lieutenant said.

Though I couldn't have said why, I didn't want Egan to know I'd arrived in California. I wanted to find him before he found me.

"No, thank you," I said.

Alta Mae gave me a questioning look. I couldn't have explained, and simply shrugged.

I went back to the garrison once two months later, in March, and again in June, each time to ask the officers if the schedule had changed. No change expected, I didn't think much about Egan for a while. What was the point, since some time would pass before he returned to San Francisco?

The months went by, and in September of 1848, I met a man on the street wearing the New York Volunteers uniform. I asked him if he knew Egan Brewer.

"He were with the company in Los Angeles. They got here a couple weeks ago. I were with the company in San Diego. We just arrived. We're all being mustered out now that the war is over."

"Do you think he'll return east?"

Instead of answering, he looked closer at me, said. "You from New York?"

I nodded.

"I can hear it in your voice," he said, smiling. He nudged my shoulder with an elbow. "Dead Rabbits or Bowery Boys?"

"Bowery Boys," I pretended, "just like Egan."

"In that case, although you're too young for anything but a scout or messenger, you should know there's a new crew called the Hounds forming up around a man named Samuel Roberts. Egan has joined up, so, yes, I'd say he's staying. Mr. Robert's will be hiring us out to some of the politicians and merchants hereabouts, you know, to control the spinach speakers, hopefully run them out of San Francisco." He laughed as if he thought it funny to mispronounce Spanish that way.

I'd got to know some of the Mexicans, especially those on the fishing crew. I also met a few Chileans, and Peruvians. Much like anybody else, they all had just as much right to the land as the Americans.

As I walked away, he called out. "Who should I say were asking after him?"

I didn't answer.

Later that day, I told Alta Mae about the conversation. "He's already joined a new gang. It's not enough that we took their land away, Egan has to hound the Mexicans out of the country too."

"Perhaps now you see why I'd rather leave him in the past," she said.

"Yes, he may be the same as he were in the Points. There's no hurry to find him, since he seems to be staying here."

Saying that, I wondered if I meant to put off finding trouble with Egan, or suffering Alta Mae's displeasure when I did find him.

"I'm certain we'll see him on the streets one day," she said.

I shrugged, and we said no more about it at that time.

—◆◆◆—

Not a month later, on a beautiful, sunny Saturday, Alta Mae and I went to join the fishing crew for the day. Florence and Zeata had stayed home. We took care walking to the dock through a neighborhood of shanties. That part of town could be dangerous. Of course, two children, we didn't look like we had much to steal, so we felt safe enough. Nearest the docks, the sandy ground in places would not support our weight. Boards had been placed to show the sturdy paths folks used, but I'd more than once stepped off into what looked solid enough, only to find my leg swallowed to the knee in the sand. The gripping mud beneath that sand would try to keep me there. Had to reach deep into one of the holes to retrieve my boot once.

The catboats sat within berths across a short pier from one another. Ivan and Paul had renamed them. The "Carla" had taken its name from our Carlotta Angelo. The "Anja" had been given Ivan's mother's name. She'd been a woman from Nassau, who had passed away many years earlier. Each boat had its new name painted in red and black at the stern and near the prow.

When close enough, we could hear a commotion to our right at another, longer pier. Smoke rose from a boat tied there, then flames climbed up its furled sail. Three men were making their way off that pier. They each carried a cudgel.

I heard Paul call out, "Miguel, your boat is on fire!"

A man shouting in Spanish came running down the slope toward the burning boat.

Paul climbed out of the Carla, followed by Ivan. They ran toward the commotion.

The three groups came together about where the pier met solid ground. Ivan caught the wrist of one swinging a cudgel at him, Paul went after another, while the man Ivan had called Miguel faced the third.

Goosecap that I was, I ran toward the fight, even as Alta Mae tried to stop me. "Stay away from those nobblers, you nimenog!" she shouted. I heard her behind me, running to catch up, still calling for me to stop. But those fellows were burning boats, and ours could be next.

Paul wrestled on the ground with his opponent. Miguel went down and the man above him struck him in the head with his cudgel.

I leapt onto the attacker's back, reached around his throat with both arms, trying to quinsey him. I hung on until he got his weapon under my right arm and pried it loose. He shrugged me off easily. I fell in the soft dirt, and couldn't get up quickly. As she'd been running, Alta Mae had gone off the path and fallen in the mud.

The man above me turned, and I saw he had Egan's mug!

I put my hands up to ward off the blows as he brought his cudgel down on me again and again. In his raging, he didn't know me, and I couldn't think to say his name. I'd never seen him like that, the frenzy, the anger in his eyes. He struck me in the shoulder and arms, pinned me to the ground with a leg.

Heard Alta Mae scream, "Egan, that's Cedric," just as his cudgel came down on my head.

Alta Mae—22

Egan recognized my voice too late. He'd cracked Cedric's skull.

Paul and Ivan, having dealt with the other two, grabbed Egan. His gaze upon me, I watched the look in his eyes change as he was dragged backwards away from Cedric, his anger swiftly turning to surprise, confusion, fear.

Ivan fell to giving Egan a lumping.

"No, Ivan!" I shouted, but the beating went on, so I screamed with all I had, "Stop!"

Crouched over big brother, Ivan looked up, his blinkers full of anger.

"That's Egan, our brother."

Ivan shuttered, took a deep breath, and let his bloodied hands fall to his sides.

Paul had gathered Cedric in his arms. "I know a doctor." He began running with him, up the slope, calling out, "Javier! Javier!"

"Wait for me," I said.

"No time," he called back, and then he was gone.

"This," Ivan said, "is your big brother?"

"Yes."

Egan choked, as Ivan had him pinned to the ground at the throat. He let up enough for big brother to gasp in a breath.

Several men hurried past us carrying buckets to put out the burning boat. Another group were tying the hands of Egan's two confederates. They also roughed them up with several strikes to the gut for each.

Concerned the men might hang Egan, I asked, "Shall we call for a constable?"

"They don't come to this shanty town," Ivan said.

From my years in Five Points, I knew too well what he meant.

Miguel, bleeding from the head, had got to his feet.

"Gracias, Ivan," he said. "You are a good neighbor. Let us take this picaro into your shack and find out who sent him."

"You need to bandage your wound," Ivan said.

"No, was a glancing blow."

Ivan hauled Egan up, and with Miguel's help, got him into the shack. They tied him to a chair, and tried to get answers to their questions. When Egan would not speak, Miguel struck him in the face.

Ivan stayed him, gestured to me, said, "This is my cousin, Alta Mae."

Miguel looked confused.

"And this is her brother," Ivan said.

He looked even more confused, but he didn't try to harm Egan again.

All three of us tried to persuade big brother to tell us why he had come to do so much harm. He didn't speak, and would only meet *my* gaze.

I suspected I knew some of the truth. To say it aloud might arouse Miguel to lump Egan more, and though he deserved it, I didn't want to see that happen.

"Allow me to speak to him alone." I said.

Ivan nodded and persuaded Miguel to leave with him.

"He called you *cousin*." Egan said after they were gone.

"Yes," I said. "I am merely dubbed so. Yet he *is* family now."

"He is *black*." Disgust showed in his eyes.

"Good, Ivan's blows have not so addled you that you cannot see."

"How do you come to be here?" he said, almost as a challenge, like I'd no right to be there. I would not let his blustering manner unsettle me.

I took a moment before answering to look at my brother. He had a harder look in his eyes than I remembered. His blinkers were green, his hair, also darker than I remembered, curled tightly, like mine and Cedric's.

Had anyone ever suggested to him that *he* was black? Or did he already know the truth, whatever that might be?

"Once we'd escaped the factory rooms at the old Brewery," I said calmly, "we found friends and crossed overland to get here."

His blinkers grew wide as I spoke, some of his blustery look falling away. "Tell me more."

"I will," I said, "if you will tell me why you are here to harm these people."

"I am a member of the hounds," he said, "an organization dedicated to driving the Catholic brown people out of these parts. I give that information freely because we are grown too strong for anyone to harm us."

Just as I'd suspected. Cedric had got as much out of his conversation with the man on the street, the one from Egan's regiment.

I told Egan our story; about Carla, Ivan, our travels by water, our time in St. Louis, Tessa, the wagon train, the North family, Cedric taking to Zeata, and us all ending up together in San Francisco.

Took so long, Ivan stuck his head in three times to see if I remained unharmed. With each, I asked for a moment longer.

When I'd finished with the tale, Egan said, "You should know the Hounds will keep coming back here until we've driven the Spanish-speaking men out of the fishing business."

"Who pays the Hounds to do this?"

He seemed surprised I knew they got paid to commit the violence, something mentioned by the man Cedric had met.

"An organization of white fisherman and merchants. I will not give you their name, and you won't find it."

I left the shack to tell Ivan and Miguel what I'd learned. Ivan entered the shack alone. I feared he would lump Egan further. Thankfully, I heard no scuffle. After a time, Ivan came back out.

"We will let Egan go," he told us. "He will take my message back to those who sent him."

"No," Miguel said. "We must take him to the policia."

"I told him to tell his gang we have our own gang with many more members. I said that we were surprised since we'd had no warning. Now that we'd had one, I said, we'll be ready next time."

"We have no *army*," Miguel said.

"He doesn't know that," Ivan said. "We will have, because Paul and I will help form one and a watch system so we can see the danger coming. Will you help us?"

Miguel looked afraid.

"My father and I have fought with men such as these. They will only get stronger if we don't stand up for ourselves. They are not coming just to rid the bay of fishermen, but all Spanish-speaking people hereabouts. They cannot abide those who ain't white

Protestants. I will help defend you and teach you and your families ways to defend yourselves."

Miguel finally agreed. They set a time to meet with other fishermen in the Spanish Shantytown.

"Where did Paul take Cedric," I asked. "He were calling out for someone named Javier."

"He is a medico," Miguel said, "I will show you."

Ivan let Egan out of the shack and told him to go. I couldn't look at him.

We then hurried after Miguel to find Cedric.

Medico Javier Delgado had a medical tent about a quarter of a mile away from the cove. We discovered Paul waiting outside, looking out for us.

"The rough that struck Cedric follows you," Paul said.

We all turned. I saw Egan some thirty feet away. We stared at each other across the short distance as people walked between us along the wooden walkway. He could have joined them and fled, but he didn't.

"I want to see Cedric." he said.

"You should go, *now!*" Ivan said, hurrying toward big brother in a threatening manner, Paul following.

Egan stood his ground.

Ivan made as if to strike him.

"Let him see what he's done to his brother," I said at the last, and Ivan turned away.

Paul and Ivan on either side of him, Egan approached. We all entered the tent, located the surgeon, and asked for Cedric.

Several of the sick lay upon the damp ground inside the tent. A few had filthy blankets. One woman had a soiled pillow beneath her head. We found Cedric in a wooden pallet, something like a large crate half filled with hay. His eyes were closed and he lay quite still, though thankfully his chest still rose and fell.

"I'll go for the buckboard and some blankets," Paul said. He went out.

"His skull is cracked above the right ear," Delgado said. "I felt it through his scalp. There's little I can do for him. He will likely recover with time, yet may have lingering problems."

I wanted to kill Egan then and there.

Big brother looked at little brother, his gaze troubled.

Good, I thought, let him suffer for what he's done.

Egan turned to leave.

"We may come for you," Ivan said.

Egan stopped, nodded without looking back, and left the tent.

We thanked the Medico and paid him for his efforts.

Once Paul arrived with the wagon, we cushioned the bed with the blankets, and I got in to cradle Cedric's head in my lap for the ride home.

—⚬⚬⚬—

At the house, resting in the bed he shared with Paul, Cedric remained asleep until the evening of the next day. All of us had stayed home, waiting and hoping for Cedric to awaken. Tessa noticed him stirring, and we all gathered round his bed.

Unfortunately, when he opened his eyes, our cheers frightened him. He cried out and held his head as if in pain.

"You should know better," Florence scolded. She ushered us out and took over Cedric's care.

The next day, he got out of bed. He complained of a headache and walked with a slight limp in his left leg. "I have a little trouble with my left arm, too," he said. His head, shoulders, and arms had turned purple with bruises.

Time passed and the limbs on Cedric's left side never got better. He seemed to find ways around the awkwardness. He didn't complain, and he didn't ask about Egan.

On occasion, I felt along the slight depression in his scalp. His skull slowly knit itself back together.

The Hounds became a powerful force in the city within the following year, yet they also inspired the citizenry to hate them. The few times they moved against the Spanish-speaking fisherman, they were sorry they'd tried. Ivan and Paul had done a good job helping the fishermen learn to defend themselves.

After the Hounds attacked the Spanish shantytown near Mission Cove in July of 1849, the city deputized hundreds of men to hunt down the members of the gang. Many got away, leaving the city. Among those arrested was Samuel Roberts, their leader. He went to prison for ten years.

While the many deputies hunted the Hounds, Egan, on the run, showed up on our doorstep, Cedric the only one home at the time.

Cedric—23
July, 1849

I didn't want to let him in. I stood in the threshold with the door partly closed, blocking his entry.

"I'm sorry for what I done, Cedric," Egan said. "I didn't know it were you."

"No, you'd have done it to complete strangers," I said. I could not hide my disgust, yet, I stayed in the doorway where I could see and hear him.

Why?

To my horror, I knew I remained drawn to him. He was my brother!

"Please Cedric, I am truly sorry. The constables are after me. If I'm seen, they'll surely capture me and I'll go to prison."

Of course, being so much bigger, he could have pushed past me, if he'd wanted.

"Why don't you leave San Francisco?" I asked.

"I have no money, so I cannot travel far..." He took his right hand out of his pocket and held it out. The fingers and palm had smears of old and fresh blood. "...and I were stabbed in our last raid."

Then I noticed the dark blood stain on his trousers.

I opened the door and let him in.

—⚊⚊—

Although none of my family wanted Egan there, Ivan showed his anger the most. He ranted and raved, and only quieted when I asked, "You would turn Egan out while he suffers with that wound?" A curious thing, big brother had been stabbed in much the same place that Ivan had shot Fletcher Carson, in the right leg, just below the hip. "Do you think the coppers will give him the aid he needs?"

Tessa prepared a dinner of pork, cabbage, and potatoes. Egan received a plate of the victuals as he rested on a pallet of blankets

Florence had prepared for him in the corner, while we all sat at the table to eat.

"If we give him to the constables, they *will* have a surgeon for him," Paul said.

"I would leave your home and look for another place to hide, rather than go to prison," Egan said. "I need time to heal up, is all. Then I'll try to leave the Bay of San Francisco."

"To find another place where you might ally yourself with bigots?" Alta Mae asked.

Egan didn't answer.

I noted that Zeata's blinkers were drawn to Egan again and again. That troubled me.

"Why do you keep looking at him," I whispered.

"Because he looks so much like you," she said almost too softly to hear. "Does he hate just Mexicans?"

"No, he hates all Catholics. Also blacks and Jews."

"He is black, in part," she said with confidence. "Why, then, does he hate us so?"

"I don't know. Perhaps *he* doesn't know."

"Cedric said you got wounded in one of your raids," Paul said. "'Twas an adventure when you faced only soft folks. Now people are standing up to the Hounds, ain't they?"

"Leave him be," Florence said. "Let the man rest."

We'd been eating in silence but a moment before Egan cleared his throat and spoke quietly. "After I harmed Cedric, some of the fight were gone from me. My heart wasn't in it. That's why I got stabbed. Were a woman done it. Foolish not to expect it, as she defended her own."

"You want us to believe you've had a change of heart?" Tessa asked. Her scoffing tone left no doubt where she fell on the matter.

Again, Egan didn't answer.

The night passed in much the usual manner; some idle talk of the day, some practice reading, Paul repairing torn togs, and Tessa cleaning up in the kitchen. Ivan read aloud a few choice stories from *The California Advance*. Zeata read aloud from a book of poetry. I didn't like the verses since I could not understand the way the words fit together. The rhyming seemed a silly device that often confused the meaning of the words. Still, her voice was musical.

Surprised to see Egan watching and listening as she read. Once done, she covered her eyes with a hand, and gave us that shy grin and giggle I loved so much. Saw big brother smile at that.

Zeata sat with me and held my hand. I thought to put her hand down so Egan didn't have cause to show disgust, but he'd already seen us that way, and hadn't said anything.

The next day, Ivan and Paul went to the cove to go out with the fishing crew. We took up our lessons with Tessa. Florence made bread dough and other preparations for supper. Egan watched us all silently. He'd never known such a home, I felt certain. I couldn't fathom what he thought of us.

A sudsday, when our lessons were done, Tessa, Alta Mae, and I turned to doing the laundry on the back porch, while Florence and Zeata attended Egan's wound.

A beautiful, sunny day, we had the back door and windows open, and I couldn't help overhearing those inside talking.

"Pull your pants down a bit," Florence said. Then a moment passed and she said, "You don't have to be modest with me, young man."

"What about Zeata?" Egan asked.

"I'm instructing her in the use of the poultice I made for your wound. She's seen a man's nakedness. Was a fellow back in Indiana tried to stick his root in her when she just seven year old."

I could not hear clearly Egan's next words, but then Florence said, "Oh, I stopped him, and he never so much as looked at her again."

Zeata chuckled at that, and so did Egan.

"Why do you help me so?" he asked.

Florence huffed. "Because Cedric brought you in, you are his brother, and he's near to being my boy now."

I liked hearing that, and I hoped Egan did too.

"Did he tell you that when we was in the wilderness, he shot and killed a man who tried to fire shot into me?"

"No, he didn't."

"He's truly brave," Zeata said and giggled. I pictured her covering her mouth.

"Saved my life, he did," Florence said. "Yes sir, I will protect that boy and whoever he claims as his own."

"You and your daughter are fortunate to have him." Egan said.

Hearing that, I believed he'd seen the Norths as deserving of good fortune. That seemed a marked difference from the old Egan.

Although we wouldn't have stood for it, he had not made any challenges to our way of thinking and doing.

Just the day before, I'd wanted to rail at him for all his lies. Somewhere, sometime, while I wasn't thinking about it, the need had gone away. I'd also noted that some of the anger toward him from others in the household had cooled too.

Something of hope turned in my breast.

—⁓—

The days passed. Egan began to heal, perhaps in more ways than one.

Since he hadn't shaved for some time, his beard started growing. I asked if he wanted to shave, and he said, "No, fewer will recognize me with the whiskers."

One day he became well enough to ask if he could help out around the house. Florence and Tessa put him to work. He attended our lessons, and Zeata made extra efforts to help him learn.

Two months later, Ivan came home one evening and said to Egan, "We lost one of our fishing crew to fever. Would you think of joining Romano Fishers?"

"I know little about fishing," Egan said.

"You can learn the ropes. Not much to that on a catboat. When you're ready, I'll give you more to do. You'll have to keep your head down until you're certain they've forgot about you, but as fast as the city is growing, and as much trouble as folks get up to here, the constables have plenty to do without worrying about you."

I had rarely seen Egan smile since we took him in. On that day, I saw the grin that won my heart as a child.

Much like the hard time I'd had shedding the false beliefs about my parents, the giant I'd made of Egan had been a stubborn notion, standing in my way, blocking a true view of the man.

Those giants no longer needed, knowing my parents mattered little, and Egan had become just a man.

Alta Mae—23

I had a large family now, and big brother had joined us. Cedric and I called ourselves Romanos instead of Brewers, though the family had Norths as well. Big brother also took up the Romano surname.

When asked, Egan allowed that of course he'd lied about our Ma and Papa being the tenements in Five Points.

"As ordinary as we knew ourselves to be, I wanted you and Cedric to feel uncommon. To be the children of giants is a grand notion."

"But you made Ma a prostitute and Papa a drunkard!"

"Had to make them ordinary enough to have ordinary children. We were very familiar with those sorts."

We had a good laugh at that.

I asked him to recollect for me his earliest memories of those who took care of him as a child.

"Several at Cow Bay, as I recall, probably all laced mutton. Those that had children spelled each other so they could get their business done."

"Were there one that took care of you that also did for me and Cedric?"

His mug pinched up as he tried to remember. "A woman named, Phoebe—no, it were… Fabienne. From Haiti, spoke mostly French."

"What did she look like?"

"Olive-skinned, black curly hair. Not particularly dimber. If you're wondering if she might have been your mother, well…"

"What happened to her?"

"Fell ill and died when I were twelve."

"When did you first know you had a sister?"

"I suppose someone said you were my sister. Later, the same with Cedric being my brother, but I don't truly know who said."

I tried to picture Fabienne. I gave her my features, of course. Her skin and hair looked a bit darker. That was the best I could do.

231

—◊◊—

Cedric and I brought home a lot of strays over the years, orphaned children trying to survive on the streets of San Francisco. When we were still young, those we chose to help were not carefully considered. The adults in our household were none to happy to be housing the waifs, especially when the guttersnipes among them caused trouble or robbed us for things to hock and then ran away.

Still, the adults knew our hearts were in the right place, and our home remained one of goodwill toward all sorts.

The family celebrated in September of 1850 as California became the thirty-first of the United States. Most important to us, it entered the Union a free state.

—◊◊—

January of 1854, I dreamt that Ma and Papa had got lost crossing the land, and arrived in San Francisco in some far future when the city appeared much grander than the one I knew. They squatted amidst the establishments south of Market Street, and looked to be at home until the ground began to shake. Warehouses, factories, and houses fell around them. Trying to flee inland to get away from the quaking, they didn't get far before beginning to crumble and fall. Glass windows shattered, chimneys tumbled, roofing scattered. Finally brick, stone, and wood framing flew apart. Mixed with the wreckage of burning buildings upon the ground, all that they had been became unrecognizable.

Frightened, I awoke. While knowing it had only been a dream, I didn't sleep again that night.

A couple days later, Tessa brought me a copy of *The California Advance*, and pointed out a story in it about the Old Brewery in Five Points, New York.

Reading, I learned that the New York Ladies Missionary Society had bought the property in 1852 as part of a plan to rid the city of that den of iniquities. They intended to put up a new mission building in its stead. In preparation for the razing of the old structures, a great force of coppers was employed to evict the tenants. They drove close to a thousand people out onto the cold winter streets, including children from the factory rooms. Some of those children had not seen daylight for many years. The newspaper didn't say what became of them.

By the score, sacks of human bones were carried out of the structure by the demolition crews, most of the remains found under floorboards, bricked up in walls, or buried in the dirt of the cellars.

The Old Brewery was demolished in December of 1853, about a month prior to my reading about it.

Awaiting construction of the new mission, the ground where the Old Brewery had stood was searched by many hoping to find treasure left behind by the evicted thieves.

No doubt nothing of value turned up. For all the criminal schemes hatched there, most living or working in the tenement seldom had two half cents to rub together.

Now that I've given up my lawless past, an odd feeling comes over me as I look back at my life in Five Points. I suppose I am of two minds about the place. I know the criminals of the points are a scourge upon the city of New York and that Cedric and I shamefully added to that with our own criminal deeds.

We believed we were surviving the best we could and that we had no better choices. Most of the poor who live there have few good choices in their lives, and they often resort to crime to get by. The laws seem to protect ownership and property first. Protection for the life and limb of common folks comes only a grudging second.

For all the squalor and the base nature of her residents, some part of me still wants to believe my mother is the Cow Bay tenement. The notion that the Old Brewery was my father remains in idle thought since no truth stands to put the falsehood to shame. Despite the callous tolerance of human suffering among those living in the tenements of Five Points, I spare a caring thought for them, because somehow they are my family too. With that deep, undisturbed well of affection, I wept to learn of the destruction of the Old Brewery. For days after, I mourned as if I'd truly lost my father.

I showed Cedric the article in the *Advance*, and spoke to him about my feelings. He said he felt much the same.

—◊◊◊—

Life in San Francisco drew me quickly from my sorrow. The tamer weather had become a comfort—the warmer, yet wet winters, the warm summers with fog until noon most days.

The city grew quickly during the gold rush years, ever wilder and more dangerous, but we'd weathered and survived much worse. The troubles that seemed to find most anyone who discovered gold discouraged us all from considering mining. Romano Fishers brought in the needed earnings.

Paul made friends with Italian fishermen who came to live in San Francisco and fish the bay. Since he spoke Italian, he helped them communicate better with the locals while their English improved. In return, they were generous with their knowledge of fishing, and Paul learned much from them that helps our own endeavor.

—⚲—

Once we were grown, Cedric and I found better ways to help the homeless children of the city through a couple of Catholic charities. We established a work program that allowed boys from St. Francis's School for Boys to go out with our fishing crews and learn the trade.

I started teaching the youngest class of women at a foundling asylum to read and write. They are girls thirteen to seventeen years considered to have been seduced but otherwise innocents, not prostitutes.

—⚲—

In 1857, when seventeen years old, Zeata came to me with a big grin on her face. "I was up all night helping Cedric with his spoon."

Rarely have I laughed so hard as I did hearing that. I had not thought of Cedric's spoon for many years. "Did he tell you he found it on the street in New York?"

"Yes, though I hardly understood him for all his laughing." She covered her grin with both hands.

Cedric and Zeata were married four months later, just as her pregnancy began to show. They would have six children, four girls and two boys, in the years to follow.

Florence remarried in 1857. Her new husband, a Mexican fellow named Bacab, had been with the fishing crew since before we bought the business.

Tessa took a teaching position with the city, and smiled more readily as the years passed. She and Ivan have remained childless. They seem as happy as they can be.

In 1858, I married an Indian fellow named Robert Tall, in part because he reminded me of the beautiful Indian man I'd seen at Fort Hall just before Ivan and Tessa's wedding there. Fortunately, I fell in love with him too. He's a good man with a head for business. During the gold rush, he bought several real properties and saw their worth increase rapidly.

Our union has not produced offspring, yet we have plenty of children in the family we call our own.

In 1870, Robert helped me open a boarding house for widows and spinsters in one of his properties, a large two-story house in Sutter Street several blocks away from the Romano home. We live in the house and let the rooms at a low rate. I must admit, my preferred clientele is a Catholic woman in her middle years.

—⚹—

Now, in the year 1873, our twenty-fifth year of business, Romano Fishers is doing well. We have more boats than ever, more crew members, and greater license to sell our catch at the wharf fish markets. I am bookkeeper, Ivan and Paul manage the boats and crew, Florence manages sales, and Egan, Cedric, and Zeata go out five or six days a week with the crew to work the fishing grounds of the bay and to help train the orphaned boys.

—⚹—

I've saved telling much about Egan for the last.

In 1855, when the Know Nothing Party rose out of nativists groups like the Bowery Boys, Egan was torn. Whilst liking their views on slavery, labor rights, and women, he despised their stance against immigration and their bigotry. What he hated most were the many lies the party told—most often tales of conspiracies to harm Americans—all meant to damn those they oppose, to sway gulpy people to their cause, and to pit people against each other.

"That were how the Bowery Boys won me over and twisted my heart," he said.

In the end, he worked against the Know Nothing Party wherever he could.

Egan married an Irish Catholic woman named Sorcha in 1856. I couldn't help thinking she looked a bit like Hell Cat Maggy. They fought a lot and I pictured him wearing his Bowery Boys red and her going after him with Maggy's metal claws.

When Cedric and Zeata were wed in 1857, Egan stood as best man.

During the Civil War, Egan joined the California 100, and traveled east to join the fight on the side of the Union. We were fortunate he returned to us whole.

For all their angry words, love has kept Egan and Sorcha together and they have had seven children, four girls and three boys. Though they live a couple of miles away, I see him nearly every day, and I'm proud that he's my brother.

I was wrong to give up on Egan, as I'd done on the journey across the wilderness.

Thankfully, Cedric had not.

§§

About the Author

Alan M. Clark hails from Tennessee, where he grew up in a house full of human bones and old medical books. At present, he lives in Eugene, Oregon with his wife, Melody. In his 35 year freelance career, he has created illustrations for hundreds of books, including works of fiction of various genres, nonfiction, textbooks, young adult fiction, and children's books. He is the author of eighteen books, including twelve novels, a lavishly illustrated novella, four collections of fiction, and one full-color book of his artwork and two books of his monochrome artwork. The World Fantasy Award and four Chesley Awards are among the honors he's received for his work. Mr. Clark's company, IFD Publishing, has released 45 titles in various editions that include hardcovers, paperbacks, ebooks, and audio books. IFD Publishing's authors include F. Paul Wilson, Elizabeth Engstrom, and Jeremy Robert Johnson.

Connect with the Author Online

You can email the author or find out more about him through the following websites:
http://www.ifdpublishing.com
http://www.smashwords.com/profile/view/IFDPublishing

IFD Publishing Paperbacks

Novels:
Of Thimble and Threat, by Alan M. Clark
Baggage Check, by Elizabeth Engstrom
Bull's Labyrinth, by Eric Witchey
The Surgeon's Mate: A Dismemoir, by Alan M. Clark
Siren Promised, by Jeremy Robert Johnson and Alan M. Clark
Say Anything but Your Prayers, by Alan M. Clark
Candyland, by Elizabeth Engstrom
Apologies to the Cat's Meat Man, by Alan M. Clark
Lizzie Borden, by Elizabeth Engstrom
A Parliament of Crows, by Alan M. Clark
Lizard Wine, by Elizabeth Engstrom
The Door that Faced West, by Alan M. Clark
The Northwoods Chronicles, by Elizabeth Engstrom
The Prostitute's Price, by Alan M. Clark
The Assassin's Coin, by John Linwood Grant
13 Miller's Court, by Alan M. Clark and John Linwood Grant
Guys Named Bob, by Elizabeth Engstrom

Collections:
Professor Witchey's Miracle Mood Cure, by Eric Witchey

Nonfiction:
How to Write a Sizzling Sex Scene, by Elizabeth Engstrom
Divorce by Grand Canyon, by Elizabeth Engstrom

IFD Publishing EBooks

(You can find the following titles at most distribution points for all ereading platforms.)

Novels:
The Prostitute's Price, by Alan M. Clark

The Assassin's Coin, by John Linwood Grant
13 Miller's Court, by Alan M. Clark and John Linwood Grant
Guys Named Bob, by Elizabeth Engstrom
Apologies to the Cat's Meat Man, by Alan M. Clark
Bull's Labyrinth, by Eric Witchey
The Surgeon's Mate: A Dismemoir, by Alan M. Clark
York's Moon, by Elizabeth Engstrom
Beyond the Serpent's Heart, by Eric Witchey
Lizzie Borden, by Elizabeth Engstrom
A Parliament of Crows, by Alan M. Clark
Lizard Wine, by Elizabeth Engstrom
Northwoods Chronicles, by Elizabeth Engstrom
Siren Promised, by Alan M. Clark and Jeremy Robert Johnson
To Kill a Common Loon, by Mitch Luckett
The Man in the Loon, by Mitch Luckett
Of Thimble and Threat by Alan M. Clark
Jack the Ripper Victim Series: The Double Event (includes two novels from the series: *Of Thimble and Threat* and *Say Anything But Your Prayers*) by Alan M. Clark
Candyland, by Elizabeth Engstrom
The Blood of Father Time: Book 1, The New Cut, by Alan M. Clark, Stephen C. Merritt & Lorelei Shannon
The Blood of Father Time: Book 2, The Mystic Clan's Grand Plot, by Alan M. Clark, Stephen C. Merritt & Lorelei Shannon
How I Met My Alien Bitch Lover: Book 1 from the Sunny World Inquisition Daily Letter Archives, by Eric Witchey
Baggage Check, by Elizabeth Engstrom
D. D. Murphry, Secret Policeman, by Alan M. Clark and Elizabeth Massie
Black Leather, by Elizabeth Engstrom

Novelettes:
Mudlarks and the Silent Highwayman, by Alan M. Clark
The Tao of Flynn, by Eric Witchey
To Build a Boat, Listen to Trees, by Eric Witchey

Children's Illustrated:
The Christmas Thingy, by F. Paul Wilson. Illustrated by Alan M. Clark
Collections:

Suspicions, by Elizabeth Engstrom
Professor Witchey's Miracle Mood Cure, by Eric Witchey

Short Fiction:
"Brittle Bones and Old Rope," by Alan M. Clark
"Crosley," by Elizabeth Engstrom
"The Apple Sniper," by Eric Witchey

Nonfiction:
How to Write a Sizzling Sex Scene, by Elizabeth Engstrom
Divorce by Grand Canyon, by Elizabeth Engstrom

IFD Publishing Audio Books

Novels:
The Door That Faced West by Alan M. Clark, read by Charles Hinckley
Jack the Ripper Victim Series: Of Thimble and Threat, by Alan M. Clark, read by Alicia Rose
Jack the Ripper Victim Series: Say Anything But Your Prayers, by Alan M. Clark, read by Alicia Rose
Jack the Ripper Victim Series: The Double Event by Alan M. Clark, read by Alicia Rose (includes two novels from the series: *Of Thimble and Threat* and *Say Anything But Your Prayers*)
A Parliament of Crows by Alan M. Clark, read by Laura Jennings
A Brutal Chill in August by Alan M. Clark, read by Alicia Rose
The Surgeon's Mate: A Dismemoir, by Alan M. Clark, read by Alan M. Clark
Apologies to the Cat's Meat Man, by Alan M. Clark, read by Alicia Rose
The Prostitute's Price, by Alan M. Clark, read by Alicia Rose
The Assassin's Coin, by John Linwood Grant, read by Alicia Rose
13 Miller's Court, by Alan M. Clark and John Linwood Grant, read by Alicia Rose

Novelettes:
Mudlarks and the Silent Highwayman, by Alan M. Clark, read by Alicia Rose

www.ingramcontent.com/pod-product-compliance
Lightning Source LLC
Chambersburg PA
CBHW032039240626
47154CB00003B/991